Also by Rebecca Denton

This Beats Perfect

A Secret Beat

REBECCA DENTON

ATOM

ATOM

First published in Great Britain in 2018 by Atom

ISBN 978-0-349-00310-8

Typeset in Janson Text by M Rules
Printed and bound in Great Britain by
Clays Ltd, St Ives plc

Papers used by Atom are from well-managed forests
and other responsible sources.

Atom
An imprint of
Little, Brown Book Group
Carmelite House
50 Victoria Embankment
London EC4Y 0DZ

An Hachette UK Company
www.hachette.co.uk

www.atombooks.co.uk

This book is dedicated to next generation babes:
Bebe Ray Campbell, Margot Franklin-Browne,
Iris McClelland, Eve Boucher, and my girls,
Georgia and Billie.

Track List

CHAPTER 1

New York, I Love You
But You're Bringing Me Down

'I'm sorry, there is no discussion to be had.'

'But, Cassie.' Alexia fixed her eyes on her mother's black pencil skirt and pondered telling her about the sale tag hanging from the hemline. 'It's a great opportunity for me. I can't work for Dad for ever. I need to grow, get out there on my own. I'm not going to learn anything more running around as personal assistant to a stupid boyband, and we agreed the full-time work on the tour was short-term!'

'Short-term because you're going to college! And for the last time, Alexia, call me *Mom*. I didn't spend twenty-four hours in labour and endure nine months of reconstructive surgery to have my only child call me by my first name. It's rude. And disrespectful.' She still managed to shout despite carefully running a blood-red liner around her lips.

'Don't blame the botched nose job on me,' Alexia said with a smirk.

Her mother closed her eyes and hung her head. 'That isn't funny. It's not botched, anyway – my surgeon is one of the best in the country.' She turned her head left and right to examine her perfectly symmetrical nose in her hand mirror. 'Botched?' She scoffed. 'It's a work of art.'

Alexia turned to her father, widening her eyes and lightening her irritated tone. 'James – you understand, don't you?'

'Well ...' Her dad eased himself up from the bar area, pulled his tuxedo jacket on and gave Alexia a weary look. 'Actually, I agree with your mother. You should finish up the next few weeks at work, then start college in the fall like we planned. What were you thinking, quitting your job without talking to me first? It doesn't just reflect badly on you, Alexia. You're my daughter.' He was disappointed in her, which was a rare thing, and Alexia didn't like the feeling it gave her.

She had quit in a hurry, it was true. But she'd had enough. The emergency call was the final straw: Alexia Falls, personal assistant and general dogsbody had been summoned. The Keep were shooting the video for their Christmas single, 'Hold My Baubles'. Singer Lee had one of his 'migraines'. He needed her. 'Now!' *He needs an aspirin and a night off the vodka tonics*, she'd thought to herself, bitterly, as she'd made her way out the door.

'I've got the thing where bright light hurts,' he'd moaned from behind his lime-green wayfarers.

'You mean a hangover,' Alexia had snapped. 'Unfortunately, you left evidence of your night out all over Instagram and Twitter, so Geoff is not going to buy it. The whole crew is waiting for you! Arghh! Enough!' Geoff was the band's long-suffering manager, and one of her father's close friends.

Her father. Who was not on her side at all right now, however carefully Alexia explained her reasons for quitting.

'I really think we should tell Geoff you're going to finish out the summer,' he said, trying to be even-handed. 'And then you'll go to NYU as we agreed,' he continued, more firmly.

'Ugh. NYU. What's the point? Four years studying film-making when I could be out DOING it.' Alexia rolled her eyes as her mom approvingly kissed her father on the cheek. 'Nobody who actually works in film thinks film graduates are any good. I need to learn on the job!'

'This conversation is over, Alexia.'

'WHY DO YOU GET TO SAY THAT?'

'Because you live in my house.' Her mother picked up her soft, tan leather Hermès handbag and turned to leave.

'But I don't want to live in this house any more. That's the point.'

With that, Cassie stopped in her tracks, the Sale tag on her skirt still swinging behind her. Her shoulders rose slightly. Alexia heard a sharp intake of breath and waited for her mother to concede defeat.

'Alexia,' her mother began, 'if you want to go to London, and live god knows where, with god knows who, with no money and no support from us, by all means buy yourself a ticket and go.'

'Thanks, Cassie.'

Her mother turned to look at her. 'That wasn't permission. It was a warning. And it's *Mom*, to you. You have everything an eighteen-year-old girl could ever want, Alexia – and if it really isn't enough ...'

'I'm grateful, really,' Alexia insisted, carefully toeing the line. She looked around the enormous Manhattan apartment – more immaculate than any Fifth Avenue showroom – and felt even more determined to get out, away from the shadow of her boring socialite parents ... and far away from Lee.

'Did Dotty do a second cleaning shift?' she smirked.

'Your father has Iggy Pop coming for cake.' Her mother stopped and sighed, catching her daughter's bemused look. 'Alexia, please.'

'I've done everything you have asked of me, haven't I? Why can't I have this one thing? It isn't fair.'

'I must get on. We have the gala tonight and I've spent all week on a client with acute spiritual narcissism and a pending divorce. Some people have *real* problems.'

'Spiritual narcissism?' her father said, kissing Alexia on the cheek.

'You know. Obsessed with his own inner god. It's so typical – he spent one weekend in some bloody forest, high on ayahuasca ...' Her mother waved the question away, looking flustered. '*He's from the West Coast*,' she said, definitively.

4

Her dad smirked at Alexia and she tried not to giggle. She was sure she'd got away with it, but then he gave her a look of gentle seriousness, his hand on her arm. 'Do go to college, darling. It's an amazing opportunity, and one that I never had. It will be a fresh start for you socially as well. I'm *sure* you'll like it more than high school. Find your tribe, as they say.'

Alexia felt a rush of blood to her cheeks. 'That has nothing to do with it. I want to go to London and work at Bright Star Productions. College will always be there.'

'No it won't. This is a one-time offer – we won't be here to pay for your tuition when you're broke at twenty-five.' Her mother plucked her keys out of an antique Japanese ceramic bowl, perched atop a real miniature Roman marble column by the front door. 'You go on this crazy fantasy trip to London and the money's gone, Alexia. I mean it. Don't try to test me.'

'It's not a test, Cassie. I'm going!' She tried to sound chirpy, ignoring the pang of guilt in her stomach. 'Have fun, you two!'

'Get some sleep. It's been a big few days.' James sighed, holding the door open. As her mother disappeared he looked over his shoulder and then back at Alexia. 'And, Alexia, please be easy on your mom. She's—'

'I know, I know,' Alexia interrupted, and with the heavy thud of their thirty-thousand-dollar front door, followed by the quietest patter of paws (courtesy of her mom's inquisitive Italian greyhound), they were gone.

'Oprah!' she called to the sleek grey supermodel. 'Come

here, little one!' Oprah trotted lazily over, her little face almost entirely eyes. 'Let's head upstairs and sort out that luggage, eh?'

Alexia made her way up to the top floor, past the hallway full of framed platinum and gold discs. The plush silver-dove carpet gently gave way under her bare toes, and the faint smell of yet another paint job lingered in the air, not completely masked by the jasmine candle her mother had lit on the top-floor landing. Alexia inhaled the scent just inches above the flame before blowing it out and waving the ribbon of smoke away.

The top floor, which Alexia had to herself, consisted of a large duck-egg blue and grey bedroom with en suite, a dressing room and a large study, which her mom had renovated the year before. *Especially for college.*

Cassie had really gone to town. The walls were adorned with framed, nonsensical inspirational quotes like, 'It's not failure, it's unfinished success!' and 'It's a good day to have a good day!' and the bookshelves bulged with old magazines, self-help and motivational books, while Alexia's own collection of film and photography books were relegated to one small lower shelf.

Her phone rang, and she felt her whole body start to tense. She just wanted some goddamn time to herself.

'Alexia!' came the warmest, kindest voice she could imagine right at that moment.

'Clint,' she said with great relief, 'it's just you!'

'Just me! How was the Christmas video shoot?'

'Heinously tragic. I can't believe I got called down.'

'Someone forget their underwear?'

Alexia groaned. Having to buy emergency underwear happened a lot, actually. It was quite something to know the boxer size of five grown men who were not her relations. She often dreamed about starting an online blog and releasing said information under an alias – *Did you know The Keep's singer Kyle is a trim 32 waist but requires an XXL boxer short?* – but she was far too loyal for such shenanigans. Still, a girl could make a quick buck with the information she had.

'So, did you do it? Are you coming?'

Alexia wondered if she *had* done it. She looked across at her suitcase, barely touched since her return from touring Europe with The Keep. It would be so easy to just chuck a few winter clothes in and go.

'I did it. I think. No, I think I did it.' She sighed. 'My parents are not one hundred per cent on board.'

'Oh well, whose parents are? Have you got somewhere to live or do you need to crash at mine for a bit? We can clear some room in the lounge. I mean, it's not pretty, but you'd be welcome.'

'I'm not sure. I haven't worked out all the details yet.'

'No worries. But you'll be here soon, I guess? We've just signed on to do another of your dad's bands – All New Wild.'

'Another boyband! I'm so sorry.'

'They're not a boyband. They play instruments, you know.' Clint chuckled. 'But yes. Same old, same old.'

Despite only being in his early twenties, Clint had been

touring with The Keep for years. He was their official cameraman, in charge of filming the bigger gigs and keeping their social media accounts looking slick by producing video diaries and so forth.

'Well, I'll message you when I book my flight. I guess I'm coming soon.'

'Okay, love. How exciting! We can't wait to have you on board officially.'

She put her phone down as Oprah curled up on a floor cushion by her feet and closed her eyes. Alexia yawned. 'Me too, Oprah. Me too.' The last few days were finally catching up with her. She popped her iPod in the dock and found Sonic Youth. Surely there was no better soundtrack for her teenage rebellion? She hit play on 'Teenage Riot', sinking gleefully into its messy, distorted guitar riff. *Stick to your guns. Thanks, Thurston.*

She flung open her luggage and began to sort through a month's worth of trash and treasure she'd picked up during the long tour of Europe. She had the dream job really – travelling the world with a superstar boyband. If only it hadn't involved being on call to five ungrateful boys twenty-four hours a day. She tossed a fridge magnet souvenir from Rome in the bin. The truth was, if it wasn't for her feelings for Lee, she probably wouldn't have lasted a week.

But as she shuffled through a selection of postcards and Polaroids carefully hidden in the satin pin-tucked top pocket of her Gucci case, she had to concede that it was fortuitous. If she hadn't been on tour she never would have met Clint and the team from Bright Star Productions, and she would have never had the offer of an internship in London. An internship that, if she worked really hard, could turn into a full-time job.

She gazed at a photo of Lee backstage, his longish dark hair hanging over his eyes, shining red from the flash but still full of magnetic wickedness. She flicked through the set – there was Lee half asleep on the plane, Lee jumping into another fountain and Lee ineffectively hiding from paparazzi by wearing a huge sombrero and comedy moustache. And, finally, one of him with his arms around bandmate Charlie at a restaurant in Rome. She turned it over and ran her thumb across the message on the back.

For eBay, with love from Lee xox

She'd never sell any of these memories. *But I can't keep them all either*, she thought with her signature practicality, tossing the blank postcards in the bin and slipping all but half a dozen Polaroids into a hat box.

She unzipped her camera bag and carefully cleaned her two most prized possessions – a vintage Polaroid camera and a brand-new Canon 5D – before repacking them. They were worth a bomb.

A couple of hours later she was unpacked and half repacked. She hid her suitcase away in her closet and closed the door, tugging her dressing gown off the hook at the back.

'I'm just going to have a quick shower, Oprah,' she whispered, sniffing her armpits and recoiling in horror. 'A long shower, Oprah. With disinfectant. And paint stripper.'

She plugged her iPhone in to charge, walked to the en suite and turned the water to hot. While she showered, she dreamily planned her escape. She would book a ticket to leave later that week. Clint would help her get an apartment. The rest she would sort out as she went. She had absolute confidence in her decision and couldn't wait to get there. A week was almost too long.

She turned off the shower and heard her phone ringing in the other room. As she reached for a towel it rang off and almost immediately it rang again. Alexia felt her heart race. She pulled her robe on and made a dash for it, but missed the call.

Lee. Lee had called eight times. Her phone beeped and a text message popped up.

> FROM LEE: Lexi. I neeeeeeeed you. Can you come now? X

CHAPTER 2

Upside Down

Alexia stood quietly at the door, ear slightly pressed against the cold wood, waiting for quiet. She recognised each tone of the muffled exchange – the clipped, sharp staccato of anger, followed by the sing-song sound of begging and finally the short, deep, calm tone of resignation. She didn't need to hear the words to know that he had lost another argument. Mind you, a donkey could win an argument with Lee – he wasn't the brightest man in America.

Luckily, the hotel corridor was deserted. She had made these visits many times before, but this time she felt unusually nervous. It was only a few hours earlier that she'd said goodbye to him at the set, and now, here she was, back again. Alexia to the rescue.

She let out a slow, calming breath and momentarily regretted the garlicky lasagne she had scoffed down before leaving her parents' apartment.

Steeling herself, she pulled her Italian cardigan around her waist and fixed it with a thin leather belt, running a hand through her dark hair, which was still damp, and frustratingly starting to frizz.

As a door slammed inside the royal suite, she jumped back, waiting a few moments for the silence to settle before she gently knocked.

Almost instantly the door flew open, and there he stood. Naked from the waist up, his belt and jeans half undone, boxer shorts billowing out, beer bottle in hand. With that perfect sly smile fixed across his ridiculously sexy face, Lee punched the air.

'Sexi Lexi.' He grinned. 'Thank god for you, you wonderful lady.'

It was talk like this that played on her mind for hours after each encounter, but she tried her best to brush his flippancy aside and get down to business.

'Hi, Lee.' She shyly smiled, pushing past him and into the lounge area of his luxurious enormosuite – which had clearly not been serviced in days – settling her laptop down on the cluttered coffee table.

'You're wet,' he noted, throwing her a hand towel. 'Can't believe you answered my text. Do you ever take any time out?'

He was, as usual, completely oblivious.

'Well, you did call, like, eight times,' she mumbled. 'Anyway, I was working late ...' she lied, her voice trailing off as she tried to gauge a reaction. Clearly her resignation hadn't even blipped on the Lee's radar, or the label hadn't felt the need to tell the band yet. 'How'd you like the shoot?'

'Okay,' he replied, looking at his watch. 'Weird without Maxx.' His voice dropped slightly and he looked vaguely serious for a moment – serious like someone who was deciding between pizza toppings, rather than someone who was contemplating their entire future.

The Keep were a band on the way out. Last year's news. The fangirls had left high school and were getting real, actual, human boyfriends. New boybands – ones that could play instruments – were being nominated for Teen Choice awards, and The Keep, at an average age of twenty-two, were no longer the sexy subjects of thirteen-year-olds' fan fiction. And now, with the news that Maxx was leaving, they were dead in the water. (Maxx was leaving because he wanted to make *real music*, and would no doubt speedily drop the ridiculous second 'x' the record label had insisted on. But also, and to Alexia's mind an even more compelling reason, he had left after discovering that bandmate Charlie was now dating Maxx's ex-girlfriend, Dee.)

Alexia had already known Maxx was going to leave, of course. One of her last jobs had been to hunt down his exit contract. When she'd seen him in Geoff's office, ready to chase his dreams, looking nothing short of exhilarated, she was inspired to hand in her own notice.

Anyway, whether the boys realised it or not, this Christmas single was the record label squeezing the last pitiful moo out of a once phenomenal global cash cow.

'I need coffee,' she said, quickly changing the subject.

She really did. The tiredness was now starting to come in waves of nausea and exhaustion. All she wanted was to curl up in her bed.

'Let me get one for you.' Lee picked up the phone, immediately outsourcing the job to room service.

Alexia opened her laptop while Lee made himself busy chatting up the concierge. She shrugged her coat off, pulled her hair back into a ponytail and took out her black-rimmed glasses.

'So whatcha want, then?' she called out to him.

'Jessica is pissed at me and I need to go to LA, like, now. And it's serious this time – even her publicist called me,' he said in a whisper, with his hand over the receiver. 'Her publicist!'

'Oh no. You're not lead story in The Buzz again, are you?'

'Something like that.'

Lee and his long-time girlfriend – Hollywood actress Jessica Stone – were on shaky ground after The Buzz released some photos of him holding hands with a girl in Japan. The photos were actually entirely innocent – Lee was touchy-feely with everyone – but out of context they looked highly incriminating.

'So, next available to LA? It's at six fifteen,' she called out.

'Commercial? What about the jet?' He winged.

'I can't for this. It will be first class though, don't worry.'

She had done this job for too long now, starting as a part-time gig during school vacations, and turning full-time this summer. She knew she went above and beyond – especially for

Lee – but she couldn't say no to him. She knew he knew it, too.

'Okay,' he said, hanging up. 'Coffee's on its way. Hang on – six fifteen in the morning? Is that the best you can do?'

'I'll book you a car,' she said, glancing up at him.

'You've got that look again, Lexi. Like I've been a naughty boy,' he teased. 'What is it? You don't believe the rumours, do you? You don't think I'm a rogue? I'd hate if *you* thought that, Lexi.'

'No. No.' Alexia felt herself blush. Perhaps he didn't know she'd quit. 'You really don't know, do you?'

'Know what?' he asked, his face completely blank.

He flashed her a smile, running his hand across his latest chest tattoo. A butterfly? Or possibly a moth. 'Mind if I jump in the shower?'

'Of course not.' She smiled, fixing her eyes on the screen and typing furiously. *First Class, 06.15. American Airlines. Jeffery Lee Bow, DOB: March 21. Confirm.*

As the bathroom door closed, Alexia felt the tension dissipate. She sat back on the self-consciously opulent velvet sofa and pulled her computer onto her lap. What was she doing here, arranging a last-minute flight to Los Angeles for Lee to see his high-maintenance squeeze after yet another fight? What was she even thinking, rushing to his side to help him out? Again.

She looked at the booking one final time before hitting *Pay Now.*

'Jeffery Lee Bow,' she quietly giggled to herself. 'J-Bow.'

As she sat there, listening to the dulcet tones of Lee singing in the shower, she looked back down at the bookings page on her computer and contemplated buying her ticket, then and there. She could be on a plane, tomorrow. There was nothing keeping her here.

By the time the coffee arrived and Lee had emerged from the bathroom, she was ready to go. He poured two cups out of the ornate silverware – both with cream and three sugars, just the way he liked it – and perched right on the arm of her chair peering at her screen.

'Here you go, m'lady. All done?'

'Thanks.' She tensed, leaning as far away from him as she could without perceptibly moving an inch. 'Yes. All done.'

'Okay, I'm going to shoot off then. Are you sure you're all right to sort this room?' he said, looking around with a smile as his phone started vibrating. He held up a finger to Alexia to keep her quiet. 'Yeah. I'm coming. I have a plane to catch but we can grab a drink.' He winked at Alexia, who was instantly jealous of the stranger on the end of the phone.

'Sorry, you're breaking up,' he lied. 'I can't hear you. Nah. Can't hear you. See you in half an hour.' Lee laughed as he slipped his phone into his back pocket.

'Don't forget, you'll be picked up from here for your plane at three-ish. Want me to set your alarm?'

'Yeah. Thanks, doll,' he said, pulling up his jeans.

Alexia realised this would be the last time she would see him. At least for a while.

'Um, so, I don't know if you know or what, but I'm leaving,' she said.

'What? But the room? My bags?' Lee pulled on his jacket, looking bewildered.

'The label. New York. I'm leaving. The band. Working for the band, I mean,' she said, looking everywhere but at him. 'I just thought you should know.'

'What? What the hell?' Lee sounded angry. 'You can't leave. We need you. I need you.'

'Nah. You don't need me. Someone else – anyone else – can do this stuff.'

'But you're so . . .' Lee struggled to find the words. 'Useful. And trustworthy. I totally trust you. The girl before was constantly getting me into trouble online.'

'Well, I might still see you now and then. I'm going to work with Clint.'

'Who's Clint?'

'Clint. Your cameraman. The guy that films your tours?' Alexia couldn't hide her sudden irritation.

'That cool gay dude?'

Alexia sighed. 'Yes. Clint.'

'Is this because of Maxx? I mean, god, I knew you two were close . . .'

'No. I made the decision before that. I guess it makes sense now anyway, with the band kind of breaking—'

'We're not breaking up.'

'Well, taking a break.' She had to tread carefully here.

'I can't talk about this now. I'll call you later.' Lee slammed the door and was gone. For the second time in the space of a few hours, Alexia had managed to piss someone off because she had shown the audacity to do what *she* wanted to do, rather than what everyone else wanted her to do.

In fact, the only person who had supported her decision was her boss, Geoff, who seemed genuinely relieved that Alexia had chosen a career in something other than music.

'Thank god for that,' he'd said before she'd had a chance to finish her well-prepared speech, filled with references to learning and growing and appreciating opportunities. 'You're out. And you're young. You're not ruined!'

'Ruined?'

'You know. Addicted to something. Dead. Wearing skinny black jeans at forty-five.'

As Alexia looked round the room at Lee's filth and faced the prospect of cleaning up his mess for the third time that day, she stopped and sat in the stillness for a moment. She looked down at her untouched coffee, which if Lee had bothered to ever notice, she actually took black or with soy milk, and never with sugar.

To hell with it, she thought, opening her laptop and rebooting the bookings page at American Airlines. *When's the next flight to London?*

CHAPTER 3

Everyday I Love You Less and Less

Greta glanced at the time on her computer. *Gah. 7.01 p.m.* Granny would be mad. She peered over the top of her screen to check for prying eyes for the hundredth time. Her boss, Lewis, was busy at his desk, and everyone else had gone home for the day. The coast was clear.

No one here at Bright Star could EVER know what she was up to, or they would freak out.

Her adrenaline was surging and she was fixated on getting this picture just right before she posted it. She searched through the tenth page of Google Images, looking for the *perfect* photo of Lee, with his soft, wavy longish hair, and fixed it against her oldest and most favourite photo of him – one from his very first concert, when his hair was cut short and spiky and was full of hairspray. Five years apart. She captioned it 'Look how far we've come. #fiveyearskeepingon'.

'Just get on with it, Greta Georgiou,' she muttered to herself. 'You've more important things to do than fangirling your life away.'

She hit *post*.

Then she slowly let out her breath.

And then she chewed her thumbnail as she closed the window on her computer.

It was like an itch had been scratched. A short-lived relief as she stepped momentarily back into the world of The Keep.

It had been so easy secretly running the UK's busiest social fan feed for The Keep when she only had boring school to worry about. But, now that she had a busy, demanding real-world job – it was murder.

'You nearly done?' Lewis shouted from across the room, making Greta jump. 'If the ingest is already pro-res no need to transcode. As long as it's h264 or higher.'

'You got it!' Greta said, hoping that nonsensical sentence was a question. Lewis always made her nervous. He was so serious. So ridiculously film-focused. 'I just have to pack the cameras away, so I guess I'm not really *that* done. Nearly done. Not done, actually, no.'

'Okay, well. One other thing – do you mind?' Lewis sat back in his chair and grinned at her from across the room. 'You know that other intern that Clint hired?'

'Yes,' Greta replied with a forced smile. She had absolutely no reason to be worried, apparently, but they *had* hired someone to do the same job as her. Someone from New York and therefore bound to be prettier, taller, more confident and better at everything.

'Well, news. She's arriving tomorrow,' Lewis said with an eyebrow raise.

'*What?*'

'Yeah, I know.' He shrugged. 'Well, can you make some space on the other side of your desk for her? I don't think she'll start until Monday, but just in case.'

'My desk?' Greta squeaked.

'Yeah. Nowhere else she can go. Neither of you will be there very often, so I'm sure you can share.'

'Of course,' she said, trying to sound bouncy and upbeat. 'That's so so so great she's coming tomorrow. It will be brilliant to have the extra help.'

'Will it?' Lewis looked amused. 'I guess. Well, Clint needs the help on tour footage and she's got a ton of experience with that.'

'She does?' Greta could hear the catch of fear in her voice and when Lewis didn't elaborate, the dread enveloped her. 'That's just great.'

Greta looked at her desk and wondered how much room to make. Fearful of appearing rude or unwelcoming, she cleared well over half the space. She moved all her paperwork into a plastic tray and found a spare chair for the opposite side of the desk. It was tight. She walked over to the stationery cupboard and grabbed a company notebook and a few pens (branded biros from the set of *Weekend Kitchen*) and placed them neatly on the desk.

'Does she need email setting up and security passes and stuff?' Greta called out to Lewis as he slipped his *Empire Strikes Back* camera bag over his shoulder.

'Oh yeah. Good thinking.' He gave her a thumbs-up, and then fitted his Iron Man bike helmet, and picked up his lime-green folding bike. 'You can do it, right? I don't want to play IT guy for anyone any more today.'

'No worries.' Greta had heard this complaint a million times. She skirted around to her computer and flipped it back open. She logged into the company's Intranet. 'One last thing though, Lewis? What's her name?'

'Um … Alexia!' Lewis called out. 'There's an HR form with her details in the personnel folder I think. If not, don't sweat it. We *can* do it tomorrow.'

He closed the main door and the office fell completely silent, except for the whirring of the machines in the edit suite and the sound of the cleaner vacuuming the corridor. Greta opened the shared drive and clicked on personnel. She noted the folder, 'Alexia', with a grimace. Created just today. Inside was a half-filled HR form and a scan of her passport.

Greta studied the photo of her nemesis with intrigue. She was dark haired with dark eyes and the fullest lips Greta had ever seen. Her hair was thrown back in a loose low bun and her eyes looked focused and fierce. She didn't look her age – she looked more sophisticated, polished and grown up – and Greta wondered how she could have so much experience 'touring' if she'd only just turned eighteen.

But there was also something distantly familiar about her. Greta stared hard at the picture, trying to figure out what it was. She quickly googled her. No online social presence to be found – at least nothing obvious and under her name. Her Facebook was private, with no pictures of her to see. What kind of eighteen-year-old has no flicker of an online identity? It was unusual and, frankly, bloody annoying.

She looked through the HR form for more clues, but there was virtually no information about her. No CV. No application form. It was clear that Clint had fast-tracked her through the hoops and hurriedly gathered just the essentials. Greta shuddered.

'I bet she's exhaustingly efficient,' she whispered dramatically. 'Like that Emily Blunt in *The Devil Wears Prada*. I'm totally screwed.'

She sent off the various emails and filled in the forms and fifteen minutes later Alexia was officially part of the team. Greta sat for a few moments in a complete huff, with her lip curled and her arms folded.

A ton of experience touring, she thought, irritated, as she began subconsciously pulling at her mousy, unruly hair and trying to smooth it out. She grabbed her make-up mirror and was aghast at the state of herself. Red-cheeked, smudged eyeliner, dry lips.

She huffed some more. *Touring*. Well that's that. She was NEVER going to go on the road with The Keep now.

She had almost been allowed to go that summer – but at the eleventh hour it was decided she wouldn't be needed. She spent the next week desperately trying to keep her professional cool in public, excusing herself to go and cry in the toilets in private. She had no choice. After all, as far as anyone else knew she was just a regular kinda-sorta-sometimes-fan – not a bona fide fangirl with an international online network of millions at her fingertips.

As a small but delectable concession, there were forty-three hours in total of behind-the-scenes footage of The Keep, plus nearly three hours of live performances, sitting unopened in a box on Clint's desk. Starting Monday she would be sitting in the edit suite, watching. Every. Single. Frame. She hadn't dared ask for a preview in case she seemed too excited. But she was. Oh, she was. She shivered with anticipation, wishing she could scream the news from the rooftops – or at least post a sneaky Snapchat of some of the material.

She remembered clearly the day that she first fell in love. She had watched Lee's *American Stars* audition on YouTube maybe a hundred times and, realising life would never be the same again, she had set up a Twitter account dedicated to The Keep – @thekeepers1.

It was a full-time job. First, she had to become more popular than every other fan account. That meant 24/7 gif and meme creations, staying on top of EVERY SINGLE update from the boys, their management, their latest girlfriends, no detail was too small; replying to other important fangirls and, since the boys were based in the USA, keeping all kinds of unsociable hours.

Her fangirl credentials were second to none. She'd been to see them nine times. Six times in London, once in Manchester and twice in Birmingham.

Online, she had by far the most interaction with the boys, and easily the most fan-to-fan interaction. She had 1.2 million followers on Twitter alone, but not a lot of real-life friends, since she was always too busy online for socialising.

But now she was at Bright Star, so close to the band's world, she had to keep it cool and tread carefully. She had so much access to confidential stuff. She felt like a recovering alcoholic at Oktoberfest.

There was only one person who knew what she was up to online, and that was her beloved granny.

'There's no art in this,' she'd scoffed, looking at a picture of the band dressed in matching white denim overalls. Not their finest hour. 'That silly looking blond one looks like he's never had an independent thought in his life.'

'But look at the dimples, Granny. The dimples! I. Can't. Even. I'm actually dead.'

'Yes. The feelings. I know.'

'THE FEELS, Granny. The FEELS! All of them.'

'Oh sorry. The feels.' Granny had rolled her eyes and poured herself a whisky. 'You're wasting your perfect youth on this garbage. Why don't *you* do something instead of existing for a bunch of halfwit boys. Women have the vote now, you know! I despair. I really do.'

'I do other things, Granny. I really do.' She'd grinned cheekily.

'Do you?' Granny had smiled at her, knocking back her drink and popping a junior mint. Her granny always smelled of whisky and junior mints. 'What happened to becoming a TV presenter?'

'I'm too fat and ugly.'

'GRETA.' Her granny had looked mortally wounded. 'Don't say such things about yourself. You'll start to believe them. I had a friend that kept saying she was going to die of cancer – and then one day WHAM, she was hit by a mobility scooter outside Wetherspoons!'

When the job came up, Granny was full of encouragement. She was pleased that something had excited Greta more than The Keep for the first time in her young adult life. But her granny didn't need to encourage Greta one bit – the advert was practically written for her:

> Intern wanted. Bright Star Productions is looking for an intern with an interest in pop music to work in their busy production department. Must be keen, organised, professional and discreet. Unsociable hours. Some travelling (touring) required. We currently work with global artists like The Keep to produce bespoke content, along with producing our own cross-over entertainment programmes like Weekend Breakfast. CVs to lewis@brightstar.com.

Greta had applied right away and a week later had a fifteen-minute interview with Lewis and his boss Kevin in the downstairs boardroom at Bright Star. And because to her it seemed like a perfectly normal thing to do, she had found both their social feeds and added/friended/liked/retweeted/messaged them right afterwards, and most days thereon in, until after a week she got the call.

'Yes. Hi, is that Greta? It's Kevin from Bright Star Productions. We've had a look through all the applications and decided that the intern job is yours.' And then he had been rather curt. 'I got all your messages, so if you could stop asking about it now.' And finally, 'Please don't contact me online again. Use my work email.'

Greta's phone buzzed her out of the memory.

'Greta. The shepherd's pie won't keep.'

'Granny, shepherd's pie is the *most* delicious the next day – you said so yourself!' she giggled. 'Anyway, I'm leaving in five.'

She realised she was absolutely starving and quickly finished up, packing her trusty brown satchel. She flicked off the lights in the edit suite and rushed out of the door to the bus stop.

It was already getting dark and Greta was happy to see the end of summer. She was definitely not a frocks and spaghetti straps kinda girl, since she hated her feet, and she couldn't wait to pull the trusty Docs out of the cupboard again.

As she wandered along the Essex Road towards Dalston and home, she pulled out her phone and felt the familiar, warm fangirl embrace, the thrill, the sheer giddy satisfaction at the number of notifications ready and waiting for her to skim through. (It was impossible to answer EVERYONE who tweeted her. IMPOSSIBLE. She had almost as many followers as the prime minister!)

But as she flicked through her mentions tonight, she felt a certain distraction. It was that bloody passport photo – it kept bugging her. She had seen this Alexia before, she was sure of it. But where? And why did she have this weird sense of dread?

'Greta,' she said to herself sharply. 'Stop obsessing.'

It had zero effect. Even as she said the words she was pulling up Lee's Instagram feed, swiping through the photos. Familiar image after familiar image flew past. Band photos, crowd shots, tourist photos, photos of fancy coffee (*ugh*), photos of beer, photos of his tattoos. What was she looking for?

Then, suddenly, up flashed an ordinary behind-the-scenes kind of snap of the band, taken in a hotel room. It was a photo from their last night on tour. Lee smiling straight into the camera, sitting next to Kyle on a royal-blue velvet sofa. Beside them a room-service trolley filled with silverware, cocktail glasses and half-eaten canapés. In the background stood Charlie, laughing along with Maxx's on-off girlfriend, singer/songwriter Dee Marlow.

And there, perched on an armchair with a bottle of San Pellegrino in her hand, smiling at Lee, was a girl. She was partly obscured, just about half her face visible – but there was no doubting who it was.

Casually sitting there.

Partying with the subjects of Greta's EVERY DREAM.

Greta's heart skipped a beat.

It was her. HER. It was Alexia Falls.

CHAPTER 4

Never Going Back Again

'Excuse me. Do you go to Angel, Islington?'

'Yup,' the bus driver mumbled without looking at her. No matter, she still had that thrill you get when you board a bona fide London red bus.

'Super!' Alexia yelped enthusiastically, giving the lethargic driver a fright.

She tapped her cash card on the yellow pad and lugged her enormous suitcase down the aisle of the bottom deck, sliding it into an area designated for pushchairs. She flopped down into an empty seat.

She looked out of the window as the bus pulled out of St Pancras station and felt exhilarated. She'd made it! It was less than twenty-four hours since she'd left Lee's hotel room, and with everything arranged in one working day, she'd outdone even herself in resourcefulness.

Her last conversation with her mother played a little on her mind, but she tried not to think too much about it. Cassie had looked genuinely wounded – something Alexia wasn't used to seeing in her usually bulletproof 'self-help guru' mom who more typically rejected all 'negative energy' (i.e. all normal human emotion) with a toothy smile and a motivational quip. It was something she'd not seen for a long time, anyway. Her mom had also reiterated the threat to cut Alexia's allowance. Well, that's something she'd just have to deal with, *if* it happened. All part of living life the life she wanted.

Her father had driven her to the airport, lecturing her on safety, the British drinking culture, regular contact with home.

'I'll be fine, Dad.'

'Life is different when there is no safety net, Alexia,' he said. 'Ultimately, Alexia, we can't stop you going. You're eighteen now.'

Alexia had looked across at him then, as they approached the familiar chaos of JFK airport, and thought she'd glimpsed a tear in the corner of his eye.

The bus rounded a sharp corner and shook her out of her daydream. She ran her fingers through her hair and tried to focus on the task ahead. She had to meet her new landlord, a Mr Tony Coleman, to pick up the keys to her apartment and get settled in. It was a Friday, so she could go to Bright Star first thing Monday.

'The Angel? Lady for the Angel?'

She looked up and realised the bus driver was shouting down the aisle at her.

'Oh, thank you!' she said, jumping up and dragging her case out onto the sidewalk. She was on a main road, with shops, restaurants and a Tube station, and suddenly she felt completely disorientated.

As the British drizzle made short work of her hair, she pulled out her phone and googled the address.

Chapel Market had sounded a lot more charming than it was in reality. She had expected a kind of cool, Williamsburg farmer's market vibe with the whiff of freshly brewed coffee and pulled pork, but instead she was confronted with stall after stall selling plastic suitcases, homeware junk and cut-price fruit in round plastic bowls. Behind the bright stripy canopy of each stall she could see a street lined with pubs, supermarkets, cafes and fried chicken shops. Many, many fried chicken shops.

Finally, she arrived outside number 65, right above 'Nail Spa', as promised. It wasn't exactly the nail spa she'd imagined; it was dim, grim and the whiff of chemicals was suffocating, even from outside. It was no wonder its army of workers wore protective masks. She rang the bottom doorbell.

The door flew open and there was Mr Coleman. He was short, easily in his sixties, but with an impressive head of thick dyed-brown hair and a bright pink pot belly. He wore little more than a pale pink terry towelling dressing gown, and stood in front of her with a mug of tea in one hand, the other holding a slice of buttered toast. White. Not a wholegrain in sight.

He looked her up and down, his eyes narrowing a little.

'Are you Alexia Falls?'

'Oh, I'm so sorry. Yes, I am. Pleased to meet you.' She smiled.

'And you're over eighteen, right luv?' he said, sternly. 'Because I can't rent this place to anyone under eighteen.'

'I'm eighteen. My birthday was back in June.'

'Well. If that's the case, dahrlin' –' he nodded, resting his half slice of toast atop his tea, shaking the crumbs off his hand and offering it out to her for a hand shake '– welcome to Chapel Place Castle, Ms Falls.'

'Oh, thank you!' she said, and confusing the welcoming hand for an offer of help, she pushed her case towards him, 'It's so heavy!'

He looked down at the case and snorted loudly. 'Awright, I'll give you a hand. Come on in,' he said, popping his tea down on the landing, stuffing the last wodge of toast into his mouth and heaving her bag up the first step. 'You got the kitchen sink in here?' he said, spitting half-masticated bread.

'I know. I was thirty pounds over the weight limit,' Alexia said grimly. 'They charge you a lot of money!'

'I only ever take hand luggage. Mind you, you only need a towel in Malaga. You ever been to Malaga? It's beautiful. Hot as you like,' he said, huffing and puffing as he dragged the suitcase to the first floor. On the small landing there were three doors and a little window, which looked out over a tiny courtyard littered with cigarette butts.

'This is the shower and loo,' he said, tapping on the door marked Bathroom. 'But we'll come back to that.' He pulled out a fat bunch of keys, spun it around to find the correct one and slipped it into the lock marked Flat One.

'Right,' he grinned, pushing the door open. 'So you've got the master suite with balcony.'

Alexia looked around her room. A double bed took up the majority of the space on the red and brown flowered carpet. There were fixed shelves on the wall beside a blocked-up fireplace and, just to the right, a tiny nook with a kitchenette. It had just enough space for a sink, small fridge, toaster, microwave and a kettle, and there was a breakfast bar for one, with a Bakelite stool folded underneath. There was a keen whiff of damp in the air, and the ceiling and far wall were stained with a faint line from what looked like a slow leak through the light fitting.

The only saving grace was its two massive sash windows, which opened out over the awning of the Nail Spa below.

'The roof terrace?' Alexia smirked.

'It's lovely in the summer,' he insisted.

'It's all great, thank you,' she said firmly. 'You can leave my bag just there.'

'I was going to, sweetheart. You want to see the toilet? It's just out the door to the right. You'll share with numbers two and three, so keep it as you wish to find it. Unless you find it after Jez has been in. He can be a right pig after a night on the whizz so give me a tinkle if it's a bitty unusable.'

'Got it,' she beamed, completely unsure what that last sentence meant. 'You said in the advert there was a laundry service?'

'No, I said there was a laundry,' he corrected her. 'Between the Nail Spa and the betting shop. You'll need coins, it's coin operated.'

'Oh, I see. And what about cleaning?'

'I have a lady who comes once a week to do the shared spaces. If you want her to do the room let me know. It's an extra twenty pounds a week.'

'Okay. I'd like that please,' Alexia said, eyeing the corners of the carpet, not daring to inspect the bed too carefully.

'So, you're going to take the place?'

'Yes. Yes, I will, thank you.'

'Okay, well, that's six weeks in advance and one month bond.' He paused for a moment, an awkward smile on his face. 'Cash. Next rent is due the first of the month and if you're late, your door will be dead bolted shut until payment is made.'

'Two thousand, eight hundred pounds, right?' Alexia pulled a white envelope out of her bag. It was really an awfully big chunk of her savings . . . but she would sort that soon enough.

'Yes, thank you. Let me get you a receipt.'

'Oh, don't worry just now. Let's do it later.' Alexia was desperate to get unpacked and organised. 'Do you know where I can get some sheets and that kind of thing?'

He shrugged. 'There's an M&S down the road,' he said, pointing through the window.

'A what?'

'A Marks and Sparks. A Markies. A Marks and Spencer. Britain's finest. Good food there, too.'

'Great. Well, that will be all.'

'Will that be all, will it?' he teased. Alexia, without skipping a beat, shoved an extra £20 note into his hand.

'Thank you for the help with the bags.'

'I'm supposed to see your passport,' Mr Coleman said carefully. 'Take a scan of it. Check your details.'

'Oh, right.' She pulled her passport out of its leather wallet. 'I'll need that back, though. I need to open a bank account.'

'No worries,' he said, grabbing it quickly and flipping to the page with her photo. 'Well, here's your keys. First of the month, remember.'

'Thank you,' she said with a salute. 'I won't forget.'

She stepped towards the door to hurry him out and when she was alone she raced to the window to check out the view of her new street. The market was beginning to shut down for the day, leaving a sea of empty cardboard boxes and rubbish. All the shops along the street seemed to house residential flats above. The balconies opposite were decorated with washing, pot plants, chairs, barbecues and broken furniture. The pub across the road had a trio of picnic bench seats outside and a group of older people smoked and drank their enormous English pints.

She took a deep breath in. She was here. And this little place – this smelly, tiny, dingy little place – was her home. All hers. Alexia laughed as she swung her suitcase up onto her bed, pulled out her wash bag and squeezed some antiseptic hand gel onto her fingers, rubbing her hands together like mad.

'First, some sheets for this bed,' she said, looking down, half expecting to see Oprah at her feet. A little voice niggled at her to text her mom, but that could wait.

Out onto the pavement and down the street, she felt light and breezy without her luggage. She made her way to M&S as advised, and up the elevator to the homeware and furnishings section. There she bought two mattress protectors, two sets of double size, 400-count, Indian cotton sheets, and four matching pillowcases. No expense would be spared on the barrier between her and that mattress. For the duvet, she opted for a nice plain white cover and cheap polyester comforter. And two feather pillows. She hesitated for a moment by a basket filled with throw cushions marked Half Price but resisted the urge to grab a gold-fringed velvet number. It was nasty, but it reminded her of something. She ran her hand across it – it was an almost exact knock-off of the ones on her mom's sofa at home.

At the checkout she did a quick tally. Realising she had blown her week's budget in one afternoon, she took a mental note to redo her sums later. There was always going to be an initial outlay – but she still needed a quick stop in the food section.

Alexia filled a trolley with what was meant to be essentials only – milk, bread, toilet paper – but turned into a huge shop including cold cuts, chutneys, chocolate, three different kinds of juice, clothes, cleaning products and an armful of ready meals she could just throw in the microwave.

After spending ten minutes convincing the security guard that she lived just up the street and would return the trolley right away, she ended up slipping him a £50 note as 'security'.

She rolled her bulging trolley back towards number 65 (only stopping to buy a small bunch of cut-price flowers from a closing stall) and wedged the front door open so she could drag her food upstairs in two trips. Then it was back down to M&S to discover the security guard had finished for the day (it was almost 5 p.m.) and had gone home with her money.

For the next hour, Alexia cleaned and dusted and wiped to the soundtrack of some of her favourite British music. The Clash, The Buzzcocks, Joy Division – all bands her mom hated – and as the noise filled the room and soared outside through the open windows she felt a surge of excitement.

She unpacked her suitcase and arranged her clothes and shoes on the shelves in immaculate order. She made her bed and arranged the slightly limp pink roses in the only glass she could find, wedged behind the tiny fridge and half full of a sludgy brown, foul-smelling liquid. She was irritated to discover she would have to buy ALL the kitchen stuff – knives, forks, pots and pans.

Her phone rang, reminding her she needed to sort out the UK sim she'd bought at the airport. It was Clint.

'I got your message. You're here!' he said excitedly. 'So quickly!'

'I know! Squeeeeeee! I'm so excited.'

'Where are you staying?'

'I got a place in Angel.'

'In Angel? A place of your own?' Clint laughed. 'Damn, that can't be cheap.'

'Well, more of what you call a bedsit, but it's all mine and it's not my parents and I'm HERE! Where are you?'

'We're just wrapping something up, actually, then we're heading to be in the audience of this new live chat show thing. Why don't you join us? If you're not too knackered. Hang on a sec, let me check on something.'

Alexia felt a surge of excitement as Clint put her on hold. She'd been to a couple of these in the States, with the boys – *The Late Show* and *Ellen* – but she'd never been out on the floor watching how it all happened. Just stuck backstage sorting out connections to Netflix and dishing out coffee to spoilt singers.

'Okay, there's room for you. Can you come to the office? There's a few drinks in the lobby beforehand.'

'I'd LOVE to come! I'm on my way. At least – I'll be there quick as I can. Just need to freshen up.'

CHAPTER 5

T.V. Eye

Alexia tried on everything in her suitcase. Every inch of her bed was covered in discarded outfits as she cursed herself for packing her newest and best clothes and nothing that remotely suited a Friday night studio filming with her new colleagues. After forty-five minutes, she opted for a pair of J-Brand jeans in black, a black denim shirt and her ten-up cherry Docs. She kept her hair tightly pulled back in a bun, and her black glasses firmly on. It should have been the perfect smart-media-type-casual look, except it was all brand new and stiff with shop folds. Her Docs were the biggest giveaway. She glanced out the window – still raining. London was delivering on its promise of terrible weather.

But rain *was* good for something . . .

Out on the street, she shrugged off her coat and walked towards King's Cross, passing a pub called the Lexington, already filling up for the night. She let the drizzle fall on her, softening the fabric of her outfit and hopefully helping it to look a little more lived in. She saw the wardrobe assistant do this for the boys once at a gig in Boston, when their outfits arrived starched to almost cardboard by the local Laundromat.

The boys. She wondered how they had taken the news that she'd gone. She hadn't the courage to check her emails – but she expected to hear from Kyle at least. He would be kind. Supportive even. Her mind momentarily wandered to Lee and she shook her head and looked up at the concrete sky.

She was excited. Bright Star were one of the biggest production houses in London, and their factual department was second to none. Factual meant everything from cutting-edge documentaries to reality TV and music. Alexia was here primarily to work with Clint, although she had been warned there was every possibility she would end up helping out on a daytime cooking show or (god help her) a reality show.

Clint worked mostly on music as a PD – Producer/Director – a role which saw him out in the field doing smallish shoots, usually on his own. Bright Star had a deal with her dad's formidable record label, Falls Records, which meant that they had exclusive access to film all the label's biggest acts. And The Keep were the biggest act of them all – for now, anyway – which meant that Clint was almost exclusively occupied by following them around, filming their shows, their YouTube videos, video diaries, acceptance speeches for award shows they couldn't attend – the lot. He had been working with them for a few years, and when they toured Europe in the summer he had taken Alexia under his wing.

She was dazzled by the Bright Star offices. A small group of people were huddled by a standing ashtray a little distance from the building's impressive glass-fronted entrance. Three men with camera equipment waited on the kerb, and production runners were waiting beside a doorman, presumably for the chat show guests to arrive.

After giving her name to the doorman, the first person Alexia saw in the vast foyer as she pushed her way round the revolving entrance was Clint, glass of champagne in hand. His bearded face was impossible to miss and his welcoming smile almost made her melt into his arms.

'Alexia Falls. How long's it been? Too long. Too long!'

She laughed. 'Less than a month – but I'm glad you think that's too long. It's so good to be here.'

'We're so happy to have you. By the way you HAVE to give me the goss.'

'The goss?' Alexia whispered, as Clint led her by the arm.

'About Max! Actually, tell me later. Too many loose lips in this place.' He grinned, waving Alexia's non-existent revelations away. 'But I *need* to know.'

The foyer was sparsely decorated. Professional. There was a huge pink-and-blue neon Bright Star Productions sign behind the reception desk (which had been turned into a makeshift bar), and a bunch of sofas in a sunken area across the room, presumably where guests sat awaiting their very important TV meetings.

'It's basically a mix of invited guests and, well, mostly producers. They're the ones closest to the bar.' He motioned to a group of well-lubricated thirty-somethings standing in a circle, faces glowing in the light of their mobile phone screens.

'Those two there are the most important. That's Kevin and Karen. Kev's our immediate boss. Head of Production, Lifestyle. He's usually off with the DIY and cooking shows, though he always finds time to harass us over our budgets. Karen runs the whole factual team. She is terrifying.'

Alexia took in Karen's tiny frame. 'Terrifying?'

'Yes, but don't worry, they know who your father is,' he teased.

'Ugh, I was hoping to have a little independence from all that.' She grimaced.

'So, I get to introduce you to the team,' he continued as they joined two people near the back of the room. 'This fine young lady is Greta. She's our original intern, assistant editor, helper, runner, life saver and the jolliest person I've ever met.'

Alexia grinned at Greta, who smiled broadly back at her, chewing her thumbnail and blushing. Greta was petite and round with a tangle of wild hair and rosy cheeks, but Alexia was not at all prepared for the thick London accent that came flying out of her mouth.

'Hey-yaaaa,' she said, her eyes darting around the room at people arriving. 'Ooooh, Davina's here! And there's Rylan!'

'Nice to meet you, Greta.' Alexia smiled back. 'You're an intern too? That's great.'

'Lewis is at the bar over there,' Clint said, pointing to a dark-haired guy in a plaid shirt.

'Oh, he's a PD too, right?' Alexia nodded.

'PD?' Greta asked.

'Jeez, Greta. How long you been here? Producer/Director.' Clint laughed. 'We're a tiny team. Everyone does everything. But roughly I do camera and often sound, Lewis directs and edits –' he dropped his voice to a whisper '– *and fixes our computers.*'

Greta nodded earnestly. 'But don't ask him unless it's absolutely necessary.'

'But honestly, as I said, we all do a bit of everything. It's going to be great to have the extra pair of hands. You want a drink?'

Alexia looked across at Greta, who was sipping on a pint of beer that looked comically big against her.

'Oh, just a water thanks. For now,' Alexia said. '*Jet lag.*'

'Sure. I can hardly believe you arrived so quickly,' Clint said, shaking his head as he headed off to join Lewis at the bar.

Neither could Alexia. She looked around the bustling foyer and noticed there were a bunch of production runners and assistants wearing headset radios and ushering people into the studio. Occasionally there was the flash of paparazzi at the front door and a murmur went round the room as someone famous came in. It was nothing she hadn't seen before, but this time she wasn't running about fetching *other* people bottled water.

'Oooh, look – Ant and Dec!' whispered Greta.

'Who?' Alexia craned her neck, though she wasn't sure what she was looking for. 'Anty Dick? What?'

'Those little men there.' Greta nodded towards them, eyebrow raised slightly. 'They're super famous. You don't know them?'

'Sadly, no. They're British stars? I'm going to be a little hopeless in that regard. You'll have to point them out to me.'

'Oh, I thought *everyone* knew Ant and Dec.' Greta pondered. 'You haven't seen *Saturday Night Takeaway*? They're the most famous people in the country, I think.'

Alexia muttered another apologetic no, more interested in the buzz of the room than anyone specific in it. There was a strange familiarity about being here – she was used to the atmosphere and commotion when celebrities walked into the room. In fact, she'd met so many over her teenage years that she was somewhat immune to it, but tonight felt different. She wasn't just James Falls's daughter – the rich-girl intern people should be nice to – she was Alexia. And she wasn't running around after five boys; she was here to work as part of a team – to create something for herself.

'So, New York?' Greta continued. 'I love New York. Although I've never exactly been. But you know, in the movies and stuff like that. I was in transit once at one of the airports. What's that airport called? No, don't tell me. It's Newark.

Sounds like New York if you say it a few times really quickly. Newark. Newark. Newark. We went to Florida though. I went with my granny when I was twelve. But you had to fly through Newark, and we could see the city in the distance. We went to the Keys. You know them? Granny had a boyfriend there. Well, it's weird saying boyfriend when she's seventy-eight. Man-friend. Gentleman friend. Not her first either, I might add. Granny is a bit of a tart, actually.' She laughed awkwardly, as Alexia looked around excitedly, taking everything in. 'Sorry. I need to learn when to stop talking.'

'So, how long have you worked here?' Alexia asked.

'Not long, me. Since I left school a few months back.'

'Ah, you're eighteen too?' Alexia clapped her hands together. 'And what have you been working on? I can't wait to get stuck in.'

'Well, between you and me – OH MY GOD, it's been so boring. I've been doing a cooking show because we've been waiting for Clint to get back from tour. I can't believe people watch shows about people cooking food.' She curled her lip. 'It's worse than shows about houses. I did a series about bloody houses during my first week here. Talk about paint drying. Literally. Three days of filming really ugly tiles being laid around a pool I could never afford. And the highlight is the bloody windows being fitted. The highlight! I nearly gouged my own eyes out. And cooking? Watching old people brown mince? I don't get it.'

Alexia liked Greta immediately. She was so bubbly and

her hundred-mile-an-hour mouth made her feel welcome and at ease. She smiled at her. 'My mother is always doing up our house in New York. I couldn't agree with you more. Soooo dull.'

She sipped her water and took in the room as Greta paused for breath. Her eyes fell on Lewis. He had to be about the same age as Clint – Alexia guessed early twenties at least. He had buzzcut black hair and dark, smooth skin, and his black-rimmed glasses almost exactly matched Alexia's. He wore blue jeans and a plaid shirt open on top of a Pokémon T-shirt, and he looked like he needed some sleep. He returned with Clint from the bar and stood next to Alexia. She got an immediate whiff of aftershave and fresh sweat.

'Hey, Alexia.' Lewis held out a water for her, then shook her hand firmly, seriously, earnestly.

'Nice to meet you.' She smiled. Once released from his firm, sweaty grasp she subtly dried her hands on her jeans.

'So, we were just saying that the gig with All New Wild is confirmed for the week after next. We're doing an interview and then filming an acoustic number with them in a hotel in the West End.'

Clint moaned. 'I hate branded content.'

'Pays the bills,' Lewis said. 'And lets us do other fun stuff, like my vinyl documentary.'

'Vinyl documentary?' Alexia piped up. 'You're a *serious* music fan. Everything I own is digital, though I used to love playing the records at Dad's work.'

'It's more about the history of microgroove recording, LPs, shellac to vinyl. It's technical really,' Lewis said. 'Although, obviously there's some music in it. For context.'

'Yes, Lewis likes to make proper, highbrow documentaries, so the rest of us get to do the glorified beer commercials to keep his dream alive,' Clint grumbled, 'and that's the real reason *she's* here too, by the way, Lewis.'

'Oh yeah?' Greta interjected, her eyes popping.

'Yes, Alexia could be in New York being super-assistant to The Keep right now, but she wants to make documentaries, so I brought her here to help film The Keep on tour instead.'

Alexia punched him in the shoulder, laughing. 'NOOO!' And then she looked at him, her eyes narrowing, tempering her sudden concern with a hint of a laugh and a finger wave. 'I mean it. No.'

'You worked with The Keep?' Greta asked casually, looking wistfully over her shoulder at a plain white wall as though it were the most fascinating thing in the room.

'Yeah. It was ... well, a lot of fun at times. But I'm happy to be doing something new. Are you a fan?'

'Oh, not really. I like all sorts of pop music,' Greta said quickly. 'So, you know them? Well? I mean. Do you know them *all*?'

'Well yeah, I guess so. I was their assistant. So ... erm ... better than most I guess.'

'Oh, for all of them? You assisted the whole band?' Greta said, her tone determinedly nonchalant.

'Yeah. Well, some more than others,' she said, looking across at Clint. 'Some of them needed a *lot* more assistance.'

'Oh, dear god, that band.' Lewis shook his head. 'But they've been a lifeline for us. The work Clint has done has kept our little music department going, really.'

'But we *also* do festivals,' Greta nodded enthusiastically. 'Lots to do if you don't want to do The Keep. We've got Ed Sheeran and Tinie Tempah this Christmas. We're also doing Music in the Park next month. I won't make you take all The Keep jobs if you don't want to. I'll share the load.' She said it with her hand on her heart.

'And when we're quiet, we all help out in the other departments,' Clint added. 'Which is more often than we'd like.'

'That's why I was doing the cooking show,' Greta explained.

'Don't worry, I'm happy with anything you want me to do. I'm *even* happy filming The Keep,' Alexia said warmly.

'Really?' Clint looked at her suspiciously.

'Anything you need,' Alexia said confidently, catching Lewis's eye. *He's impressed*, she thought with relief. She was determined to make a good impression and let it be known she would do whatever it took.

'Okay, then,' Clint shrugged. 'Monday morning you can go over the rushes from the tour. There's no one better equipped really – you were there at every gig, appearance, interview . . . '

'Sounds great. It will be like I never left,' Alexia said.

'But . . . ' Greta looked concerned. 'I thought I was—'

49

A booming voice calling out to Clint cut Greta off, and Alexia became aware of a kind of hushed commotion in the room as a slender-framed man marched towards them.

'Oh god,' Clint mumbled, forcing a smile. 'Look alive people. Here *it* comes.'

Chapter 6

Hanging with the Wrong Crowd

Theo Marlon was one of the most notorious gossip columnists in the world. London-born, celebrity-world bred, there was no private life off-limits and no subject too taboo for his website, The Buzz. He was responsible for almost all the major exposés of the past few years. He had destroyed and made careers while building an online empire unrivalled in the world of digital and social media.

'Well? How is last week's biggest boyband?' As Theo sucked back on his e-cigarette, Alexia felt a cold sweat come over her. She knew all about Theo Marlon and how fiercely everyone in the music business despised him. And he'd messed with Lee – so he was the devil.

'Hello, Theo. How's things?' said Clint, warily.

'Oh, you know – great. Got a really big exclusive coming out next week. On Drake,' he added, his eyes dancing. 'We've got new offices by the way – we're in Old Street now. You should come by, Clint. We're hiring a video production arm right now.'

Big, and brash, Theo managed to be both slender and soft in that unhealthy, too-much-alcohol-and-cigarettes way that kept your eyes dull and skin grey. His T-shirt was a little tight round the middle and he kept awkwardly pulling it and stretching it every time he moved, as if it was restricting him.

'I'm happy where I am.' Clint was being good-natured, but his manner had changed dramatically. Alexia could almost see him closing up. 'Things are great, really. Super busy.'

'So, any news from the road?' Theo raised his eyebrows at Clint, and shot a quick look Alexia's way, which made her immediately uneasy. But this was a game Clint had played before.

'Nothing to report. Straightforward tour.' Clint rolled his eyes at Lewis, who had pulled his phone out to mindlessly scroll through Twitter. Both DPs were doing everything they could not to engage.

'Must have been a bit of drama, Lewis?'

'Not that I'm aware of, I wasn't there,' Lewis sighed.

'True that the last two gigs weren't sold out?' Marlon was nothing if not persistent.

'I don't know. I was busy filming,' said Clint. 'Anyway, I'm sure if the gigs weren't sold out that would be public knowledge.'

'Yeah. They didn't sell out. I mean, not by much, but

usually – well, *in the old days* when they were able to get a number one hit – you had to sell your mother to get a ticket.' Theo laughed again, this time rubbing his nose with the back of his hand and rubbing it on his jeans. 'Not any more though.'

'Well, it was a great tour,' Clint said, trying to put a full stop on the conversation.

'But The Keep,' Theo pushed. 'Is it true, are they breaking up?'

Alexia's ears pricked, her heart beginning to beat.

'The Keep?' Clint said casually.

'No, they're not!' Greta piped up, red-cheeked, her beer spilling a little.

Oh yes they are, thought Alexia.

'I heard they're breaking up. For good,' Marlon said. 'Maybe even before this last Christmas single comes out: the dream is finally over.'

Alexia felt a sudden surge to protect. Theo was speaking as if it didn't matter, as if the lives of the boys, their staff, the record company – all the people Alexia had worked with and cared about – didn't matter. She didn't often have a strong emotional response to people, but Theo Marlon was an exception. She hated him instantly.

'Ahh, I don't know anything about that.' Clint shook his head, ramming the point home. 'And if I did? Well, Theo, you know I'm not going to tell you – I'd lose my job.'

Theo laughed, leaning forward and lowering his voice. 'Well, you know that there's a rumour that Lee is leaving the band and that's the reason for the split. He's doing a Zayn Malik – making "real music".' Theo was searching Clint's face to find any hint that he was on the right track.

'Lee's not leaving the band,' Alexia scoffed suddenly, the words flying out of her mouth before she had a chance to stop them. 'He's perfectly happy in The Keep. He's got no interest in going solo.'

'Oh really?' Theo eyes widened as they fixed on Alexia, who stared straight back at him, defiantly.

'Theo, meet Alexia,' Clint said warily, giving Alexia a 'look' as he nodded in Theo's general direction. 'Alexia, this is Theo.'

'Ah, Alexia. I wasn't sure of your name,' Theo continued, his tone turning gentle and sing-songy, verging on sleazy. 'How do you know that Lee isn't leaving the band? Did he tell you?'

'I just know, okay?' She wouldn't be bullied by this guy. 'It's none of your business.'

'Ah, you see, Alexia,' Theo said softly, slipping his e-cigarette into his back pocket, 'what's none of my business, is, in fact, *exactly* my business.'

He gave the group a smug grin and half-turned to leave, before adding, 'Good luck with All New Wild, by the way. They're nice guys. I met them last week – they gave me the exclusive on the single. Should be a good gig for you once The Keep finally give it up.' He winked at Alexia. 'Have fun, kids.'

Ugh. Her dad's label had given Theo an exclusive,

despite what a horrible person he was. *But that's the game*, thought Alexia.

'Well, welcome to the world of Theo Marlon. We hoped he'd piss off out of the area when his offices moved, but obviously not.' Clint sighed, and turned to Greta. 'If he or anyone from The Buzz gets in touch – which they probably will – my advice is just ignore them. Don't even reply. They might come across all friendly, but Marlon and his minions just want information, as you can see.'

'Okay.' Greta nodded earnestly.

'He's repugnant.' Alexia shook her head. 'And believe me, I've met some sleazy dudes in my time.'

'There was this guy who worked at Image Management – you know, the talent agency?' Lewis chipped in. 'Chris or Craig or whatever? He got involved with Theo. And, well, Theo outed him as a source over some story that got serious blowback online.'

'Oh god, yeah. I remember that story,' said Clint. 'Ruined his career. I mean his own fault, but ...'

'Well, I guess for Theo it's work, isn't it?' Lewis said. 'Look, guys, I've got to split. Going to see my folks for dinner. And then Avon, twenty-eight, from Battersea! Wish me luck.'

'Lewis is trying out Tinder,' Greta whispered. 'But he's never had a second date.'

The noise increased as drinks were set aside and chairs scraped back. The crowd were being ushered into the studio area to take their seats for the talk show.

'Come on, let's go in and watch the show,' Clint said. 'Alexia doesn't need all the London gossip in one night. She'll run screaming.'

'I'm not sure how long I'll last tonight,' Alexia cautioned him, realising she was starting to feel queasy from the jet lag.

'I understand. You can sneak out any time, don't worry. To be honest, this show is going to be so awful I encourage sneaking out.' He turned to Greta, who was glued to her phone. 'You coming?'

'Sorry! Yes, coming.'

They made their way with the crowd to the audience bleachers inside what was a surprisingly small studio. There were four cameras set up – three huge ones across the floor and one on a crane that could fly across the audience's heads. Alexia strained her neck to see what equipment they were using as she was ushered to a seat near the back.

The set was made up to look like a real man cave, complete with tartan throw rugs on the couch, a pool table and massive TV screen to the side. There was a neon sign fixed above the stage which read 'The Friday Late Show with Ant and Dec'.

'The little people,' Alexia whispered.

'Yes. Very famous here in Britain,' Clint whispered back.

'So I've been told.' She tapped Greta on the leg, smiling.

'Don't worry, I'll show you all of this on Monday. It's a great crowd tonight because it's mostly staff – first live night and all that.'

A guy came onto the set with a microphone and some very

loud music began to blare across the speakers as he walked up and down, urging the audience to clap along in time.

'ARE YOU READY TO HAVE SOME FUN?' he shouted into the mic, and the audience clapped loudly in response.

Alexia sat up straight.

'He's just the audience warm-up,' Clint whispered. 'I thought you would have seen this stuff before. You must have been to heaps of TV show filmings in America with the band?'

'Yeah, I have, I guess. But mostly I was out back, so I never got to see anything.'

'It's true, isn't it?' Clint looked straight at her. 'I mean, not about Lee. But Max is going solo?'

Alexia swung her head around to look Clint in the eye. 'How do you know?' she said steadily.

'He was in London recently, we caught up. I kinda thought that's why you were able to leave so quickly and come to London. Will they break up? Is Theo right?'

'I don't know,' Alexia replied, suddenly feeling like the walls were closing in on her.

'I'm not one to gossip, usually,' Clint said, 'I don't want to put you on the spot. It's just, you know, my job might depend on it.'

'I don't feel very comfortable talking about it. I feel like I'm betraying them.'

'Fair enough,' Clint said reassuringly.

'How does he know? Theo?'

'That guy has people on the payroll everywhere. He pays

well for the information, too. When Max was in London The Buzz managed to get a video of him playing his own music at a local pub. You must have seen it? Honestly, I have no idea how he moves so quickly.'

'Oh yeah, I remember that. Well, you don't need to worry about me, Clint. I am extremely discreet.'

The lights faded and Alexia took a moment to calm herself. The excitement of the day had left her feeling physically and emotionally exhausted.

It was not long ago she was boarding a plane to London, running away from The Keep, her parents, her old life and responsibilities. She was in a new bedroom, a new city and a new job, and there was very little to make her feel grounded. Even the talk of The Keep and Clint's familiar face were no comfort – in a way it was a bothersome reminder of everything she'd left behind. It was almost too overwhelming to think about, and she realised she needed to rest and be alone. Suddenly, she wanted nothing more than silence. She closed her eyes, drew in a deep breath, and felt her lip quiver.

'Are you okay, Alexia?' Greta whispered.

Weary, she accidentally snapped back her reply, 'Fine.'

Greta looked away quickly, and Alexia, too tired to apologise, turned to Clint. 'Oh my god, the jet lag. I have to . . .'

'Go,' he said, moving his legs to let her squeeze past.

58

Chapter 7

Beast of Burden

A week or so later, Greta and her granny sat in the dimly lit booth at Deniz's Diner awaiting their meal. Deniz, who had served them there for almost eight years, was slyly watching football on the TV hung above the counter. Dalston's early nightlife shuffled past outside, some in search of fried chicken and kebabs, the more recent arrivals looking for 100 per cent grass-fed bison burgers with applewood-smoked bacon and house-made pickles on a brioche bun. The wankers.

Granny always ordered the same thing – lamb kofta with a half portion of salad – no cabbage – smothered in the hottest chilli sauce, with a glass of wine – some kind of red that Deniz kept on the menu specifically for her.

'COME ON YOU SPURS!' A drunken young man had appeared in the doorway, his white Tottenham shirt splattered with a cocktail of mystery stains. When wasted meets sober: awkward silence.

'Thank you very much, young man. Now, off you go.' Granny waved him away like the queen, and, like a loyal subject, he gently pulled the door shut and skipped off into the night.

She was a curious creature, Greta's granny. Not elegant or beautiful exactly, but what they used to call handsome. She was tall, almost six foot, and towered over Greta, who was barely five foot two and must have got her height genes from her dad's side of the family. Granny had bright, grey hair cut into a sharp bob, with a short fringe, brown lipstick and round red-rimmed glasses, thick, from years of detailed work, sketching and painting. She had the long, dexterous fingers of a pianist, and her precisely manicured nails were painted a bright green.

She was flamboyant and outspoken, creative, highly educated and the smartest woman Greta had ever known. So much so that she used to make Greta feel embarrassed at the school gate – Granny's look-at-me fashion sense and doesn't-give-a-damn attitude contrasting with her own painful self-consciousness.

Greta had once longed for a more conventional upbringing, if only to help her fit in more at school. She was humiliated when her granny met her at the gate, like a brightly painted giraffe in a sea of neutral sweats. She hated standing out and wished she lived in a simple flat in north London with IKEA furniture and a cat with its own Instagram account, like normal people. Instead, they lived between Granny's canal boat and Dalston flat, which occupied two floors above an old clock shop.

'No wonder *you're* such a freak,' Kyle Sunderland had declared in front of half the class one summer, pointing at her grandmother. 'Look at your mum.'

No wonder she hung out online.

Long weekends and school holidays had been spent with her father and his girlfriend at their dairy farm outside Colchester. Greta's mum had died when she was two, something that she rarely dwelled on. It was hard to feel loss when all you'd had was a photograph and a bunch of stories told over and over for sixteen years. She could have lived with her dad, but apparently toddler Greta would scream and cry for hours on end when her granny wasn't holding her, and at some point temporary turned into permanent.

'So, how's the job since that American arrived?' Granny asked, before shouting, 'Deniz, this lamb is overcooked!'

'Go to hell, Maggie,' Deniz replied.

'I hate him,' Granny said in a stage whisper. Deniz gave Greta a wink and a wry smile over Granny's shoulder.

'We both know you and Deniz are secret soulmates.' Greta rolled her eyes as they tucked into their dinner. 'Work's not been great, to be honest.'

'What's she like?'

'Perfect. Beautiful. Efficient. Totally relaxed and confident. I feel like a big, bumbling fool next to her.'

'So, she's Grace Kelly and you're Bridget Jones. Got it,' Granny said with an eyebrow raise.

Greta flinched. 'Yes, Granny, it's true. You should see her. She's always talking with Lewis about serious film-making stuff. And Clint and her are always having their little "chats" and it's always ME who has to do the support jobs – like fetching coffee, and looking after the talent. She doesn't even wait for them to be split. She just takes all the filming jobs with the boys, and I'm left to be the general dogsbody. Entitled or what?'

'Well, perhaps you need to speak up if you want to do more of the filming?'

Greta slumped back. 'Well, I don't really want those filming jobs anyway ... and I like looking after the talent, but that's not the point.'

'I like that Lewis.'

'Yeah, he's cool. I'm always a bit on edge around him.' Granny had met Lewis once, much to Greta's embarrass-ment, at the Westfield in Stratford, outside Boots. Granny walked out with a box of tampons for Greta and made a big, obvious song and dance about how there was no room for them in her M&S Bag for Life and Greta would have to carry them because she wasn't paying another five bloody p for a plastic bag. Lewis had been utterly gentlemanly when Greta had managed to shut Granny up long enough to make an introduction, even obligingly kissing the back of Granny's hand when it was presented by way of greeting.

Greta hadn't seen Lewis as relaxed and breezy as he was that day – she'd almost got over her embarrassment about the tampon announcement, until Granny declared that Greta should ask Lewis on a date before he was out of earshot.

'But, anyway, I guess Alexia *did* work for The Keep, so her and Clint are friends from that. I just feel a bit left out.'

'Well, can you at least get lots of great insight into the band?'

'No. Not really. She's like a closed book. She NEVER talks about them, except to make stupid in-jokes with Clint that I don't get. Oh, and Granny, The Keep announced they were taking a "break" this summer, which made her even more tediously sneery and secretive.'

'A break, huh? How have the fannies taken the news?'

'Stop calling them fannies.' Greta pouted. 'There's been a sort of collective DEEP BREATH and togetherness, actually. We're keeping each other's spirits up. There haven't been any specifics about how long the break is, so it's a time for reflection, you might say.' Greta caught her own reflection in the front window and grimaced. 'Granny, can I tell you something? And can you promise not to say "I told you so" or anything like that?'

'Of course, darling.'

'I'm actually relieved that there isn't much happening with The Keep right now. I am finding it, like, so hard to juggle work and the fandom and keeping it secret is exhausting as hell.'

'I told you.'

Greta sighed. 'And some days I can't even be bothered any more. *And* Alexia's arrival has meant that I don't even do a lot of actual work Keep stuff any more. She's doing all the edits from the tour. I mean it makes sense – she was there – but I've been working on the bloody cooking show again.'

'Ooh I love *MasterChef*.'

'It's not *MasterChef*.'

'The Australian one is utterly forgettable. You'd rather have a meal out with the bald one, he's the personality.'

'Are you listening, Granny? It's not *that* cooking show. It's a Saturday morning one. It's so crap. The celebrity guests are cyclists and authors and boring people like that.'

'Hmm. What about Lee? Are you still going to marry him one day or have you finally rid yourself of that pointless infatuation?'

Greta cringed. She had been in love with Lee since she was thirteen years old, but at eighteen she now found at least *some* of her obsession embarrassing. At thirteen she thought she might love Lee forever. She fantasised about him pulling her out of the crowd at a show. About him spontaneously asking her out while being interviewed live on air by E! news. About being his girlfriend and having an H&M store card with no limit. About being picked up outside school in a pink Hummer like the one from the 'Baby, You're Humming' music video.

But now that she was eighteen, she just wanted to meet him. Just once. That would do. And maybe kiss those lips. Or go on a date. *Arghh*. Who was she kidding? She was as obsessed as ever.

'No,' Greta lied. 'I'm over him.'

'Well, this is good news. He's just a *poundstore* Mick Jagger anyway. Oooh, now there's a band. Bands in my day were far sexier, Greta. Have you listened to "Beast of Burden"?'

Greta held her hands out. 'No, no – Granny, no! Please!'

But it was too late. Granny had already taken a deep breath . . .

'*I'll never be . . . your . . .*' She belted it out in her raspy voice as Greta shrank deeply into the booth, wishing she could be swallowed up immediately.

Please don't start dancing, Greta thought, cramming her eyes shut.

Louder and louder Granny sang, standing up in the booth, swinging her hips, arms in the air. On it went, humiliating, explicit lyrics about sex and . . .

'*Am I HARD enough . . .*' Deniz chimed in from behind the counter, emphasising the mortifying lyrics with X-rated hand movements.

Christ. Greta literally died.

They both wailed together, only stopping when the door opened again and a couple wandered in, looking for a meal.

Granny laughed until she started coughing. When she caught her breath, she put her hand gently on Greta's. 'Music is great. But you can't be a "fan" for a living. You need to figure out what to do next, Greta. And if it's not this job, then throw yourself into something else rather than moping around that office waiting for snippets of info on that band. Sounds like it's not getting you much closer to them, at any rate.'

'Seems like you might have been a bit of a fangirl yourself,' Greta said pointedly.

'I was a fan. But not like you. You're consumed!'

Greta put down her knife and fork and sat back in her chair. She knew her granny was right. What point was there in being at Bright Star beyond covert-extremist fangirling?

'Surely there's something you like doing at that office?'

'Well, they gave me all the social media accounts and I'm looking after them.'

'Ugh, more fannygirling.'

'No, it's different!'

'How is it any different to what you already do for The Keep?'

'Well, it's official. I don't hide. But yeah, I do all of that same stuff. Well, someone looks over it and tells me what to write, but I do more and more on my own now. You can make a whole career out of it.'

At that moment, Greta's phone beeped. She looked up at her granny guiltily.

'Oh for heaven's sake.' Granny wiped her mouth with her paper napkin and folded her arms. 'I thought you'd turned all those bleep bleep bleeps off?'

Greta quickly unlocked her phone.

There was a notification from Theo Marlon's online gossip site, The Buzz. She had set the app up to get any news on The Keep, and since his site was notorious for breaking BIG salacious stories, it was bound to be something of interest.

She blinked. And then blinked again. It couldn't be! She opened up Twitter, holding a finger up to her granny.

'Sorry, Granny, I need to get home and make a quick ... um ... call.'

Granny slammed down her fork and glared. 'Call? To whom?'

'Okay, okay – I need to get online and speak with my people. Lee's at the Taj Mahal and everyone's losing their minds.' Greta shrugged, standing up. 'It's in my bones.'

CHAPTER 8

Bone Broke

'It's not possible,' Alexia said firmly, confusion not yet giving way to panic.

'DECLINED,' repeated the impatient delivery guy, handing back her card. 'It doesn't work. No money. You're skint,' he said, trying to make a joke of it.

Alexia looked over her shoulder at Lewis and Greta, who were exhausted by their early start, laden down with camera gear and looking embarrassed on her behalf.

'I can get it. I should have offered anyway,' Lewis said, reaching for his wallet.

'No. It's fine. I can get it – I just don't understand.' Alexia handed across her credit card. 'Can you try this one?'

The guy looked at Lewis with a sigh. 'It's the third one,' he said plainly.

'This is actually ridiculous. There must be something

wrong with your machine,' Alexia said, offsetting her embarrassment and growing concern with a stubborn tilt of her chin.

'Please, Alexia.' Lewis handed the man a £20 note. 'Don't worry. It all gets expensed anyway. Interns shouldn't be shouldering ANY costs, and you've already brought your own computer, and all that equipment.'

'I never pay for anything,' Greta offered proudly. 'Like, ever.'

Alexia grabbed the bag of burritos and tray of drinks, ushering the delivery guy out the door. 'I just don't understand though!'

'Well, we don't pay you guys much,' Lewis said with half a laugh.

'Yeah, but I should have plenty of money in there,' Alexia said, before pondering the thought like it was a new taste in her mouth. 'I think?'

Alexia had been in London for less than two weeks and had still not called her parents. Her mother had sent her nearly a dozen emails, all breathless rants about how disappointed she was in Alexia's life choices, all replied to with perfectly cutting one-liners like: 'Mom, it doesn't need to be your problem. I'm gone now.'

She was too busy loving London to dwell on her parents' meddling. The team at Bright Star were all warm and welcoming. Lewis had been paying particular attention to her, given their mutual love of film-making – he'd passed her small edit jobs and let her do some of the filming. Clint was almost always on location, filming different bands, but today he was helping them out.

Greta had also been a welcome addition to her life. Alexia had never met anyone like her, a bit annoying and childish, but endlessly bubbly and totally unrestrained – she would have never survived high school in NYC. But her altruism – letting Alexia take the better tasks, the little cups of tea, surprise deliveries of slightly burned homemade cupcakes, and the as-yet-unaccepted invitations for a walk-and-talk lunch to something called 'Tesco's' – had certainly helped Alexia feel part of the crew.

'Must be a problem at the bank or something. I'll call them,' Alexia said quickly, feeling a little ashamed of herself and feeling the first stabs of panic. *She's actually done it. I'm actually cut off.* She turned to Lewis and Greta and smiled broadly. 'Sorry! How hopeless to offer to get lunch and now this.'

'Forget it. We have to get the rest of the gear set up.' Lewis motioned for her to hurry and they all turned to lug the last of the gear into the hotel room, where Clint was moving around all the furniture. 'The band will be here soon and we've only got two hours with them.'

They were filming an interview with All New Wild, followed by a short acoustic performance. The British quartet were pegged to be bigger than The Keep, and more respected, since they played instruments and wrote some of their own songs. Alexia thought the content would be 'dull as dishwater', a phrase she's picked up from Greta, but she used every job as an opportunity to learn how to use the camera and sound gear, and how to frame the perfect shot to tell the best story.

Greta and Alexia were wrestling with a light reflector when there was a sharp rap on the door. Lewis clambered over their kit and when he swung the door open a familiar face appeared.

'MEL!' Alexia ran forward and threw her arms around her friend, plunging her face into the huge red afro and inhaling its familiar smell of jasmine and cigarette smoke.

'Sweetheart!' Mel squeezed her tightly. 'What on EARTH are you doing here?'

Mel had managed The Keep's European tour, and had been Alexia's Tour Mother throughout. It could only be a month or so since they'd last been together, but to Alexia it seemed like an age.

'I left Falls Records. I'm in London now,' Alexia said, proudly. 'I work at Bright Star. But . . . what are *you* doing here?'

'Well, I figured since the boys were taking some time out, I better take another job.' Mel grinned. 'I'm taking these guys on their promotional tour. Can't say no to your dad.'

'It's so good to see you.' Alexia let go of the hug, wiping away a tear in the corner of her eye. She was surprised at how emotional this tenuous connection to home and her past life had made her.

'Have you been in touch with the guys since you left? I bet they miss you.'

Alexia was suddenly aware of Greta hovering next to her. 'Mel – this is Greta. She's also at Bright Star, we do the same job, kind of. Greta, meet Mel – Tour Manager for The Keep and now … All New Wild.'

'Nice to meet you, sweetheart.' Mel smiled warmly.

'Hi, I'm Greta. I work with Alexia.'

'Yes, darling, I got that. Aren't you absolutely gorgeous.' Mel knew how to make anyone feel at ease. 'So, you want to be a film-maker too?'

'Oh, no. I just want to meet famous people,' Greta said, laughing. Alexia and Mel looked at each other. 'I'm kidding! Who would want to do that? How tragic.'

'Well, I think it's just gorgeous you're here and chasing your dream, Alexia,' Mel said. 'Don't you worry about your parents.'

Alexia felt relieved to have Mel's support, particularly considering how long Mel had worked with her father. 'Anyway, I thought the boys would be here already and I'm really just saying hello. I'll head down to the lobby and catch them there. Let me get out of your way and we can catch up afterwards. Can I take you for dinner?'

'Oh, yes please.' Alexia smiled, hugging Mel again. 'A girl can't exist on microwave dinners and takeaway Sushi alone.'

'Oh, you mean ready meals? I love ready meals.' Greta piped up. 'Specially the posh ones from Markies.'

'Alexia!' Lewis called out from across the suite. 'I'm setting up.'

Alexia nodded goodbye to Mel and was quickly at Lewis's side, earnestly helping with the camera set-up while Greta worked with Clint to ready the area where the band would be sitting.

'You know a lot of people in this business,' Lewis said, helping Alexia unpack the boom mic. She plugged the large headphones into the camera and found the correct cables to attach to the microphone and fastened the whole thing onto the pole.

'Oh my god, you have no idea. Like, seriously. Pick someone famous – and I bet I've met them,' Alexia sighed.

'Sounds like a real drag,' Lewis said with a smirk and handed her the spare batteries for the camera. 'Can you check these are both charged?'

'They're charged.' She smiled at him. 'Sorry. It's weird to explain unless you've grown up in ...' Her voice trailed off.

'A rich, white, privileged bubble?' said Lewis, teasingly.

'No. I mean yes. I just mean that I don't really get what the big deal is with "meeting" a famous person.' She blushed, feeling annoyed, before adding quickly, 'I was really lucky to have the opportunities I had.'

Alexia had learnt the hard way not to complain too much about her life, even if she wanted to all the time. It was that kind of talk that isolated her at school.

'Must have been a riot being on tour for so long with The Keep.'

Lewis had a way of making her feel slightly embarrassed

about her time with The Keep. Like most guys, he didn't understand the appeal – they were strictly for teenage girls.

'My little sister is obsessed. I tried but failed to get her into John Williams.' Lewis smirked again, standing up to check the way the shot looked through the camera. He moved the tripod backwards and raised everything up a few inches, then, after a couple of moments, looked back at Alexia. 'She's obsessed with *this* band, I mean. All New Wild. Between you and me, she thinks The Keep are boring.'

'Well, they've been around for a long time.' Alexia shrugged.

'Greta, can you go and sit on the sofa so I can check the lighting,' Clint shouted across the room. Greta had made her way over to the burritos and was leaning over the table, ready to pounce.

'Sorry!' she said with a jump. 'I'm starving!'

'Let's set up. Then we can quickly eat,' Lewis said sternly.

Greta always seemed a bit disinterested in the filming, but today she seemed even more tired and distracted than usual. They'd all had an early start but she looked like she hadn't slept a wink.

On almost every job, Greta would offer to do anything that didn't involve the technical stuff. But when the talent arrived she really came alive – she was bubbly, warm, efficient and attentive, and they all adored her. It suited Alexia just fine too, since the last thing she wanted to do was deal with the 'talent'. She was done with that. Alexia watched Greta put a burrito back on the table and caught the look of humiliation on her face.

'I can sit in shot,' Alexia offered. 'If you're starving, Greta. Go ahead.'

'Thanks, Alexia.' Lewis and Alexia shared a smile while he taped cables to the carpet.

Alexia plonked herself down on the sofa, which was surprisingly hard, causing both her UK and US phones to bang hard into her butt. She pulled them out and set them next to her, before picking up the All New Wild limited-press vinyl from the table in front of her. Lewis and Clint fiddled with the lighting.

'Look up at me,' Lewis ordered, peering into the camera. His face was stern and focused.

She looked up and straight down the lens but, feeling a bit uncomfortable, shifted her focus past him to the mirror at the back of the room. Her phone vibrated, but she didn't dare move to look at it.

'Can we do something about the shadow under her eyes?' Lewis said to Clint.

'No.' She smirked.

'Yep,' Clint said, adjusting a huge circular reflector until the lights were just on the edge of uncomfortable.

'Look down the barrel,' Lewis said. 'No. Right down.'

He leaned over and peered into the viewer, turning the lens on the front.

'Perfect,' he said, standing up. 'That's the shot.'

Clint burst out laughing, and Alexia felt suddenly flustered and self-conscious. 'What?' she said. 'What's so funny?'

'Lewis thinks he's Christopher Nolan.' Clint laughed some more. '"That's the shot,"' he said, mimicking Lewis's faint Irish accent.

'Oh, piss off,' Lewis said with a hint of embarrassment, flicking off the camera. 'Let's eat, for christ's sake.'

Alexia picked up her US phone, flicking through the dozen or so notifications she had received this morning. And there it was – another missed call from her dad – *Probably a heads up about the allowance being cut*, she thought. Just as she was about to put her phone away it buzzed again. With a deep breath, she answered.

'James,' she paused. 'Dad.'

'Alexia. Hi. I've been trying to call.' Alexia could imagine her dad on the other end of the phone, twisting his black hair into little spikes, playing with his coffee cup. It was 7 a.m. in New York – he would be down in the kitchen having his protein shake in his stupid bike shorts before cycling off to CrossFit.

'I know. Sorry. I can't talk long.'

'It's okay, I'll be quick. We … well, I just wanted to check in,' he said, the slight echo on the line giving away his supposedly stealthy use of speakerphone. She could picture her mother disapprovingly listening in, lips pursed, arms crossed.

'Your mom is upset, darling. Please get in touch with her.'

'She made you call, right? Is she there?' Alexia tapped her foot on the ground, rolling her eyes at the predictability.

'No. It's just me.' He lied so badly. 'Although we both want to know how you are.'

'Riiiiight,' Alexia said. 'Well, I'll be fine. I have enough money of my own, so do stop the allowance and credit card, if you haven't already.' She hoped she was a better liar than her dad.

There was a pause. 'How are you enjoying London?'

'It's great. I'm working lots. And I've got a cosy flat above a cute little market. I couldn't feel more at home.' She delivered this practised sound bite with acute nonchalance. Then, after holding up a single finger to Lewis and mouthing 'one minute' across the room, she tossed in a casual, 'How're you?'

'Good. Well. We're holding auditions for a new band. A girl band, actually. There's a real gap in the market. Geoff calls it a thigh gap.' Alexia could hear him placing a cup into the dishwasher, then shifting it again, no doubt after drawing an admonishing frown from their housekeeper, Dotty, for not 'filling from the back'. Oprah's bark sounded in the background, causing Alexia a brief pining flutter. 'To be honest, we're all worrying about how we're going to compete with K-pop. Everything's going Korean. You can't swing a fork in this town without hitting a side of kimchi.'

'A girl band sounds great,' Alexia said wearily.

'Well, we hope so. The board are worried since The Keep are on their way out the door – but it's been coming for a while.' He sighed. 'And now, with Lee AWOL.'

'LEE?' Alexia yelped. 'What's happened with Lee?'

'Are you not in touch? Huh,' he said shortly. 'You really don't know?'

'What's happened?' Her heart began to quicken.

'I thought you'd know. I believe Jessica finally broke up with him. Just after you left, actually. And he's taken off to India on some kind of soul-searching madness. We're not sure. No one is.'

'Really? But he can't even book an airline ticket. He can't even PACK A SUITCASE.' She turned her back on the room, aware that Greta was staring. 'I had to show him how to use a toaster,' she whispered.

'Yeah. He's gone. It was in all the newspapers, all over the Internet. You didn't see?'

'No. I don't follow them any more, and it's not like I have any buddies into them enough to alert me,' she said, her voice breaking slightly as her mind raced. Lee and Jessica broke up. The moment she had dreamed about had finally happened and it wasn't the exquisite delight she'd always expected it to be. She felt a little light-headed.

'Well, we've been trying to keep things quiet but some pap snapped him at the Taj Mahal sitting alone on that Princess Diana seat.'

'Poor Lee.' Alexia could hear the anxiety in her voice and wanted out of the conversation. 'Sorry, I'm super busy, James. I have to go.'

'Okay, Alexia. Promise me you're okay?'

'Yeah. I really have to go.' She quickly added: 'Hi Mom. Bye Mom.'

She hung up the phone and took a moment to breathe, the silence in the room behind her making her immediately uneasy. How much had they heard?

She turned around and looked from one gaping face to the other.

'Sorry. My dad,' Alexia explained coolly, walking over to grab her lunch. 'There's always a drama.'

'Was that news about Lee?' Clint asked, Greta coughing loudly into her burrito and knocking her Fanta all over the carpet in the process. She realised that it must have been common knowledge to everyone but her.

'Because, OMG. The papers.' Clint raised an eyebrow. 'I was going to ask you later if you knew anything.'

'Yeah. He was just wondering if I'd heard from him because they still contact me sometimes to ask for help with stuff,' she mumbled, playing the game. She was not about to show she cared.

'Oh yeah, I'm pretty sure I saw a photo of him moping about at the Diana seat,' Greta piped up. 'Maybe, in the paper or somewhere. I wasn't really paying attention. I mean, who can keep up, right? Is it true him and that actress broke up?'

'I guess so,' Alexia said, the words making her stomach leap, 'though they've broken up before ...' she added, reminding herself more than anyone.

'I always thought they were a weird pairing,' Clint said,

screwing up his wrapper and tossing it into the bin, 'she's like this statuesque, posh, red-haired beauty-queen bore and he's a bit . . . fake rock-and-roll, boys-on-tour-party boy. He wasn't exactly faithful, either. Not on tour.'

Alexia shot Clint a look. 'Well, I never saw anything.'

'He took what he wanted. They all do.' Clint shrugged. 'You'd have to be utterly bonkers to date someone famous. I guess that's why they always end up together.'

'Probably,' said Alexia, feeling suddenly down. 'Guys, I'm really careful – as you know – about what I say about them in public. Can I trust you all to keep this to yourselves?'

'Are you going to call him?' Greta said, suddenly sounding anxious. She was on her hands and knees, mopping up Fanta, face flushed, bum in the air.

'Probably. After this.' Alexia nodded to the empty interview set-up as her nerves began to settle and a wildly annoying maternal concern crept in. He'd lost his band and his girl-friend. She hoped he was okay, even though he *was* prone to dramatics.

Just at that moment, the door swung open and in sauntered All New Wild. Alexia felt transported back to every press interview she'd ever attended with The Keep. They were made-up, puffed-up and 'on' – Alexia rolled her eyes as she quickly wrapped up her untouched lunch and tucked it into a bag.

Greta was up on her feet, greeting the band immediately. All the smiles. All the sweetness. The singer, Nav, even got a hug from her.

One of the boys swaggered over and pointed to Alexia's cold can of coke, which she was dying for and just about to drink.

'Is that mine?' he asked, without looking at her.

'Sure.' Alexia's teeth were gritted behind her smile.

CHAPTER 9

Run the World (Girls)

It was earlier than Alexia would normally arrive, but there was much to do. Lewis had promised her she could cut the first version of documentary on The Keep's European tour, a huge deal. It had been commissioned by ITV and was due to air before the release of their Christmas single later in the year, and she wanted to get ahead. She came out of the lift and headed for the main door . . .

'Alexia,' a voice whispered loudly. Greta stuck her head out from behind the door of the accessible bathroom and shower cubicle in the third-floor foyer, opposite the mercifully unmanned reception desk. 'Alexia, I need to speak to you. It's an absolute catastrophe.'

One side of Greta's hair was scrunched up and frizzy and standing near vertical, her red lipstick was smeared down one cheek and she had a white line of dry dribble down the side of her mouth. She was shielding her body with the door, but Alexia could see a purple bra strap on a very bare shoulder.

'Where is your shirt? Are you just in your bra?'

'Quick! Before someone comes,' Greta begged, as the lift behind Alexia dinged to signal it was about to open.

'What happened?'

'QUICK.' Greta ducked back behind the door as the lift doors opened. 'PLEASE.'

Karen and Kevin came out together, deep in conversation. Karen looked briefly over to Alexia, taking her in completely in a split second. It was unnerving. Alexia smiled at them both, pretending to head for the lifts, and when they were out of sight she slipped into the accessible toilet cubicle.

A large rug from the photocopy area had been dragged in and rolled into a makeshift mattress. Greta had nicked two cushions from Kevin's office couch as pillows and the crudely painted white sheet that was used as a filming backdrop was her blanket. Greta had clearly slept there last night.

'I know how this looks, but it really isn't as bad as you think.'

Greta held her hands across herself to cover the ratty old bra she was wearing. Thankfully, she still had her skirt and tights on.

'Oh my god, Greta. What happened?'

'It's kinda hazy after JJ's.'

'What's JJ's?'

'That nasty dive of a nightclub at the back of Sainsbury's.'

'The what?'

'It doesn't matter now,' Greta said. 'I need my top.'

'I can see that.'

Greta picked up one of the cushions and held it to her chest. 'This is comfortably in the top ten worst things I've ever done.'

Alexia burst out laughing. 'It'll be fine. Did you go out after the filming?'

'Can I fill you in later?' She jumped every time the lift bell went. 'It's nearly nine.'

'Okay. Where's your shirt?'

'It's in Kevin's office.'

'Oh god.' Alexia giggled again.

'Stop laughing.'

'I can't help it. Why is it in Kevin's office?'

'I spilt beer on it and took it off to hang on his radiator. Oh my god. This is a disaster.' Greta's mortification was so comical that Alexia was struggling to keep a straight face. 'Stop laughing at me!' Greta said, bursting into laughter herself. She flushed the toilet to hide the noise, her voice dropping to a whisper. 'Shhhh,' she pleaded. 'Oh god, Alexia. Please help me. Quickly.'

'Okay.' Alexia looked around. 'Give me the rug and I'll do some recon – see if Kevin is in his office. Give me five.'

'We need a secret knock,' Greta said.

'What for?'

'For when you come back. A secret knock. A bloody *knock* so I know it's you,' Greta said, freaking out. 'Sorry.'

'Don't worry,' Alexia said, 'I'll do this.' She knocked three times quickly on the tiled wall and then twice slowly. 'Got it?'

Greta nodded. 'Thank you. What do I do if you get caught up?'

'I'll text you.' Alexia tried to be serious. 'Please don't worry. I've handled much worse than this before. I once had to sneak Lee out of Tokyo airport naked, and with no passport.'

Greta opened her mouth to speak, but instead sat back down on the toilet seat, looking utterly dejected. 'Did you contact him?'

'I called, but his phone was off,' she replied. 'Now, sit tight. We've got this.'

Alexia rolled up the rug and slipped it under her arm. She pressed her ear to the door, waiting until the foyer was quiet, and slipped out. She heard Greta slide the lock as she strode assuredly through the office to drop the rug back by the photocopier. The more confident you looked, the less people were likely to question you. 'Fake it till you make it,' her mother used to say.

Next, she swung by Kevin's office. He was sitting alone at his desk, stroking his beard with one hand, clicking his mouse with the other. His glass door was shut, and it was better to leave it that way for the moment. She needed a plan B-top for Greta.

She strode off towards the art department. Luckily, they were all late in as usual. Quick as a wink, she slipped through to wardrobe and grabbed a plain white T-shirt off a hanger.

Then she grabbed a hand towel and some make-up remover from make-up. She swung by her desk, collected her own make-up bag and a large camera bag, and was back out in the foyer by the lifts. She'd been gone less than ten minutes. Steady streams of people were arriving now, but she was able to quickly dispatch the secret knock.

'Have a shower,' Alexia said, pointing to the cubicle, 'here's a plain shirt from wardrobe – they won't miss it – and here's my make-up and hairbrush.'

Greta's huge eyes were full of gratefulness. 'Oh, Alexia.'

'Hurry up now. Maybe wash your hair – it kinda smells of cigarettes.'

'Their manager,' Greta explained. 'At least, I don't remember smoking. I'd better hurry.'

'I'm going to sneak off with the rest of this stuff now. Kevin is busy and I can pretend we borrowed them for a shoot,' she said, tucking the white sheet and cushions under her arm and picking up the camera bag. 'See? I look like I've been working.'

Greta smiled meekly. 'What can I do to thank you?'

'Take me to lunch at Tesco's, I've earned it.'

Greta threw her arms around Alexia. 'Oh my god, you're like a miracle.'

For a moment Alexia stood still. She wasn't used to warmth like this from someone her age. She pondered the situation, before returning the hug. 'See you in a bit. And you have to tell me what happened.'

*

A few hours later the two of them were sitting on a bench by the green outside Jamie's Italian, eating a Tesco meal deal, waving away pigeons and watching the world go by. Greta looked completely fresh and had even helped herself to a full face of Alexia's make-up, which, despite being rather hastily applied, looked fab on her.

'This is pretty good, and just a couple of quid!' Alexia enthused. 'I need to be more frugal like this.'

'Frugal? This is a treat. I normally reheat leftover dinner,' said Greta.

'Oh, that's the smell from the kitchen?' teased Alexia, making a mental note to do a thorough budget. If she could budget a shoot, she could budget her dwindling finances.

'Ha. Yes, reheated fish really does stink. I'm so sorry! You know, the British say sorry for everything. Even if we haven't done anything wrong. Like if I bang into you,' Greta explained, shoving Alexia with her shoulder. 'Like that. *You* would say sorry as well as me. It's all in the tone. And if someone says "it was lovely to meet you" it means the conversation is over and they don't want to speak to you any more. And *maybe* always means *no*. *Always*, mind. Like if you asked me to go for lunch and I said *maybe*, that means no. And never make a northerner a tea, you'll only get it wrong. In fact no American should really ever make a British person tea.'

'Is *that* why you guys never let me make tea then?'

'Absolutely.'

'Brits are weird,' Alexia laughed.

'Americans are,' countered Greta.

'This is just like *The Princess Diaries*.'

'Oh my god I love that film. It's my very very very secret pleasure.'

'Never tell anyone, but I might just have it on Blu-ray at home.' Alexia giggled. 'I truly delight in any "American girl comes to England to learn how to make tea and be posh" type films.'

'Well, I can help with the tea, but oh god I'm not posh. My mum was from Essex and my father is from Durham ... so.'

'What does that mean?' Alexia asked, genuinely confused. 'Where are your parents?'

'Dad makes cheese in Colchester with his new wife. I see him heaps though, but who wants to live in the country? And Mum, well, she died.'

'Oh, I'm so sorry.'

'It's okay, I was two.' Greta smiled. 'You can't be upset about what you don't know.'

Alexia's mind drifted to thoughts of her own mom again, interfering in her life at every given moment. *And yet to not have her at all ...*

'So, what happened last night?' Alexia tucked her dry, half-eaten egg sandwich back in its plastic wrapper and opened her bag of sea salt and cracked pepper crisps.

'I went out after the shoot. Look, full disclosure: I haven't been to a wrap party before. Or an after party.' She swung around as she spoke, so she was facing Alexia. 'Anyway, I drank too much. It was ridiculous. They brought out these drinks in hollowed-out pineapples. You can't say no to a pineapple drink. And there were a lot of really great power ballads. And that's all I remember clearly. Nav helped me back to the office, for reasons I hope to one day understand. I think I might have told him I lived there.'

'He's the singer, right?' Alexia said, raising her eyebrows.

'Yes. He's dead nice. And from near where I live. Like old socks, as my granny would say.' Greta paused for a moment. 'But he wasn't drinking ... Oh god.' She put her head in her hands. 'I might have danced inappropriately to "Pour Some Sugar On Me". You know how you just get flashes of things you did?'

'No, I'm not much of a party girl.'

'I bet you went to some really lush parties in New York.'

'I went to a few.' Alexia shrugged. 'I kind of rejected all the music industry stuff though, cos Mom and Dad rammed it down my throat. Not the fun stuff. No. They wanted me to learn about the business side. You won't believe this but Mom actually refused to let me learn the guitar.'

'What?' said Greta, aghast. 'That's so weird, considering ...'

'I know. Tell me about it. I think Dad's seen too many girls get chewed up and spat out or whatever. To be honest, they don't really respect the music very much. God. Don't tell anyone I said that. My parents wanted me to go to college so badly, Greta. Dad never did, and even though their very success kind of negates the argument that I *need* to go, they just won't let it go.'

She hunched her shoulders, feeling the frustration rising. 'And I just want to film stuff. I want to be a film-maker. Ever since I saw the first music video being shot – I was like, I don't want to be anyone else on the set but that dude in the cap sitting by the monitor.'

'Who's the dude?'

Alexia laughed. 'The director!'

'Oh. Right. Of course,' said Greta, looking confused. 'That's great that you have a dream, or goal or ... an idea of what you want.'

'Don't you?'

'Not really. I don't think I'm good at anything, really.'

'Everyone's good at *something*,' said Alexia firmly. 'My mom drilled that into me from really young. Find what makes you sing. As long as it isn't singing!'

They both burst into laughter, Alexia momentarily relaxing.

'So your mum is in music too?'

'She was. She had a kind of ... emotional timeout, when I was thirteen.' Alexia grinned at Greta.

'What do you mean?' Greta's face was so full of genuine concern it was disarming.

'A mid-life crisis or some crap,' Alexia said, dismissively.

For a moment they sat in silence. Alexia knew there was an expectation she would expand on this, but she couldn't. She still didn't really understand to this day what had happened – she was simply told that Mom was sick, and she would be leaving work for a while. Her mom, who had never sat down or relaxed a day in her life, was suddenly home all the time, though not exactly present. Alexia received no explanation, other than 'Mom is sick', or sometimes Dad would say 'very tired'.

Her mom would try, hopelessly, to make Alexia her first ever packed lunch one day, and the next, just sit on the balcony in a robe, staring motionless out across the Manhattan skyline.

In the year following, Alexia started high school, got her period and had her first kiss. Her mom was either too tired to listen to her stories or too disengaged to *really* listen. Though Alexia was told she shouldn't take it personally, it still did hurt, and when her mom tried to properly engage, it made Alexia feel uncomfortable anyway. Like it was forced – something her therapist told her to do to help make things feel normal at home. Alexia stopped inviting people over because it was too weird to explain all the strange rules designed to keep her mother calm which had become a normal part of Alexia's life.

A year or so later, she remembered the sound of the ensuite shower running as she passed by her parents' bedroom. It was 7.30 a.m. Her mother was up well before lunch. There was coffee on. Her dad was smiling.

'She's fine now,' Alexia said quickly.

'Oh, I'm sorry.' Greta gave Alexia's leg a quick squeeze.

'Well, she reinvented herself as a life coach afterwards. So, you can imagine how supportive she is of me chasing my dreams.'

'That's great!'

'I'm being sarcastic. She only wants me chasing the life she's planned out for me,' Alexia said flatly. 'Anyway, I'm not much of a fan of the music industry.'

Alexia had never said this out loud before, but it was true. She could see Greta gawping at her from the corner of her eye. 'I mean, don't get me wrong, no one wants to complain when Justin Timberlake and J-Roc are sitting in your lounge. But it wasn't as fun, or, like, the social currency at school you'd expect it to be.'

'What?' Greta threw her hands up. 'Oh my god, you would have been SO POPULAR at my school.'

'Never seemed to work out that way. The other kids were jealous of me.'

'Or they thought you were a bit up yourself,' Greta teased, but her relaxed and easy delivery did not stop Alexia from feeling a bit hurt.

'Excuse me?' said Alexia, sharply.

'I'm teasing. Up yourself was the wrong way to put it,' Greta said hastily. 'Sorry. Oh, I'm sorry, Alexia, I didn't mean to be hurtful. I was teasing. And anyway, you're not the only one who didn't crowd-surf through school.'

'It was exhausting, actually,' Alexia said, scrunching up her crisp packet as the pigeons began to descend.

'Is it okay to admit *I'm* a little bit jealous?' Greta smiled at her, her mouth starting to run off, as it did when she got nervous. 'I mean, I'm not going to be an arsehole about it, but it's rather glamorous. Oh my god. I can just picture all the cava and cashmere. And I'm glad you joined Bright Star, despite the fact you're a huge threat with all your bloody experience. But yeah, it's been nice to have another girl in our tiny team, even if you're American and you can't make tea.'

Alexia softened. She felt a surge of warmth for Greta, and a momentary feeling of belonging. She reminded herself why she had broken out, and why she had come to London, and it was this – to escape New York and to find her place. A large seagull flapped his wings right by the remains of Alexia's sandwich. 'Crap! We're surrounded!'

'Seagulls attack people in Cornwall. You know, if you have chips – fries – they swoop. Can take an eye out, I heard.'

'What?' Alexia said, starting as a pigeon jumped up and sat next to her on the bench, trying to get at her sandwich.

'I like pigeons,' Greta said. 'Everyone hates them, but I like them. I heard that rats eat their feet while they're asleep. Imagine that?'

'Shall we get back?' Alexia said, feeling 100 per cent grossed out. 'I really need to get on with my work.'

'Sure.' Greta brushed her crumbs onto the ground and looked on happily as the birds gathered at her feet.

CHAPTER 10

Harvester of Hearts

Greta knocked on the small bathroom cubicle while the canal boat swayed gently from side to side. She had squeezed her ankles into a pair of strappy sandals, with a heel just big enough to be difficult to stand in on an unstable surface. She was going to be late for work if her granny didn't hurry.

'Granny, can I get in there? I need to do my eye make-up.'

'Yes, dear. Sorry, it was time for an emergency foot exfoliation. My right heel was hard as a paddleboard,' Granny said, opening the door as she dropped her filthy foot file into the bin, before adding proudly, 'I finally wore that thing out.'

She squeezed out of the doorway wearing a silk dressing gown, followed closely by Teal, her black-and-white cocker spaniel, who limped down the hallway of the boat on his three remaining legs. 'You don't *need* make-up, darling,' Granny called as she flicked on the kettle.

Greta hardly ever wore make-up, and if she did it would be a two-hour affair with a YouTube tutor at her side, guiding her through every stage. Today, she had just eight minutes.

She attempted a kind of Amy Winehouse cat's-eye flick, but in her hurried excitement she ended up looking more like a dog with an eye patch. In a panic, she rubbed and spread the black line further round her eyes.

Bloody hell, Greta, you look like you've been beaten up! GET A GRIP.

She went on rubbing until the effect was more of a smoky eye. It was hard to tell how it really looked in the dim light of the canal boat, but it would have to do. If she didn't leave soon she would be late for work, and given that she already looked a little more dressed up than usual she didn't want to stand out any more.

'Where are you meeting him?'

'I'm not *meeting* him, he's just coming to see Alexia and I want to make sure I don't look like trash.'

'Well, you know what they say. Don't meet your idol.' Granny handed Greta her satchel and gave her a kiss on the cheek. 'I mean to say, don't be disappointed, will you?'

'I won't.'

Granny gave her a squeeze and smiled. 'I'm kind of excited for you. I admit it. He's going to love you.'

Greta jumped out onto the towpath, dodging the morning joggers as she hot-footed it to the bus stop. The bus crawled along at a snail's pace towards King's Cross and she jumped out early, knowing she'd be faster on foot, but then somehow ended up in a Costa ordering a caramel mochaccino with whipped cream and a cinnamon swirl.

The Monday after their Tesco lunch, she and Alexia had been sitting across from each other at the tiny desk when the return call finally came in. Greta had put her headphones on, pretending to listen to music while she eavesdropped on every word. Alexia seemed jumpy, frustrated by the call, but was obliging.

'What the hell's going on?' Alexia had almost shouted. 'Everyone's looking for you. What were you doing at the Taj Mahal? You hate spicy food! No, I've not been to Goa. Which guru? Yes, of course I know The Beatles! I heard she broke up with you. Well, no I'm not surprised, you kept lying to her. I can't hear you over the train. Yes. No. Is that a goat?'

Some of it was hard to decipher, but then, as the conversation became more and more surreal, Alexia dropped a bombshell.

'Okay, fine. When do you want to come? Where do you want to stay? I'm in Angel. No. There's no room. You'd have to sleep in the bathtub with Jez. My neighbour. I didn't think so. This week? Can't you book it yourself? How did you get to India then? Argghh. Okay. I'll call you in a second.'

Alexia had hung up and scowled while Greta tried to look as casual as possible, despite her fingers trembling and her knees jiggling violently under the table.

'I couldn't help hearing. Was that Lee?'

'Yes. Lee. I wish I'd never called him now.'

'Why, what's happened?'

'He wants to come to London. What's that banging noise?' Alexia had said, irritated as she peered under the table. Greta froze.

Every sound, every plan, every person in the world disappeared from Greta's vision in that instant. Lee wants to come to London? BINGO! She instantly pretended to sort through the invoices in front of her as her heart thumped in her chest.

'Oh, that will be nice. To catch up. Will he come here? To work? That would be good, to see where you worked. Maybe. I guess he doesn't really know what work is like. I mean, he *works* right, but not *works*. Work like this. I like work.' Greta had found herself increasingly unable to keep cool around Alexia, especially when Lee was mentioned. It had taken all her will to hold in the excitement. She'd have to excuse herself and go to the bathroom to silently scream in a cubicle, because she couldn't give Alexia an inkling of how she was feeling, especially after she'd revealed how much The Keep and music-biz stuff annoyed her.

'I don't know. I'll just book him into a hotel and hopefully he'll have something to do. Honestly. He can be such a pain in the ass,' Alexia had said, her cool, upbeat perfection ever so slightly ruffled.

'Were you close?' Greta had asked, hardly able to hold her

now-cold cup of tea without shaking, using all her fangirl superpowers to remain chill.

'Well, we spoke, but I was staff, so that's the job, right? Max was probably the nicest, but even he still asked me to do ridiculous errands for him from time to time.' Alexia had stopped for a moment, and cleared her throat, sipping on the large bottle of Evian she always kept next to her computer. Greta had momentarily fixated on this extra expense for a moment. And the ten quid's worth of sashimi box next to it. Perhaps this was why she never came to lunch with her? She had more expensive taste? Maybe she should stop asking her to walk to Tesco's for an egg sandwich.

'Anyway. You'll meet him I'm sure, I'll get him to come by. If you want to?' Alexia had looked straight at Greta; her face gave nothing away but for a short moment Greta had been terrified she'd been sprung.

'Oh sure,' she'd said casually. 'I've worked on the band stuff long enough – nice to finally say a quick hello, I guess.'

It was enough. Lee was arriving and today was the day. The day of Music in The Park. Greta didn't even mind having to work on a Saturday. Lee was popping by to pick Alexia up and then she was taking him for coffee. And whether Alexia brought him upstairs to say hello or not, Greta was going to make damn sure she happened to be outside when his car pulled up.

But it wasn't going to be easy.

When she arrived at work everyone was in a bit of a fuss. Though they were thoroughly organised for the shoot, Bright Star had been roped in at the last minute to cover the main stage, not just do the usual crowd shots and promotional material. It was a big deal, and they were under some real pressure to get things perfect.

'Greta – you're late,' was the only greeting from Lewis as she clip-clopped into the production meeting. 'What happened? What happened to your eyes? Have you been crying?'

Her eyes. She forgot to check them in the daylight.

'I was cutting onions,' she said quickly, pulling out her phone to check her look in the camera. He was right, these were not gentle, smoky eyes; they were the eyes of a girl with two left hands trying to apply make-up on a swaying canal boat.

'Onions for breakfast?' Clint said, suspiciously.

'Yes. An omelette. With cheese. And onions.' She licked her finger and rubbed the underneath of her eye. 'For Granny,' she added, remembering the breakfast she was carrying.

'Love the lipstick, really matches the shoes.' Alexia smiled, nodding approvingly before pulling a concerned face. 'Did you bring a spare pair for the shoot? Sneakers?'

'Oh, yes, of course,' Greta lied, immediately panicked. 'What's the plan?'

'Guys, we've really gotta hurry,' Lewis interjected. 'The van is coming in twenty minutes. Where were we?'

'Running through the timings,' Clint said, holding up the production schedule that Alexia had put together.

Greta felt humiliated and slipped into her chair, meekly opening the Costa bag to liberate her cinnamon swirl from a brown bag, which crackled at a million decibels every time she tried to open it a little. Then the swirl crackled when she bit into it. Then she spilled her coffee trying to gently take the lid off. And there was no napkin in the bag. She used the edge of her shirt and looked up to see Alexia watching her with a bemused grin.

You're wearing make-up too! Greta thought, irritated. *I would never draw attention to it on you! Even though I want to know what that beautiful caramel shade of lipgloss is! It looks so expensive. So New York.*

'Clint and I will head down to meet the other production company who are covering the acoustic and smaller stages and all the major interviews. We're supporting THEM, remember, so we have to be at our super-efficient best. Their producer is going to go over the set-up on the main stage. I'll meet the team at eleven – we have three cameras confirmed, and the sound.' Lewis smiled at Clint.

'Yep.' Clint nodded.

'So, Alexia, you'll be down at three p.m.?'

'Maybe earlier,' Alexia said. 'I'll get my friend settled and come straight by. But you'll have Greta.'

'You will?' Greta quickly scanned the production schedule. 'Yes. Oh yes. I'm there all day setting up.'

'Well, not setting up exactly, but we need a runner for the morning.'

Greta's heart sank. She hadn't bothered to read Alexia's stupid colour-coded Excel schedule last night, she'd been too busy thinking about Lee coming into the office and how he would see her and be bewitched by her awkward beauty. Instead, she would be getting coffees and holding cables for these stoooopid guys. And why was she always the bloody runner? Alexia was an intern, too. *AND SHE IS STILL NEW.* Greta swallowed her huff.

'Okay, great,' she said flatly. 'Can't wait.'

'Well, we have to go. Cabs and van will be outside in ... fifteen minutes,' Lewis said. 'This is gonna be fun!'

Greta avoided eye contact with everyone as they all stood up, pretending instead to be reviewing the production schedule as they filed out into the corridor. She wouldn't be meeting Lee. No sparks would fly. No dreams would come true. As the last person left, she sat, with smudged black eyes, a coffee stain and croissant flakes down her front, and decided it was probably for the best.

CHAPTER 11

Here You Come Again

TO ALEXIA: Just come and meet me and we can
take it from there.

Theo Marlon again. She wasn't sure how he'd got her number, but she wished she'd never entered into dialogue with him. The call had lasted less than a minute, and instead of replying 'piss off, you total bastard' to his invitation to come and chat about The Keep, she'd replied 'I'll think about it.' *Classic, Alexia. You just can't say a firm no, can you? Always leaving a toe in the door.* And now he wouldn't go away.

She slipped her phone into her back pocket and gazed out across the grassy field beyond the backstage fence at Music in the Park. The sun was low in the sky, but its gentle warmth radiated against her skin. No. As tempting as it was to rattle off a few secrets to Theo to get her out of her financial bind, she would have to take some paid night shifts at work, ingesting footage and transcoding rushes and that would be that. She could make this work. Maybe she could stay with Clint in his London Fields flat, if it came to it. Borrow some money off someone? No, it wouldn't come to that. She could scrape by to the end of the year and secure a full-time paid job.

'Sexi Lexi,' Lee said, arriving back with a couple of beers and a smattering of small coins. 'Here's your change. Twenty per cent tip was enough, right?'

'Thanks, Lee,' Alexia said, letting out a huge sigh as she lay back on the cool, damp earth. He hadn't had cash, of course. And now Alexia didn't either.

He'd arrived at Bright Star in a black cab with two small leather totes and no money to pay the driver. His skin was tanned yet somehow sallow and he was skinnier than usual – and when he gave her a bony hug he smelt vaguely of sandalwood and whisky. A combination that was, unfortunately, still heady and wildly attractive to Alexia.

She was used to seeing him tired, hungover, red-eyed, but this was not the impossibly sexy, care-free Lee of last month.

India had been amazing. He'd surprised his mother's side of the family in Pondicherry, to much excitement. Went to the Red Fort. The Golden Temple. Got high in Goa. Hooked up with an Israeli student. Caught giardiasis and shat himself on a train. Visited the Taj Mahal after a really hard night. A monkey stole his iPhone. The stories were colourful, but the tone of his delivery was grey and tired.

Alexia assumed she would be dumped as soon as he was settled, but after she got them 'a decent American meal' (a Big Mac and fries) and they ate it in the relative privacy of the Bright Star roof terrace, he started angling for a pass to Music in the Park. Alexia realised he didn't know where to go.

'Thanks for showing me around London,' he said, undoing the second last button on his shirt so it was almost open to his navel. It was no longer actually functioning as a shirt.

'It's okay, Lee. My colleagues were very obliging, luckily,' Alexia said coolly. She felt that irritating little flutter in her stomach as he gazed at her. She wouldn't be fooled – this wasn't fondness, it was survival.

Lee rolled over onto his side and leaned over her. 'Aren't you just a little happy to see me?' he said, with less of his usual swagger. Alexia looked up at the oak tree beside them, its beautiful mass of rounded yet pointy leaves waving gently with each light north-westerly gust. *Hints of fall.* She examined the small goose pimples on her forearm and tried to think of an answer to his question.

'It's nice to see you,' Alexia said, trying to keep her tone neutral. 'But I need to work today, and for the rest of next week. You know Max is around, don't you?'

'Yep, yep. We're in touch. I've been hassling him about leaving. A sustained campaign of sad emojis and photos from the last tour, but it's not working, Lexi. I think he's done. Anyway, he'll be here later I think, so I can try in person. And I want to go to Abbey Road. Properly, this time. I think Max might go too.'

Alexia remembered their last trip to Abbey Road, strictly for a zebra crossing photo shoot on the way to the airport – they never even went inside, but the photo ran with some bogus story about the new album being inspired by their time there. They were there for literally ten minutes. It was such rubbish. *So many little secrets.* She thought again about Theo Marlon's offer.

'That's great. I'd like to see Max too, actually.'

'Apparently, there's a girl.'

'Yeah? That's great. I'm happy for him.' Alexia smiled – she really was. ''Bout time he met someone new.'

'You never asked what happened with me and Jessica,' Lee said with a wry smile. 'Wanna know? Wanna know what that last-minute flight to LA you booked had me walking into the middle of?'

'You broke up, my dad told me.' She had to steel herself, focus on being sympathetic. Compassionate.

'Yeah, but you wanna know why?' Lee grinned. 'It's pretty funny.'

Alexia didn't, but she braced herself – she'd hear it all either way. Another girl? Or had poor Jessica finally had enough of the rumours of Lee's infidelity?

'She's pregnant,' he blurted out, with half a laugh.

For a moment, the statement hung in the air. Alexia shook her head, staring intensely at the oak leaves, one after another, counting each point, trying to steady her mind. The music from the main stage suddenly blasted as a new band began their set. She sat up, looking out across the field, clutching her untouched beer.

Alexia shouted over the blare of the music, 'I don't understand.'

'Well, it's a simple matter of biology . . . ' he said playfully.

'What? Lee! Please.'

'It's not mine. It's that dude's in that Marvel movie she was in. The French cowboy from Montreal. Wore tights in the movie.' Lee laughed, swigging on his drink and shaking his head. 'It's too damn funny.'

'I'm not sure I understand the joke.'

'Don't you see? *She* ended up being the cheat.'

'Are you sure? That doesn't sound like her,' Alexia said, shaking her head.

'Oh, I'm sure. First she balled me for cheating, which, as you know, I've *hardly* ever done. Only right at the beginning, anyway. Oh, and Australia. And I think Hawaii.' He smirked. 'Then she tells me *that*.'

'Jesus, Lee,' Alexia said, standing up and nodding towards the main stage. 'I have to get back to the team. Sorry.' She picked up her cardigan and shook the leaves off it, slipping it around her shoulders. 'I get the trip to India now – you needed some time to recoup.'

'No, I just wanted to party in Goa,' he said, tossing his empty bottle in the wrong recycling bin. 'Jessica was a drag, really.'

Alexia looked over at him as he rearranged his shirt again to show a little more tattoo and nipple, and pulled his wide-brimmed hat down over his nose. She watched the fidgeting – tugging at the legs of his skinny jeans, smoothing his long hair – and she knew he was hurting. He had really loved Jessica. She knew that only too well. He was upset – lashing out and acting his role at the same time. She wanted to give him a hug and try to soothe his pain, but thought better of it.

'She *was* a drag. Always giving me a hard time when she was screwing Mr Canada the whole time. Bitch.' He spat the last word out, and Alexia flinched.

'Lee!'

'What? Hey, forget all that crap. Let's go party!' he said. It was clear he'd moved on from the conversation, a smile creeping across his face as two girls from a Jägermeister promotional team wandered past sporting a tray of shots and very little else. 'London's full of ass.'

'Ugh. I can't party. I have to work. I'll walk you to the backstage bar though. I'm sure you'll know plenty of people.'

As soon as they reached the VIP bar, he strode straight over to chat with a par-drunk indie band Alexia recognised from New York. He turned to wave at her, a flash of the usual Lee sparkle returning. 'See ya soon, Lexi. Hey, get in touch with Max. We should all hang. Maybe go party together?'

She watched him dishing out man hugs and high-fives to the band as if he hadn't a care in the world. She felt angry. Whatever he was doing here, he had to go. Her phone rang.

'Hi, Greta. I'm on my way. Tell Lewis I'm so sorry,' she shouted as loud as she could, unable to hear Greta through the blaring music in the background. She must have been right near the sound desk.

'It's okay. He said you brought Lee with you?' Greta shouted back.

'Lee's in the backstage bar. I'll introduce you later, okay?'

'Whatever. Sounds neat. If I've got time. Whatever. I'm cool.'

Alexia hung up the phone and shook her head. Something was up with that girl, but she couldn't quite figure out what. She bounced from super friendly, to a bundle of nerves, to a sort of faux-cool, to latently hostile, all in a day. It was hard to keep up. She strode to the backstage area gate and flashed her AAA badge at the security guy.

'Only need that on the way in, love.' He winked at her, and she made her way out into the field towards the sound desk. It could have been any festival anywhere. Girls in denim shorts and Hunter boots, feathered earrings and floaty fringed tops flapping as they danced in circles or on the shoulders of bare-chested boys in low-hung shorts and flip-flops. The music was loud and distorted but the crowd didn't care – they were too buzzed on extortionate beers and sunstroke.

As the crowd thickened towards the main stage she had to push past a few groups of people to reach Lewis and Greta.

'Alexia,' Lewis said, a warm smile on his face, 'Clint's over there, filming. Can you see him, to the left of the stage?'

'Oh yeah. Does he need me?'

'No, stay with me,' Lewis replied. 'I need someone to help with the kit, and Greta keeps— Greta's not as familiar with it as you.'

'Okay,' said Alexia, giving Greta an apologetic look. 'We'll work it out between us.'

'It's fine. I'll just go back to handing out release forms,' Greta said cheerfully. 'Fun day so far then?'

'It's been okay.' Alexia shrugged, putting in a pair of ear-plugs for protection from the massive speakers.

'It's very screechy, isn't it?' Greta said, fidgeting with her own earplugs and watching Alexia intently, as if she wasn't sure she had them in right.

'It's distortion, not screeching – it's Songhoy Blues,' laughed Alexia, rearranging the mess Greta had made of the camera bag.

'How was your friend?' Lewis asked, peering through the camera.

'Oh, he's a mess.'

'Oh yeah? Must be a bit weird to be in the biggest pop group in the world and then—'

'Yeah,' Alexia interrupted. She didn't want to go into it. 'Unfortunately he's going to be hanging around today.

I dropped him at the backstage bar, though. He found some friends.'

Lewis took his headphones off and looked at her. 'It's not going to be a problem for you that he's here, is it?'

It already was.

Chapter 12

Hey

Greta followed Lewis and Alexia around, moping. Totally, unequivocally moping with all her might. Her huffs and pouts and sighs fell on deaf ears, even when they got to comical, theatrical levels – yet she still diligently handed out release forms to everyone they interviewed, walking endless loops of the festival ground, the whole time knowing Lee was in the backstage bar. Not 100 metres away. Lee. LEE! It was pure torture.

The ridiculous shoes she was wearing were also torture. The soles of her heels burned, as did the back of her calves as the mini heel sank into the soil with every step.

The sunset was in its last throes – blazing red and orange against the azure and purple sky as the first stars began to appear overhead. The peripheral stages were winding down and the crew was getting less stretched. Magic hour – the time when the light is most beautiful for filming – was finally over. Greta knew they were nearing the end and she would get her chance to go backstage. But then Alexia efficiently pulled out a top light and fixed it to Lewis's camera – even darkness wouldn't stop them.

'Do you need me to get the spare batteries?' Greta tried. Their kit was all stored in the backstage area, so it was as good an excuse as any.

'No, Alexia has them,' Lewis said as they ploughed on through the field, Greta weighed down with everything he needed but didn't want to carry, including an open parasol wedged under her armpit that she kept accidentally poking people with.

'Sorry,' Greta said earnestly to a girl in an Indian feather-head dress and a T-shirt that said 'Beer is My Spirit Animal'. Greta saw another way out. 'Shall I go get us some complimentary water?'

'I've got some.' Alexia held her bottle up.

Just as Greta had run out of excuses to catch a glimpse of Lee, Clint came running over, camera packed down. 'Guys, I'm done. I've had enough! Do you mind if I head backstage? Julian's been here all day and I want to see him. We only got a few minutes earlier to say hello. A dear friend of ours played today, it was a big deal.'

'We're almost done,' said Lewis. 'The other production company are finishing up the main stage.'

'Alexia, Max is here.' Clint smiled. 'Aaaand ... I think he found Lee.'

'Oh, brilliant. I really wanna catch up with Max.'

Lewis turned to Alexia and nodded towards the backstage area. 'Fine, go. I think we're done.'

They pulled over between Lucky Chip burger stand – the king of all East End burger stands – and one selling retro lollies in small retro bags for five quid a pop. Lewis checked something on the viewfinder of his camera and nodded to Alexia. 'Yep. We got everything we're going to squeeze out of this mess.'

'Well ... if we're done, I might ... well, I could use a drink,' Greta said, looking at Alexia and Clint, but there was no response except a nod from Lewis, which could have meant 'yes, off you go', or 'yes, I want a drink too, let's go', or 'yes, I agree, but you have to stand here until I'm done which will be never'. Greta could have actually screamed until Alexia said, finally, 'Do you want to come meet Lee and Max?'

'Sure,' she squeaked. Alexia was immediately her new best friend and all of the day's little injustices were forgiven. 'It's just that it's so great to finally put a face to a name, you know?'

'I *think* you know their faces,' Alexia teased.

'You know what I mean, though,' she replied, a fierce blush exploding across her cheeks.

'Come on then, you two.' Clint set off as Greta put the parasol down and frantically finger-combed her hair into some semblance of a style.

This was finally it. *Summon your chill*.

The backstage bar was set up to look like an old English

pub, but in a big white marquee lit with tiny fairy lights which sparkled in the late evening light. There was a makeshift bar in one corner with pints of local pale ale and craft lager on tap, served by a girl with purple hair and an old guy in an AC/DC T-shirt with a massive tattoo of a snake crawling up his arm and out onto his neck. Opposite the bar was a pool table, which was currently being used as a seat by members of Deerhunter. The floor was covered in woodchip and various mismatched armchairs and leather couches were scattered around. On one of the latter, reclining with beer in hand, sat Lee, and opposite him were Max and a girl about Greta's age, who looked strikingly familiar to her.

Greta's heart began to quicken as they approached. Lee looked exactly like his pictures, except maybe a little thinner. She took in everything, as fast as her brain could compute it all – his hair, the flicks of dark red and brown under the fairy lights. The way his hands moved around his beer bottle as he picked at his nails. The way he kicked at the coffee table. The fold of skin that hung like an empty roll over his belt. And then the way he looked at Alexia as they joined them at the table. And the way Alexia almost ignored him in return.

'Max!' Alexia walked forwards, smiling.

'Alexia!' Max was up and gave her a gentle hug, and they immediately launched into animated conversation. His voice was deep with a thick southern twang, but he spoke slowly and quietly – such a contrast to the high-octane, energetic 'Maxx' from The Keep's videos. Even though Greta could hear the hushed murmur of news and secrets being passed between the two, she was more interested in watching Lee run his hand down his aggressively bare chest.

'Oh, how rude of me,' Alexia said. 'Lee, Max, this is Greta. The intern at Bright Star. And obviously you know Clint.'

The intern? Greta tried not to frown. *You mean the other intern, right? Your fellow intern?*

'Very well. Clint! How ya doing? Hey, Greta.' Max stretched out his hand and shook hers firmly. Greta looked down at her hand and then at Max and managed a nod before she quickly wiped her hand on her denim skirt. *This is actually happening, Greta. SAY SOMETHING HILARIOUS.*

'I am Greta,' she said. Her voice sounded like a wailing fox in the height of mating season, or a squealing microphone at sound check. Or maybe it didn't, suddenly she couldn't really hear anything.

'Yeah, I got that.' He winked. 'Nice to meet you.'

'And this is Lee,' Alexia continued, smirking at Greta with one of her eyebrows slightly raised.

Stop smirking at me, I am totally normal.

'Hey there, Greta,' Lee said, standing up. Greta looked over at him, it was happening too fast. Way too fast. 'Don't leave a guy hanging.'

She looked down at his outstretched hand and felt hot all over, impossibly hot. *I'm freaking out. No chill. Be cool, Greta.* She focused on shaking the hand. She farted. Quietly. The hand. *Shake the hand really, really normally. Not for too long, not too short. Just a normal shake. Oh my word, I'm shaking Lee's hand. Oh crap. That was too long.* She pulled away. She realised she was struggling to be in the moment. The fangirl in her was watching this play out like a movie, but the Greta who was here, standing right in front of them was real. She needed to take charge.

'Hello, Lee. Hi.' She realised he was still looking at her, and quickly shifted her focus to the girl standing just behind Max. 'Hello.'

'Amelie,' she introduced herself with a smile.

Now Greta recognised her – she was the girl who had been briefly linked to Charlie from The Keep a couple of months ago. Greta's followers had been up in arms. She cringed a little as she remembered partaking in some rather intrusive online stalking of the girl. It had turned out she was their sound guy's daughter, and Charlie had said there was nothing else to it, but still – it was a big fandom drama for a few days.

Greta was quietly pleased with herself. She literally knew EVERYTHING about this band. 'Ahh! Well, it's nice to actually meet you.' She grinned. Then panicked. *'Actually'?! Too familiar.*

'Um … you too?' Amelie said, casting a bemused sideways glance at Max.

'How long are *you* staying in London for?' Alexia asked him.

'Oh, I'm not sure.' Max smiled, gazing over at Amelie again as they all exchanged knowing looks. 'Some more studio time, I guess, then … who knows?'

'You suck,' said Lee, kicking his shin gently. 'The one that leaves the band first always gets the best record deal.'

'I have to go get my guitar . . . ' Amelie said to Max. 'Enjoy the reunion.'

'Sure, sure.' He nodded, smiling at her as she disappeared from the tent into the darkness.

'So, you're publicly "out" of The Keep now?' Clint asked.

'Yeah. Well, should be in the news Monday. *Sun* exclusive, Geoff told me,' Max said, shrugging. 'It's not like people don't know already, but yeah. I'm out of the band.'

'Everyone thought you were suffering exhaustion and "recuperating" in Memphis.' Lee laughed, as Greta's brain went into full-on fandom overdrive. Maxx had left. He had left the band. And it would be public knowledge in two days.

'Good for you, Max,' said Alexia.

'But what will you do?' Greta asked, trying to hide the concern in her voice. 'Are you single now?'

A silence passed between everyone. Greta could hear the echo of her words in her head for a few moments, until she cringed and quickly corrected herself. 'I mean, *solo*. Ha. Not single. Is that what you're recording? Are you doing a solo album?'

'Maybe.' Max looked over at Lee and rolled his eyes, before quietly adding, 'But yeah, something new – that's another thing being announced next week. The other big break-up.'

'Ah, that's good though. 'Bout time. For them and every-one concerned,' Lee replied, as Greta struggled to follow the covert communication going on between them all. Lee started looking around the bar and Greta could feel the conversation drying up. She'd hardly made herself known.

Lee. Lee was *right there*, single, breathing, and despite knowing he was exactly 169 centimetres tall, he seemed shorter than expected. She put her hand in her front jeans pocket and considered asking for a photo, but she couldn't think of a way to make it sound cool. This moment was going to slip through her fingers any second.

'We're heading off now,' Max said as Amelie returned with a backpack on and guitar case in hand.

'What are you guys doing? Shall we hook up later? I'm hungry,' Lee asked. 'Or . . . no?'

'Nah. Not tonight, buddy. I just arrived and . . . ' Max shook his head and smiled at Amelie as they both turned to leave. 'Well, got stuff to do. This week though, yeah? See y'all soon.'

'I can't go out for dinner,' Alexia said flatly. 'I've got to go and do an overnight shift at Bright Star. I need to leave soon, actually. But maybe another night?'

'What?' Greta and Lee spoke in unison, causing Greta to half laugh, half snort.

'I'm also extremely broke,' Alexia said matter-of-factly, ignoring Greta's desperate eyes. 'Can't just expense things any more, Lee.'

'I'll pay,' Lee pleaded.

'I'm doing paid shift work, Lee,' Alexia said, sighing. 'So I need to show up and, you know, work.'

'Julian and I are meeting his parents for dinner,' Clint said, shrugging apologetically. 'There's a bunch of restaurants up there in the village?'

'Ah, damn, you guys suck,' Lee said, finishing his drink and waving towards the crowd. 'I don't fancy the hassle.'

Greta could imagine. It didn't matter that the crowd at Music in the Park were literally the last few thousand people on earth that would ever buy a Keep record, he would easily be recognised by the drunken mob.

'I can take you out,' Greta blurted out. At first there was silence, as she felt Alexia's eyes burning into the side of her head. She braced herself as the words hung in the air. 'I mean, dunno if you've been out in Dalston, but I know a place that literally no other human being will bother you. If you like Turkish food. Do you like Turkish?'

'Well, well, Greta,' Lee said, threading his arm through hers and grinning at Alexia. 'My *new* best friend.'

CHAPTER 13

Blindsided

TO ALEXIA: I hope it's okay? I just thought it might help? ☺

TO GRETA: It's fine! Thanks for taking him out.

TO ALEXIA: Taking one for the team. ☺

But was it fine? She wasn't sure. She cursed the editing suite and plugged in the next memory card and set it off to ingest. She hated this work. Even though technically, a girl with her limited experience *should* be doing the ingesting, she'd been doing so much interesting stuff at Bright Star that it felt depressing being alone prepping edits for someone else. Especially at this time of night. And especially this night in particular, when she knew that Greta was taking Lee out for a meal. Greta, who was warm and friendly and open, and, as it happens, a bit of a party girl. Out with Lee, who was freshly single.

> TO ALEXIA: I'm just taking him to this place in Dalston called Deniz's. It mostly does lamb. But does he eat lamb?

> TO GRETA: He does. Yes. He hates chilli though.

She slammed the camera case shut and shoved it under the desk. Realising her laptop was back with the rest of the kit at the festival site, she strode over to her shared desk to fire up Greta's. Everything was an irritation tonight.

> TO ALEXIA: Sorry, one more question. Does he mind people knowing his name? It's just in case I have to introduce him. Though there's no one here. But Deniz will ask. He owns the restaurant. I know him. He'll ask. BTW, I know you don't do 'social' but you should definitely download Whatsapp.

> TO GRETA: I'm sure he won't mind.

Jesus. Why not just ask the guy? He's right there. You do know how to speak human. She walked over to the vending machine and fished out the last of her change. She pressed the button for a lemonade and waited for the mechanical arm to move up and down. It selected a Fanta, which thumped its way down into the hole below.

'NO!' Alexia shouted, banging her fist against the glass. 'Ugh.'

Alexia wandered back to the computer, which was asking for a password. She sighed. This work didn't want to be done. She looked over to the edit suite and could see the side of the screen as the footage rendered, shot by shot, into Apple ProRes, ready for its import into Final Cut.

She opened the can, which fizzed and spurted out all over her, staining her white T-shirt with orange splashes. *Damn Fanta. Who drinks this stuff?*

She typed in 'brightstar' to Greta's machine, but it was the wrong password. That was the default password for all machines and most people never bothered changing it. She looked around Greta's side of the desk, hoping the answer might present itself. It was a huge mess of release forms, invoices, receipts, chocolate wrappers, Pret napkins, plastic water cups, business cards and more. There was an old *Sun* newspaper open on a page of celebrity gossip. She thought of Theo Marlon again as she scanned the stories. Drake had a girlfriend. A Kardashian had lip implants. *X Factor* was back on TV. She flipped the page over, and there was a photo of Lee sitting on the Diana seat at the Taj Mahal. The page had been endlessly scribbled on with notes– phone numbers, reminders, Greta's signature. The girl was a world-class doodler.

TO ALEXIA: I really hope it's okay. Going in!

TO GRETA: Fine. Really. What's your password?
I forgot my machine, it's in my backpack with all
the kit.

Alexia watched the little bubble appear on her screen, and disappear, and then reappear, the way it does when someone is deciding what to write. Alexia set the phone down and sipped at her drink. *Not too bad, actually.* A few minutes later, there was still no reply from Greta. Alexia tried again.

TO GRETA: Password? I only need to open the
shared log. Won't check your browser history,
don't you worry. ☺

While she waited, Alexia looked back at the newspaper clipping and suddenly the image of Lee seemed strange, as did the multiple signatures of Greta's around the photo. They clearly read 'Greta Bow'.

That was Lee's last name. At first, she laughed out loud, but then as she looked more closely, she saw some of the scribbles resembled hearts. It was like a fourteen-year-old fangirl had scribbled on the page. *What the ...?*

Alexia's stomach lurched. She held her hand over her suddenly dry mouth and picked up the Fanta, hastily swallowing the thick sugary sweetness. She looked down at her phone again and read over the messages.

But Greta's not a fan of The Keep. She looked up at the computer screen once again, suspicion creeping. She picked up the phone and called Greta. It went straight to answerphone.

> TO GRETA: Are you there? Greta can you
> call me back ASAP. I just need to do some
> logging! Thanks.

Alexia looked at the screen again and shook her head. She typed in the password 'Leebow', but it was incorrect. She knew the machines would allow ten attempts and she was at two. 'Gretabow' didn't work. 'Leethekeep' didn't work. She tried simply 'thekeep' and, unbelievably, she was in.

If Greta had wanted to hide her secret, she had done a terrible job. As soon as Alexia opened the browser the default tabs came up, fully logged in to all Greta's different social media channels. It was all *right there* for Alexia to see, and it was shocking.

At first she felt intrusive and her instinct, despite what she'd found, was to close Greta's accounts, but she just couldn't. She stared at the screen, trying to make sense of what was in front of her.

She clicked on the tab that opened Greta's Twitter feed.

She knew the account of course – the boys talked about it all the time, since it was their biggest European fan feed. Greta read through the tweets, grimly noting that some were from just an hour earlier.

> @thekeepers1 Big news from The Keep coming on Monday.

> @thekeepers1 Sometimes I love my job and the fandom so much. #keepers #keepfam

> @thekeepers1 RT if you just want to MEET THE BOYS, Like if you've already met them. ;-)

As the reality of the situation sunk in, Alexia became furious. Greta ran The Keep fandom but had been working at Bright Star at the same time – who knows what confidential information she could've overheard or dug up on the shared drives? A Keeper. Most of whom were awesome. But Greta was one of those extreme fangirls who took their love of the band too far. Who camped outside hotels and venues, even the boys' own private homes – *just for a glimpse*. Who stalked the band's friends and families online and – more worryingly – in real life. Who threatened terrifying things when they didn't get what they wanted. Who trolled almost any girl photographed with them. One time, a girl had thrown herself at Alexia outside a radio station, threatening to harm the band, then harm

Alexia, and then, even more worryingly – harm herself. This was not only bizarre fan behaviour, it was dangerous.

All the things she'd discussed – Lee, the band, the boys' conversation today about Max leaving. She felt betrayed. And now Greta had managed to wrangle herself into a night out with Lee. He was with her now, clueless as to who she really was. This was a total disaster.

Alexia trawled through all the accounts – Tumblr, Instagram, Facebook, all of them – forensically looking for any whisper of anything private or secret Greta may have shared. She looked at her phone. It was now twenty minutes since she had texted Greta to ask for the password, and more than an hour since she'd left her with Lee outside the venue. Her heart was thumping in her chest.

She checked the direct messages.

@thekeepers1 Thanks for the follow! Don't forget to turn notifications on.

@thekeepers1 Thanks for the follow! Don't forget to turn notifications on.

@thekeepers1 Thanks for the follow! Don't forget to turn notifications on.

Alexia pored over everything from the last month and eventually sat back in the chair, not as relieved as she would have liked, but reassured that Greta had not shared any private information or secrets. In fact, it was all innocuous, basic fangirl-type stuff. Memes. Polls. Promotion. *Could this whole thing be harmless? Was it really so strange that a fan would end up in this job, with all the access? But why the secrecy?*

She glanced over at the edit suite. The import was finished but she still hadn't logged anything. She *could* come back and do it tomorrow, though. It was Saturday night – surely no one would start editing the rushes tomorrow. She picked up her phone and took some photos of the open feeds as receipts and sent a direct message to herself from Greta's Twitter feed.

She had to get to Lee.

Alexia shut down Greta's machine and marched over to the edit suite, shutting everything there down as well. A quick google gave the address of Deniz's right away, and she booked a cab on the company account. She'd deal with the expense later – surely this was a business trip?

As she nodded goodnight to the security guard and made her way out onto the street she tried to weigh up the best approach. How was she going to play this with Greta? And with Lee? As she slipped into the back of the cab and it pulled away, Alexia realised that she was furious.

Be kind, Alexia. She just wants to be loved, like everyone else.

It was her mother's voice that niggled in her ear. That was the kind of thing she would be saying. The kind of thing she'd trot out every time Alexia had been left out of a party invitation or left out of some stupid party by those girls at her school. Who did that kindness serve? It never served Alexia who smiled and forgave like a complete mug with no spine. *Be kind?* What good was kindness if it didn't help someone learn? This idea of kindness as a cure? It was a fallacy. Kindness doesn't change behaviour. Kindness forgives it. Be kind? Utter crap.

At that moment, Alexia was certain her mother's mantra of 'compassion and forgiveness' was weak in times of crisis.

CHAPTER 14

Fit But You Know It

Greta was sweating. When she took an inconspicuous sniff she realised her armpits were funky as hell. She tried to sneakily run an antibacterial wipe across them, but her shirt was too tight across her boobs. She needed a bathroom trip, but was convinced Lee would make a run for it as soon as she was out of sight.

The anxiety and excitement was too much. She was with Lee, ordering a kebab, in Dalston. Things like this just didn't happen. Particularly at a kebab shop. When she'd fantasised about her first date with Lee, it had always been somewhere exceedingly posh. And generally in west London, not Dalston. It didn't matter that he'd been on his phone since they got in the taxi. And it didn't matter that he'd made no eye contact since they got here. All that mattered was that she was here with him.

'So, how do you know Alexia?' Lee said, absently staring at the menu, then his phone again. 'Where are we again?'

'Dalston. And, um ... we work together?' Greta said. Her eyes flicked from his neck tattoo up to his glossy if somewhat greasy hair. He was missing his hat. Had he left it in the taxi? That was her favourite Lee look. She wondered if he still had the brown one he wore in the 'Golden Rain' video.

'Ah, sure. Of course you do. She's fun, right?'

'Yes. Well, I don't know her super well. We only ever went out once, really, outside work,' Greta said. 'I mean, I took her to Tesco's for a meal deal the other day after she saved my actual life and job and dignity. But, yep, it's usually just work with us.'

Lee glanced over her shoulder to Deniz's huge front windows, which, due to the overhead lighting and gathering dark outside, acted like enormous mirrors. He brushed his hair to the side, eyes shifting around. *He's on edge.* Greta narrowed her eyes. *But why?*

Greta looked down at her own phone, which she'd hurriedly switched off after the password question from Alexia. She would just say her phone died and Alexia would use Lewis's machine or something. Easy. There were plenty of other machines in the building and she felt sure Alexia would call Lewis or Clint if she was truly desperate.

'Can we order?' Lee said, sitting back. 'I need a beer.'

'Sure. I'll go up. What do you want to eat?'

'Nothing.'

'Nothing?'

'Well, a beer will do. I don't really fancy this kind of food.'

Greta cringed, looking over to Deniz, who had been fiddling with the cables at the back of his TV since they arrived. Mercifully, he'd been distracted enough not to say anything too embarrassing yet, but if Lee didn't eat, there was no way he wouldn't say something.

'Okay. One beer coming up. But you did say you were hungry. Are you still? I'll order you something anyway, you don't have to eat it.'

'Sure.' He was distracted, and Greta got a sinking feeling in her stomach. The evening was already taking a nosedive.

He's bored. Take him somewhere else.

'Would you prefer a pub then, if you just want a beer?'

'Sure. A pub. Where are we?'

'Still Dalston.'

'Are we near Waterloo?' he said, still looking at his phone.

'Not really,' she replied, and when he didn't elaborate, 'Do you need to go to Waterloo?'

'Maybe,' he said.

'You two lovebirds gonna order or what?' Deniz shouted across the room.

Lee looked up from his phone and smirked. Greta giggled, turning red. 'Oh no, Deniz. No. It's not like that. This is just business. I mean, for work. He's my work. Arghh. I'm coming to order.'

She walked over to the counter and whispered, 'Shhh, please.'

'Don't you worry about me,' Deniz said, pinching her cheek really hard.

'Can I have two lamb, fries and two beers? No chilli.'

'Put your money away. My treat!' Deniz said, nodding at Lee, who was *still* glued to his phone. 'He should be paying, anyway.'

'This is a business dinner, Deniz.' She tried to sound firm, but she had thought it was odd that he'd let her pay for the taxi and now dinner. *Well, he only wants a beer*, she reasoned. She slid back into the booth with the two beers and subtly craned her neck to see what he was doing on his phone. *He must have to field emails from agents and managers and stuff all the time.* She craned her neck a little more – he was playing Candy Crush.

'So, how long are you in London for?' she asked. He didn't respond, so she picked up the menu and pretended to read the dessert section again, while peering around the plastic edge to drink in his beautiful face.

'Damn it,' he barked, slamming his phone down.

'It gets annoying, doesn't it?' Greta smiled. 'Candy Crush? My granny plays it sometimes.'

Lee looked her in the eye at last, a wicked grin on his face. 'Don't tell anyone I play that.'

'Your secret's safe with me,' she said, before wilting under the eye contact and staring down at her hands. 'So, London. How long?'

'Dunno. Guess I'd better get back to New York, really.' He sat back, eyeing up the huge lamb Iskender kebabs that arrived. 'I have to be there. A million band things going on. Okay, these look great. Thanks, man.'

'No worries, *man*,' said Deniz, shooting Greta a wink as he walked off.

'You want my hot sauce?' Lee asked as he tucked in.

'No. I'll take some of the yoghurt, though.' Greta took a bite of lamb and felt a surge of pleasure as Lee nodded in approval with each mouthful of his kebab.

'So, what are you, like, eighteen?'

'Exactly,' Greta took a second bite of her dinner, but found herself unable to properly eat. She was still sick with nerves. She watched Lee, who was holding his fork upside down and clumsily gripping his knife in his whole fist, as if he were nine years old. She felt an urge to correct him.

'You like doing music TV and films?'

'Yeah, I guess. I like meeting all the bands.'

Lee laughed. 'Ha! That's pretty honest.'

'Don't you like it? You must meet so many interest-ing people.'

'Yeah, and a lot of assholes.' He grinned at her. Greta could sense he was relaxing at last. She wished she could do the same.

'Well, I enjoy meeting people. I like people,' Greta said, 'even the assholes. Everyone's interesting if you take five minutes to ask a few questions. Well, most people are anyway. There was this gym teacher at my school – Mr Dicks. He was from New Zcaland I think. He wore the same black Adidas tracksuit with those yellow lines, every day. Every day. Well, *he* wasn't very interesting. All he talked about was rugby, rugby, rugby. I went to school in Hackney! We don't do rugby. We didn't see eye to eye about a lot, him and I. He gave me detention because I refused to do the climbing wall, but I'd forgotten my gym shorts and there was no way I was climbing the wall in my school uniform. You don't have school uniforms in America. *Soooo* lucky. But Mr Dicks's son was nice. He was in my class. Richard. Richard Dicks. Get it?'

OMG Greta shut the hell up!

'Huh?' Lee looked bemused.

'Dick Dicks. That was his name.' Greta blushed. *Christ!*

'You're sweet,' Lee said.

Sweet? Wow! She choked on her beer as the little bell on the door rang and a gust of wind accompanied Alexia's entrance. She looked strange, stressed perhaps, even angry? Greta felt a deep sense of dread. *I should have answered my phone. Is this about the computer? It can't be. Why is she here? OMG, did Lee call for backup? Is she the backup? Am I one of those disaster dates? Is this a date? Am I on a date with Lee? He's so good looking.*

'Hi, Greta. Lee.'

'Hello, Alexia! So good to see you. Would you like some of my kebab?' Greta held out her fork, a piece of cold, greying meat impaled on it. Alexia actually recoiled.

'No,' she said sharply.

'Sexi Lexi!' Lee sat up a little in his chair. 'I knew you couldn't live without me.'

'Well,' Alexia said quickly, 'I finished early at work.'

'You did?' Greta's nerves jangled some more. She'd been sure Alexia had a solid night's work ahead. 'Did you try to call? I'm sorry, my phone died . . . '

Alexia looked at Greta with such contempt that Greta's heart started pounding.

'I called that bar you like – Mahiki,' she said to Lee, 'and turns out some of the bands from today are there, for an after party.'

'Awesome!' Lee almost bounded out of his seat. 'We were just finishing here.'

'Ooh that sounds awesome,' Greta gushed.

'I could only get artists' names on the door, sorry,' Alexia said bluntly. 'There's a car waiting outside if you want to go, but you'll need to go now. It's going to be rammed.'

And with that, Lee stood up, slipped his phone into his back pocket and strolled out of Greta's life.

'I'll come with you, actually, you can drop me in Angel on the way.' Alexia turned to leave. 'Thanks for looking after him.'

'Ummm, it's okay.' Greta sat, utterly alone and downcast, in the now-empty restaurant. Lee was gone. *LEE*. And Alexia had just treated her like dog crap on the heel of one of her fancy pairs of brand new Docs. *What the hell just happened?*

CHAPTER 15

She's Lost Control

Theo Marlon was utterly unashamed of his decrepit, disgusting behaviour. Alexia had caved and agreed to meet him at a greasy spoon just off Old Street. It was called the Shepardess and reminded Alexia of an old American diner – it had that 1950s vibe, albeit one that was super English. Lots of green and white Formica and chrome shining brightly under the tube lighting, and the smell of dirty frying oil hanging in the air. It was almost better when smoking *was* allowed in these places – the pungent stench of stale fat was nauseating.

Most of the other diners were sitting alone with enormous English breakfasts of bacon, beans, eggs and fried bread. On the table, a *Sun* newspaper was folded open on the gossip section. Theo had pointed at a story about an actress whose brother was in hospital after a horrific car crash.

'I broke that story,' he'd said proudly.

'That's ... great?' Alexia had muttered in response.

'I mean, you don't become a celebrity without wishing to court *some* attention,' he was saying now, wrapping his fingers around the edge of a cup of very dark-brown tea. 'There was this one time we got a sex tape featuring a certain London singer who shall remain nameless, but let's call him Carl. The sex tape was completely limp, if you'll excuse the phrase – but it was the room you could see in the background that was really exciting. Let's just say it made Christian Grey look like a frigid teenager.' He belly laughed.

'I'm not sure I understand.' Although she did. Perfectly.

'No offence to teenagers,' Marlon continued, as he dunked a sugary chocolate cookie into his tea. He sucked the liquid out of it, then licked off all the chocolate before taking a soggy bite. 'But anyway, we digress. Are you clear on how this is going to work?'

Alexia looked out of the window and tried to block the dull ache that had been present since Lee had left town. If there was one thing to be said for this kind of heartache, it was that it made the anxiety of being broke pale into insignificance.

That twisty, stomach-churning ache of saying goodbye to Lee – again – wasn't about to leave her without a place to sleep. She'd been stupid. London was expensive. Living on her own was expensive. Obviously, she couldn't beg her dad to send her money or reinstate her allowance – not after she'd made such a big deal of doing things on her own. And she couldn't tell anyone at Bright Star – they wouldn't understand how she'd let this happen.

Though she still felt some loyalty to the boys, they didn't really give a damn, did they? Charlie had asked her not two days ago to book him a haircut – she hadn't been working for them for over a month! She was lost at sea, and right now Marlon was her only life raft.

'Sure. I get it.'

'Okay, let's do it,' Marlon said, pulling out his phone and setting up the voice recorder.

'Oh, I'm not comfortable with that,' Alexia said, eyeing up the big red record button on the screen. 'You said you would pay me for some fun, anonymous information, but that's a bit FBI. Also, it's leaving kind of a trace, isn't it?'

'Okay. The old-fashioned way,' he said, pulling out a leather notebook.

'What do you pay the most for? Boxer size? Embarrassing ailments? Strange quirks?'

'Affairs,' he said shortly. 'Or anything worse than that – sexual assault allegations, hard drug use, that kind of thing. Sexual depravity is kind of the jackpot these days.' He smiled, raising both his eyebrows as Alexia fought the urge to run out the door. This man was vile. 'But any Keep story pays well, really. They're so protected, so *stage-managed*. And they've closed ranks even more since Max chucked it in. Any little thing on them is golden, really. That's why we're here, right?'

Alexia considered some of the secrets she knew. There were

so many little things she could tell him about those boys. Little things she would quite enjoy spilling – things they probably wouldn't really mind being spilled. It wouldn't do too much harm.

'Well, Kyle won't drink tap water, so you have to have room temperature bottled water on standby all the time. It has to be room temperature!' She laughed with the joy of a friend recounting a friend's silly habit. 'That could be funny.'

'Um, you'll have to do better than that. Unless you can give me a huge list of things Kyle doesn't like, so we can do a story on how difficult he is.'

'Kyle isn't difficult. He's a dream to work with.'

'Okay, well, that isn't going to get me hits.'

'Which band member then?' she asked.

'No one cares about Art, unless you have something totally spectacular about him, he's far too dull. A tell-all from one of Kyle's lovers?'

Alexia winced, knowing how much Kyle protected his private life. 'Um, what about Max?'

Theo grinned, lifting his eyebrows conspiratorially. 'Well, have you got the real story behind him leaving the band? He's not "taking some time out with friends and family", is he? And did Dee and him break on amicable terms? There has to be more to *that* story.'

On Monday, an article had run, just as Max said it would. Max had left The Keep, and he had broken up with his girlfriend, Dee. It had been big news for a couple of days, but

Alexia had barely noticed after the Lee and Greta fiasco. She'd been pretending to have the flu so she didn't have to face Greta at the office, while also hiding from Mr Coleman, who was chasing her for rent and threatening to toss her out on the street 'with the pigeons and the badly organised recycling'.

'I can give you something on that,' Alexia said quietly, turning her hand over to inspect her nails. She'd never worn them so chipped and chewed. The ruby polish was the last remaining mark of the flush days before she lost her allowance. And her integrity.

'Okay,' Marlon said, his eyes sparkling with anticipation as best they could through the red lines that snaked through them.

'How do I know what it's worth?' She reasoned that the news was not so big – she wasn't even revealing anything new. Just a little bit of a correction to the status quo.

'I won't rip you off. I'm fair.'

She took a deep breath. 'Well, Max and Dee actually broke up months ago. Maybe close to a year now, I can't be exactly sure.'

'Really?' Theo said, scribbling. 'I need details. Places. Arguments. Anyone else involved?'

'I don't know the full story, but I know that Dee broke up with Max and it wasn't amicable. He was pretty heart-broken, actually.'

'How do you know? Did something happen?'

'No, no. I don't know the details.'

'Okay, so they only announced the break-up now, but they actually broke up ages ago.'

'Yes. Because of touring and her album and stuff. They wanted to delay the news.'

'And Dee broke up with Max and he was upset,' Marlon said flatly. 'So all you're basically saying is that they broke up earlier than they officially announced.'

'Yes.'

'Like almost every famous couple who have PR stuff to work through.'

'Um, if you say so,' she said.

Theo sat back in his chair. 'Alexia. That's not how it works. I need more than that – a story that ties it together. Why did she dump him? Did he cheat on her? Did he do anything bad to her? Was he abusive, that kind of thing.'

'Jesus. No.'

'Well, it's not a story.' Theo sighed. 'It's just a sentence. I can't spin it without more.'

'Okay, okay, but you shouldn't be nasty about it. Remember, they fell in love and Max is okay now, he's moved on. They're all decent people in the end.'

'I'm sure they are. Come on, Alexia – if you don't spill it someone else will. Why don't you be the one with the money in your pocket?'

'She met someone else. Well, she already knew him. They both did.'

'Okay. Who?'

'Charlie.' It was out, and she felt immediately ashamed.

Theo's eyes widened and he licked his lips before a sly smile crawled up one side of his face. 'Now we're getting somewhere. A bandmate betrayal!'

'Charlie and Dee have been dating for months, but everyone's cool with it. Max found out a while back. Just before he left the band.'

'Were those things connected?'

'No, no. He was cool with it.'

'You said he was "heartbroken".' Marlon made an exaggerated point of reading the exact word from his notebook.

'He was, when they first broke up, but like I said, that was more than six months ago. He's met someone else now, anyway.'

'Was there an incident?'

'I don't know.'

'Is this why he left the band, Alexia?'

'I don't think so,' she said, starting to wonder. 'No. No. It's not connected. Max and Dee broke up ages ago. Dee started dating Charlie but I guess they waited a while to tell Max. I think he was cool with it because he has a new girl. He's here with her now in London.'

'I don't think that part is important, for now.'

'But I'm just trying to put it into perspective. I mean, everyone's cool now.'

'Okay, but let's focus on Dee and Charlie. Was there any chance of crossover . . . ?'

Once the story was out she couldn't put it back in. She spent the next ten minutes trying to soften the details, smooth the edges, but Theo had a way of putting things that led her into telling him more than she meant to.

'I mean, when they were on tour, Charlie and Dee were super careful not to upset Max.'

'So he didn't know that they were secretly sleeping together when they were on their European tour? The one this summer?'

'No. Everyone kept it quiet. There were no dramas.'

'So everyone knew except Max.'

'I mean, I guess so. But it didn't feel like some big thing. Remember they weren't together any more. It was kind of no one's business.' Alexia shrugged, frustrated. 'You make it sound like a big conspiracy. Dee and Charlie just fell in love. They're not bad people. It made sense if you really looked at it. They're way more suited. Max was never into the limelight ... he never made a good half of a celebrity couple.'

As Theo scribbled on the pad, his hand partially obscuring his notes, Alexia thought of the money. It wasn't the worst secret she could tell. It wasn't news of Lee's girlfriend's infidelity and pregnancy. It was more of an exclusive reveal. All she'd really told him was that Charlie was dating Max's ex-girlfriend. It was going to come out anyway. But why did it feel so awful?

'So, how much?'

'For this?' Marlon said with a deeply satisfied smile. 'It's pretty good. A few thousand?'

'Okay. I have to wrap things up.' She cleared her throat and sat up a little straighter.

It was over. Rent would be paid for another month, the wolves were no longer at the door. She almost felt relieved – there was something about stepping away from the inner circle of The Keep that felt like a breakthrough. Or a breakaway. She glanced across the table at Marlon as he slurped the last of his tea and licked his lips.

She watched as he slowly shut the notebook, caressing the leather spine as he handled it. She'd betrayed them, and she'd betrayed her ethics.

And right off the back of judging someone simply for keeping their own secret.

'It'll be up tomorrow, probably,' Marlon said, leaning back. 'Your first story! You should feel proud. Don't look so worried. I bet you get a secret thrill out of it. It always gives me a buzz anyway. That's why I called it The Buzz.'

CHAPTER 16

Caught

Not even one bloody photo of us together.

Greta huffed as she walked to Oslo, one of Hackney Central's more upmarket dinner and live music venues. With a gastro menu and 'under the railway' vibe, it was perfect for inviting all the music influencers along for a showcase of the band. And it was a great setting for the batch of diary videos they needed to film and populate All New Wild's YouTube channel with before their launch.

As she arrived, she saw the band pre sound-check, scattered around in the bar area tucking into beers and burgers. Just like The Keep, they were all young, handsome boys – only their look was slightly more edgy. More tattoos and slightly more *hipsterish* haircuts. They also dressed more like an indie band – well, an indie band dressed by an army of stylists with no budget restraints. The effect was, even to Greta's star-struck eyes, highly orchestrated. A perfectly ripped jean. A purposefully oversized T-shirt. A far-too-new sneaker.

But there was no doubting the fact that Greta got a thrill seeing famous people, and it was even more thrilling getting to know them. She waved across at them, cursing her choice of cropped top that exposed too much midriff. She put her arm down immediately and tugged at the hem.

'Hey, Greta!' called out the singer, Navid. Or Nav, as he'd insisted she call him. He was definitely the most handsome of the bunch – Iranian, dark stubble, not too tall and with that perfect, thick north London accent.

'Hello, Nav.' She smiled calmly back, trying to keep it professional. Last thing she needed was another Lee in her life. 'I'm sorry about the other night.'

'What? No, you were great fun. I particularly loved the Abba table-top dancing . . . '

Greta drew a blank and blushed. 'Not my finest hour.'

'I dunno.' He grinned. 'I thought you were pretty fine.'

Greta gawped at him for a moment, then decided the best course of action was to ignore the comment. 'Everything okay for you guys?'

'Yeah,' he said, pulling out a seat and offering it to her. 'But, can I ask you something? You just had so much good advice about my career the other night.'

Greta cringed. She was prone to lying, exaggerating, lecturing and life coaching after a few drinks, but seriously, she had no memory of which way she went with Nav that night. 'Okay ...'

'And all that work you do with The Keep ...' He smiled. 'You really know this business.'

'Well, I mean, mostly Clint does, or Alexia. You should ask her.' *Christ, Greta!*

'The label,' he said glumly. 'You really sell your soul. I mean, I knew what I was getting into, but damn.'

'What do they want you to do?' She was going to have to wing this.

'Well, we have our first music video shoot coming up. I hate the concept. I hate the director dude. He wants us to be gritty and real.'

'Well, isn't that a good thing?' she asked.

'Gritty? No. I want dancers. I want colour. I thought we'd at least have dancers. This isn't the pop band I signed up for.' He ranted, shaking his head in disbelief.

Greta stifled a giggle. 'So it's too, um, real? Not pop enough? Is that what you're saying?'

'Exactly.' He smiled at her. 'I knew you'd get it.'

In all her dealings with bands, she'd never once heard someone say they wanted to emulate the manufactured vibe. She'd always enjoyed the dress-up feel of The Keep's various videos and live shows, but that was always the very thing that serious musicians baulked at. 'God, what an actual, real-life nightmare,' she said with complete sincerity. 'What can we do?'

He smiled at her. 'I dunno. If we can't have dancers, can we at least do some kind of dancing ourselves, rather than just walking around moodily and playing our instruments? I'm not a choreographer, but without any dancing isn't it all a bit . . . indie?'

'I think you have to just voice your concerns,' Greta said seriously, trying to remain diplomatic. But then she broke into a grin as an idea came to her. 'You're filming at London Fields, right?'

'Yeah.'

'Why not ask to be filmed in the *actual* playground there? You could play your guitar on the swing? Unplugged, of course. Quite fun really. And Alex could play drums on the roundabout? That would look awesome, actually.'

Nav smiled. 'Yeah, that would be funny.'

'Mention it to the producer. I bet they'll do it, if you go along with most of the other stuff. And just do the moody walking bit. You know The Keep did that video for "Alphabet S'up" where they just walked and sang through Central Park?'

'The Keep are so cool,' he nodded. 'You like them?'

'Oh, I love them,' Greta said enthusiastically, spotting Lewis out of the corner of her eye. 'I mean, you have no idea.'

'Thanks, Greta.'

'I'd better . . . ' She motioned to Lewis and Clint, who were waiting for her to help set up, and shyly smiled. 'See you in a bit.'

'Is Alexia coming?' she asked Lewis nervously, and she scuttled across the bar and dumped the gear she'd been forced to lug halfway across Hackney. 'I need help. I left the tripod on the side of the road.'

'Yes, I think she's feeling better.' Lewis was running a cable along the length of the bar as Clint fixed it down with silver tape. 'Clint?'

'Yep, just spoke with her.'

'Oh, that's good,' Greta said, trying to stifle a yawn that was, frankly, as involuntary as it was inevitable. 'I'm glad she's be-ahhhh-better.'

'Late night?' Lewis asked.

'No, just didn't sleep that well.' Greta had slept for around four hours, in truth. Even that was double what she'd managed for a couple of nights previous. But it was crisis time for Keepers all over the globe after the announcement that Maxx had left the band, and as one of the fandom's chief cheerleaders, she had to try to keep everyone calm. Plus, she'd had since Music in the Park to prepare herself – an extra forty-eight hours can work wonders for your sense of perspective. Tell that to the fandom though – there'd been every kind of freak-out imaginable, from social-exhibitionist type stuff to the usual giff-riddled faux meltdowns – and responses that were frankly frightening.

Greta hovered around the camera bag, wondering what she could do to help Lewis, but was too intimidated by his busyness to ask, so she pretended to sort the filters. She was really good at sorting the filters.

She thought back to Alexia's rude interruption at Deniz's and her strange, agitated behaviour. It was almost like she had wanted to get Lee away from her, that she didn't think Greta was safe for him to be around ...

'Don't be paranoid, Greta. You're totally cool here,' she said, trying to drown out the niggling concern.

'Talking to yourself again, Grets?' Clint winked at her. He'd caught her talking to herself on many occasions and always gave her a good-natured prod when he did.

She helped Clint arrange some chairs into a row and pretended to reposition some of the huge retro espresso machine paraphernalia that would serve as the backdrop to the showcase. All New Wild's debut album was called *One More Pint of Coffee*. Perhaps she needed a coffee. She couldn't focus on anything.

'Good afternoon.' Alexia's restrained greeting cut through Greta's sleep-deprived haze.

'Hi.' Her heart immediately quickened as she turned to face her. 'Glad you're feeling better ... You must have been really bad to be off all week.'

'Thanks,' Alexia mumbled, without making eye contact.

'You left pretty quick the other night,' Greta said, smiling sheepishly. 'You didn't even stay for a drink.'

'Well, yes. I had to.' Alexia looked fierce. Maybe even annoyed?

Greta decided to go and pretend to run over things with the band's management. Anything to get away from having to do any production work, and to get away from Alexia's weird mood. *DO NOT BE INTIMIDATED*, she repeated to herself, while creeping backwards out of the room.

Their boss, Kevin, made a surprise appearance under the guise of making sure everything was going okay. Lately, he'd been poring over Greta's budgets and double-checking everything she'd been doing, and she had been kind of glad of the guidance. The others were far more interested in pointing a camera and taking light readings than paying for taxis and making sure the talent were on time.

'Hi, Greta.' Kevin smiled broadly, his beard bushier than usual. 'Do you know where I can find the others?'

'In the back.' Everyone always wanted the others. Greta did what she often did at shoots, where the setting up seemed to go on for ever and nobody spoke to her unless they wanted a glass of water – she went and sat in the loo cubicle and checked her phone.

There was another Keep alert on her screen. *Oh god help us, not another one.* She dreaded any more Keep drama after the last few days.

Backstab Boys: The Real Story Behind Maxx leaving The Keep.

Greta read, her heart racing. *What was the* real *story?!*

The Buzz has learned that the real reason behind Maxx's departure was a secret affair between his then girlfriend Dee Marlow and bandmate and friend Charlie Childs. Our source said, 'Maxx was heartbroken. Dee and Charlie were together in secret during their recent tour around Europe and he only just found out.'

Maxx and Dee were the on-screen lovebirds who captivated the country with their sweet romance on reality TV show American Stars, but our source said the relationship had soured months before the recent announcement of their split, and that the couple had been keeping up appearances to help boost sales of Dee's upcoming album.

Greta was shocked. She felt angry, and then totally creeped out.

The band's glossy veneer had been peeled back and underneath was the usual kind of debauched, tacky behaviour usually reserved for Justin Bieber and the like.

There was something about the fandom game that suddenly felt gross. She loved to play when the boys were clean and untouchable – it was like interacting with a TV show, or a film. A constructed world that always delivered exactly what you wanted, with no surprises – the ultimate reality TV played out in real time across multiple platforms. But now, she had a backstage pass to the real action, and it was all a bit too ... real.

So, Maxx had left because of betrayal by another band member. It was hardly surprising – stealing a guy's girlfriend was bad enough in the playground, let alone in something as tightknit and intimate as a band. *Ugh. Yuk.*

She slipped her phone back into her pocket, flushed the toilet and left the cubicle to pretend to wash her hands. Alexia walked in through the swinging saloon doors.

'Greta,' she said uncomfortably, 'we need to talk.'

'I know. The article, right? I just read it.'

'What article?'

'About Charlie and Maxx and why he left the band. It's really sad. Did you know?'

Alexia seemed to flinch ever so slightly. She tucked a loose tendril of her glossy, beautiful hair behind her ear, and her newly manicured nails, painted the palest of pastel blues, ran across her face and stopped over her mouth while she considered her next words.

'I don't mean about that,' she said, finally.

'Did I do something wrong?' Greta blurted. 'Is this about the night with Lee? Because I didn't answer when you needed my password? I'm sorry – my phone died.'

'No, it's not about that. Well … it is a little,' Alexia said, cryptically. She seemed to be feeling her way into the conversation. For once, she didn't seem any more self-assured than Greta.

'I shouldn't have taken Lee out, should I? I feel so bloody bad, Alexia. I really didn't think you would mind … I mean,

I just thought I was helping. Was it terribly unprofessional? Or – oh my god – do you *fancy* him or something?'

'Of course not,' Alexia snapped, jerking her chin up. 'Don't be ridiculous. Of course I don't.'

Greta wondered at the fierceness of Alexia's protest for a moment. 'What is it then?'

'I know about your other ... life.' She waved her finger downwards, as if Greta's life might be found somewhere on the toilet floor. 'Your secret life.'

Greta inhaled sharply, hot dread building. *No. Please, no.*

'Wh – what do you mean?'

'The Keep?' Alexia looked upset, and Greta's dread reached boiling point.

'What?' Greta looked over Alexia's shoulder – everyone was well out of earshot. She felt sweat begin to bead on her upper lip.

'I know,' Alexia sighed, 'that you run that fan feed.'

'Whaaa ... ?' The small bathroom suddenly closed in on Greta. She could hear the sound of her heart, amplified and reverberating in her ears. 'I don't understand.'

'I cracked your password,' Alexia said. 'It wasn't hard.'

'Oh god,' Greta whispered.

Alexia raised her eyebrows and pursed her lips.

'You broke into my computer?'

'Well, I don't think that's the bigger crime here.'

'Is that why you took Lee away in such a hurry?' Greta replayed Alexia's arrival at Deniz's place through a different filter – her slightly wired, agitated manner as she shut the conversation down, gently coaxing Lee into heading to the bar. And the way she bundled him into a taxi, standing between the two of them on the pavement like an overprotective parent, so Lee had to smile and wave goodbye to Greta almost in secret. Lee had given her a wink. The greatest wink a girl could ever know.

'Of course. I realised you were the damn queen fangirl, and I wasn't sure it was a good idea to leave you alone with the object of your infatuation. I was extremely concerned.'

'But it's just harmless—'

'Harmless? Harmless? No it's not. I've seen first-hand what fans like you will do to get what they want. To "connect" with the band.'

'I'm not like that. Like those ones,' Greta protested. 'There are some fans who take it too far, but ninety-nine per cent of us just like the band. We like the camaraderie. They were kind of my family.' The words fell flat as a flash of pity crossed Alexia's face. 'Alexia … I …' Greta continued, stumbling on the words. 'It's not what you think. I mean, I would never do anything. I'm not some stalker or spy or something …'

'I know you haven't been spying, as such,' Alexia said with a sigh. 'But you kept it secret.'

'I'm sorry, I didn't think I was hurting anyone. It wasn't my intention to betray anyone and I've kept work and fandom stuff separate – you must know that if you've seen the feeds. I haven't leaked anything.'

'Intent and impact are a different thing. I don't trust you any more.' Alexia's face reddened when she said these last words, looking past Greta into the mirror at her own reflection. She shook her head and looked to the floor.

'Alexia ... please.' Greta was dying inside. She wanted to disappear, to run away, to hide. 'Please ...'

'I won't tell them,' Alexia said, softening. 'You could lose the internship and I don't want that to happen. I mean, if my father knew that someone at Bright Star was ... an obsessed fan ... a liability in this way, there's no way he'd award any more work to the company. This gig, the filming contract with All New Wild. That would be pulled in an instant. Discretion is so important, Greta. What were you thinking?'

Obsessed fan. She made it sound so disgusting. So shameful. So desperate. Greta felt her eyes begin to sting as the tears came. 'I'm sorry. I didn't think of it that way ...'

'Well, I won't say anything,' Alexia said quickly. 'It will be okay. Don't cry.'

'Oh, okay then. If you say so,' Greta said with uncharacteristic sarcasm, a large glob of snot starting to spring from her nostril. She wiped it with her sleeve.

'Please don't be upset, I don't want you to feel bad.'

'Why are you telling me, then?' Greta said, the tears now flowing uncontrollably. 'You already make me feel useless at work.'

'*I* don't make you feel anything,' Alexia said. Her look was tough, but she did seem a bit concerned. 'You don't seem to enjoy the work – that's not *my* fault. I guess that's what happens when you take on a job for the wrong reasons.'

Alexia stood for a moment, thoughtful, and then leaning forward a little she lowered her voice to a barely audible whisper. 'Do you even want this job? I mean, if it wasn't for The Keep?'

Greta sniffed. 'I like running the social media accounts. And I like dealing with the bands.'

The door flew open and Lewis stood there, flustered. 'Guys? What the hell? We need to get moving. What's wrong, Greta?'

'Nothing,' Greta said, wiping her nose and quickly drying her cheeks. 'Sorry. I'm just tired.'

'You also look unwell. Go home and get some sleep. We can manage here without you. We don't actually *need* you.' His words sliced Greta through the stomach.

Alexia turned to leave. 'Go on, head home, Greta. Get some rest. It's going to be okay,' she promised.

Why? How? Greta looked up at her through her heavy, tired eyes and gave her a desperate, frantic nod – half in thanks and half in defiance.

Then she quickly turned and fled, pushing through the crowd that was beginning to form in the bar and barging right into Navid on her way out the door – losing her footing and spinning sideways. Quick as a flash, he grabbed her round the bare skin at her waist to stop her from falling face first into a standing ashtray. She couldn't look at him or he would see her eyes red with tears. 'Sorry, I have to rush. There's an emergency. At home. My boat. My boat home. A catastrophe, really. I can't stay.'

She peeked up at him, and he was staring at her, his brown eyes full of kindness. He simply smiled. 'I hope you're okay. See you soon?'

CHAPTER 17

Use Somebody

'What do you think?' Alexia bit her lip, looking nervously at Lewis. The edit suite was hot and the machines whirred as they worked hard under Alexia's nimble fingers. 'Shall I play it again?'

The money from The Buzz had allowed her to stop taking on the evening admin shifts and keep Mr Coleman, that sweariest of wolves, from the door. It also meant she had time to spend on honing her craft. Making documentaries was the whole reason she was here in England, cut off from her parents financially and geographically, and why she was selling her soul to Theo Marlon. It was a high price – so she was going to make damn sure she got the most out of this internship.

'It's good.' His head pitched. 'But maybe . . . do you mind?'

Lewis gently touched Alexia on her hip, urging her to move slightly so he could squeeze into the tiny edit suite chair.

Alexia had cut together the short film they had been commissioned to make for The Keep. It was called *The Keep UNKEMPT*, and was supposed to be a behind-the-scenes look at the boys' last European tour as a five piece, using the rushes that Clint had filmed and some 'found footage' the boys had shot on their phones. 'Found footage' in this case was all knowingly filmed, so it was far from candid. It was a Christmas special, commissioned by ITV to play late in the evening just before the premiere of their Christmas single and their first appearance as a four piece.

It opened with a shot of Charlie on a plane, filming Lee asleep in a first-class bed.

'Lee wears pyjamas to bed every night,' Charlie whispered, turning the camera phone on himself. 'Even when we're flying – look.' He turned the camera back around and tugged at Lee's PJ bottoms, pulling them down slightly to reveal his bum crack.

Lee woke up immediately. 'Charlie! Eff off.' The expletive would be replaced with a bleep later in the process, of course.

Immediately, the film cut to the band on stage, music loud, followed by a montage of shots. The titles faded up:

The Keep – UnKempt
Starring
Cut to Art taking photos of the Brandenburg Gate in Berlin.
Art
Cut to a shot of Lee jumping into the Trevi fountain in Rome.

Lee

Cut to Charlie and Kyle playing chess on an enormous life-sized board in Prague.

Charlie

Kyle

Cut to camera creeping up on Max through the door as he plays guitar on his balcony overlooking Rome.

and Maxx

He shakes his head at the camera, and puts his hand up to obscure himself. Fade to black.

Lewis hit the spacebar and stopped the film.

'It's very MTV. You're on the right track. It's bouncy and fun and all those things a good Keep film should be. But . . . '

'But?' Alexia repeated.

He hit play again, and the boys were at rehearsal in Berlin. Lee was sitting on the edge of the stage, swinging his legs.

'We have to spend every afternoon at rehearsal. Sometimes it just takes an hour or so. Like we have to fix a dance routine or find out where to stand during the songs.'

Lewis hit fast forward, past some of the rehearsal footage, and then stopped on Max talking to camera.

'I have to hold this Perspex wand, and we basically cast a spell on the audience during the first chorus of "Magic Man".'

Off camera, Clint asked, 'And then what happens?'

An uncomfortable pause.

Max shrugged.

Lewis hit fast forward again and stopped on a shot of Kyle

and Art leaving the venue. Behind them Charlie was doing the old press-the-button-and-pretend-to-go-down-a-lift gag.

'And that's a wrap. Back to the hotel for a shower and some interval training.' Kyle smiles broadly.

'And I'm going to finish a re-read of *The Grapes of Wrath*,' Art enthuses.

Lewis hit stop.

'There's got to be some more interesting stuff?'

'Ha! Have you seen the band?' Alexia joked. 'Part of the stage collapsed in Prague, but Clint was filming in the Old Town at the time, so ...'

'Does Kyle say anything else? Jesus.'

He spooled through the rushes and pulled up the whole interview with Kyle. They watched it in full. Alexia knew she had pulled the only coherent and vaguely interesting line from the clip, but sat through the nine minutes of inane chitchat for the third time.

Lewis sat back in his seat. 'Lord. They really are dire. Let's take a break. Coffee? Actually ... lunch?'

'Sure. It's on me, though. For the help.'

'We already talked about that,' he said, putting his coat on. 'It's on Bright Star. We've earned it.'

As the front doors of the office opened, it was clear autumn was on its way. Warm summer air had been replaced with a feisty cold wind – the promise of winter gently pulsing through the air, gathering the first of the fallen leaves and a few discarded cigarette butts and blowing them into

Alexia's face. She braced herself, and pulled her wrap around her shoulders.

'Yikes,' she shouted. 'The weather changes so quickly.'

'Welcome to England,' Lewis said grimly. 'At least it's not raining . . .'

Before he got a chance to finish the sky opened on them, and it was run or be soaked. They bolted down towards the station and found shelter outside an all-you-can-eat Asian buffet.

They stood in silence as the downpour drummed on the awnings. Alexia was grateful for the diversion. She'd been editing for three days straight to get the film finished and, though it had kept her mind off other things, there was a churning sense of dread that appeared when her focus on work waned, if only for a moment. Selling the story to Theo was meant to have removed the anxiety of having no money, but it had only replaced it with a new kind of disquiet.

In the edit suite, she was learning how to craft a story out of pieces. She understood what it took to create an appealing narrative – but what Theo had done felt manipulative. Mean.

Max had left the band because Dee had an affair with Charlie and he was heartbroken.

It wasn't what had happened, but since the outcome fitted the story, it was difficult to dispute. Also, the PR people for The Keep were not going to let the truth ruin some much-needed column inches, whatever hurt they caused.

She worried about Max. She worried about Charlie and

Dee. And she worried about Greta. And she worried about her parents. And her bank balance.

'You're miles away.' Lewis shook the rain off his jacket as they took a seat in the all-you-can-eat buffet place.

'Yeah, I guess I am.' She forced a smile as the memories of her conversation with Theo Marlon flooded back. The dread was constant. 'I'm not hungry.'

'You should eat,' Lewis said. 'Sorry, I shouldn't say that. You should do whatever you want. I feel this overwhelming need to give you food.' He smiled. 'That's creepy, right?'

'No, I know.' She pulled at her jeans waistband and looked down at the gaping hole. It was incredible what a little anxiety could do to an appetite. 'I think I need to eat more.'

'Come on. Everyone likes a sweet and sour chicken served on chips with a side of pad thai, right?'

'Is there any fried rice?'

'With reconstituted, unidentified seafood and/or white meat?' Lewis said, grabbing her plate and smiling. 'You bet your ass there is.'

She laughed. It was rare to see Lewis so relaxed, and so light-hearted. He was often so earnest, so serious, so focused, it was easy to let a week pass without any small talk. She reached forward and touched his forearm. It was beautifully smooth, with just a sprinkling of dark hairs along his skin. Lee's skin was always cold and a little clammy. 'Thanks, Lewis.'

He looked at her hand for a moment and nodded, pulling away to go pile up two plastic plates with the restaurant's finest.

As she watched him filling their plates, he looked back and for a moment their eyes met. Alexia looked away immediately.

'So, you still want to make documentaries?' Lewis said as they both picked at the truly horrendous food in front of them. He doused his noodles in own-brand chilli sauce. 'You are so much better than I was at eighteen. I had just started my media diploma.'

'You went to college?'

'Just a year-long course. But yeah. I mean, how else do you learn? You can't get internships without something to get you in the door. Well, unless you know the boss.' He grinned.

'I worked hard,' Alexia countered. 'I started taking courses when I was fifteen. I learned photography from a friend of my dad. He used to take me to some of his shoots, for like *Teen Vogue* and *GQ*. It was pretty cool. My parents hate it, though. They want me to go to NYU and I'm deferred, so I have to at some stage. I guess, come Christmas, I'll probably have to head back.'

'Don't tell me, that's when the money runs out?' he teased.

'My parents aren't helping me,' she said defensively.

'Okay, okay,' he said with a smirk. 'It's just that it's an internship. Most people's parents have to help them out. It's nearly impossible to live in London without some help.'

'Sorry.' Alexia put her plastic fork down and wiped her mouth with the paper towel. 'I'm a little on edge today.'

'On edge?' She watched as he weighed this up. 'Do you need to talk to someone?' he said, awkwardly.

'Not really.'

'Well, I'm here.'

'Thanks.' She managed a weak smile. 'If you ever go to New York I know the best place to go for Chinese.'

He took another mouthful of noodles and washed it down with some Coke. He curled up his nose and shook his head. 'It's remarkable. It has the texture of hair.' They both laughed. 'If you want to make documentaries, you should start thinking of shooting something yourself. It's great to cut up the footage from The Keep, but that's not why you're here, is it? Why do you want to make docos?'

'I guess because people fascinate me,' she said. 'My parents are kind of shallow – Dad's all music and showbiz and CrossFit and Mom does this kind of skin-deep therapy that's basically life coaching. Do you know what life coaching is?'

'No idea. It sounds like exercise, which I'm firmly against. Unless it's exercising my thumbs.' He held up his invisible game console. Alexia could totally imagine him at home playing *War Thunder* with Internet friends until the wee hours.

'Same. Anyway, I've always felt removed from their reality. And I love watching people. Living with my parents was kind of a front-row seat to an incredible psychology show. And I read that film-making takes the photographic eye to its ultimate end. That documentaries indulge that voyeuristic tendency.'

'*I* read somewhere that under the guise of truth, documentaries entertain us with lies,' Lewis said.

'Everything's about agenda, right?' Alexia smiled.

'What's yours?' he said.

Alexia sat quietly for a moment. She didn't know what that question meant, nor how to answer it. Her agenda was to make a documentary – but what about? What did she want to say? What was her story? As if he could read her mind, Lewis continued.

'It's a pretty personal journey. You need to have a story in mind, or at least, something that interests you. Sheffield Doc Fest is coming up. You could submit something. A short maybe? Or speak to big-boss Karen about moving into the docs department? They're working on some proper feature-length stuff at the moment. Lucky buggers.'

'Yeah. I have a good idea I'm thinking about, I guess,' she sighed. She didn't have a good idea. She had nothing. Nothing but the gnawing anxiety of her dealings with Theo Marlon, anyway.

'That's great. Oh, and on that note, I have something for you.'

He pulled out a leather Moleskine notebook, still in its plastic wrap. 'I didn't wrap it or anything, sorry. But I just thought, every film-maker needs a leather notebook.'

Alexia wanted to reach out and hug him but she felt sure he would freeze like a lamp post. She stared at the beautiful book and hugged it to her chest. 'I'll treasure it!'

'Well, fill it with ideas, and then it's a real treasure.'

For a moment, they sat in comfortable silence. Alexia stared at the group of fashion students from St Martin's who had piled in for a cheap lunch, and Lewis played with his empty Coke bottle absent-mindedly.

She watched on as they laughed, easily, tossing off their coats and huddling down together to eat, one girl chattering loudly about her dissertation while the others leaned in supportively.

'Can I ask you something?' Alexia said gently. 'What do you think of Greta?'

'She's great,' Lewis said plainly. 'Kind, considerate, fun. Maybe a little bit crap at the technical and creative side of things, but you're here to do that now. I actually think she'd be a great producer, or, if she wanted, an excellent PR or marketing type.'

Alexia looked out at the rain, which was starting to ease, though the air had certainly thickened. 'Do you think she's all she seems?' she asked.

'No.' Lewis laughed. 'If there's anything I know for sure, it's that Greta has definitely got some other life outside Bright Star, but lord knows what it is. I'd believe anything. Did you know she lives on a houseboat most of the time? Have you met her grandma? She's like this incredible artist and she's totally hysterical.'

'No, I've never met her,' Alexia said glumly. She didn't know Greta lived with her grandmother, or on a houseboat. She realised she'd never even asked after Greta had revealed she didn't live with her parents. She'd guessed it might come out in time, but the stuff with Lee and the impact of discovering

Greta's secret had been surprisingly acute and cast any other background into shadow. Not just because of The Keep or any of that fangirl stuff, but because she'd thought Greta was becoming a real friend. The betrayal felt personal. And yet, she had her own secrets.

Lewis pushed his empty plate forward, grimacing. 'Is there something wrong? Are you two not getting on?'

'Oh, no. I really like Greta. There was just something that bothered me, but it's not important,' Alexia said with a smile. 'Coffee then? A real one?'

He nodded, tossing a £10 note on the table. 'But let's get a takeaway – go back and finish up this god-awful job. I was going to try to turn that turd you cut into a diamond, but I realise we're never going to make it good. You need good source material ... and *they* are not good source material.'

'Okay,' Alexia said. She buried her hands in her pockets and followed Lewis out of the restaurant.

Lewis turned to her once they were back on the street. 'Just so you know, and so you're clear – you're doing great. Better than great. Kevin has been asking lots about you. I think if you keep on, maybe you won't need to go back to NYU.'

'A full-time job at the end of this?' Alexia felt a pang of excitement in her stomach, briefly pushing down her anxiety.

'I hope so. The rain's stopped – let's make a run for it before it starts again.'

CHAPTER 18

London Calling

'Broadway Market is ace,' Clint insisted.

'Oh, I don't know, I'm right above Chapel Market you know, and I kinda don't think I need to see another London market.' She thought of Tony Coleman, marching up and down the street cursing the stall owners for not obeying the rules about how to display their products. She'd seen him kick at a pile of suitcases that had inched slightly onto the footpath, waving his arms in mock fury as the stall owner came over and they engaged in a proper cockney shouting match, featuring all manner of strange but weirdly cheery-sounding insults.

'Yes, you do. Chapel Market isn't Broadway Market. Trust me. Why you chose to live in Angel I'll never know.'

'It was close to work ...' Alexia laughed. 'I don't know London. Also, who wouldn't want to live in a place called Angel?'

The question went unanswered as they turned the corner of Regent's Row. Alexia was instantly glad she'd come. Stall after stall of gourmet food ran the length of the street, with small terraced shops flanking each side. She'd walked down this street before, but never on a Saturday. Clint had dived straight off to a stall and returned with a paper bag, grease already turning it translucent.

'What on earth is this?' Alexia asked.

'A scotch egg,' Clint said. 'Don't be fooled by its exterior. That is British culinary excellence.'

'Hmm.' Alexia was unconvinced.

'It's literally a meat-wrapped egg snack. How much better can it get?'

'I don't want to peak too early, this is the first stall.' Alexia screwed her nose up.

They walked past Ghanaian curries then deep, rich Bolivian hot chocolate served with gooey handmade marshmallow. Aromatic Persian stews bubbled next to brightly dressed sides of beetroot and aubergine and feta. Delicate handmade underwear was displayed on a gilded clothes line. Eco toiletries. Records. Meats. She'd never known Cheddar could come in so many varieties. 'The really orange one?' She pointed at a huge chunk of luminescent cheese.

'Red Leicester.' The stall owner sliced off a hunk with his knife for her to try.

'Oh my, I want to have them all.' *Happiness!* Alexia hadn't spent nearly enough time just 'being' in London. She was so focused on making this trip work professionally she'd not spent any time just hanging out. Or hanging out with cheese. She definitely needed more English cheese in her life. 'I think I'm in love with cheese.'

'You gotta try these gourmet toasties,' Clint said, motioning to a huge queue that had formed in front of a stall crafting hot sandwiches of bubbling French cheeses crushed between sourdough.

'Oh god, nine pounds for a sandwich?' Alexia bit her lip. She was trying to stretch the cash that Theo had given her, but she wasn't good at living with the feeling of deprivation. The pennies had never pinged on her radar before the last month or so.

'Come on.' Clint pulled her down the line of stalls. 'Let's go get a pint, eh? There's a pub called The Dove, they do pints and Thai food. It's actually the perfect combo.'

'No! I can't really afford to drink, either,' she said glumly. 'Ohhh goodness, warm cider!'

'I'll buy you a drink,' Clint offered.

He led her down the footpath, weaving in and out between the trendy coupled-up Londoners doing their weekend shopping, sipping their flat whites, nursing hangovers with indecent portions of bacon.

'Okay, this place is great,' Alexia said. 'I wish I'd moved to Hackney now.'

'Told you. And you still could. How are you enjoying things?' Clint said, as he handed the lovely Dorset cider stall owner a twenty-pound note. This was the ultimate people-watching place, and Alexia was in observational heaven. Just ahead an old rocker was playing 1960s rock and roll, thrashed at full, distorted volume on his guitar and tinny little battery-powered amp, his voice like a raked field of stones. It was brilliant.

'It's good, you know. I'm enjoying.' She smiled.

Clint winced at his first sip of cider. 'Jesus, this is a bit sweet for me.'

'Nothing's too sweet for you, Clint.' Alexia smiled at him, feeling more carefree than she had in weeks, months maybe. Her dealings with Theo were fading into the background, and a little of her regret and anxiety were fading with them. *Until next time, at least.*

'Are you okay for money? You can always live with me and Jules for a bit. That offer stands.'

'I'm okay. I've never had to worry about money before.' She bit her lip. 'I know that sounds bad, but I think it's probably good for me.'

'It can't be good to live like the rest of us,' Clint said with a laugh. 'You should see our flat – it's falling apart. We're probably moving, actually. Looking for something smaller but nicer. What we'll lose in square foot, we'll make up for in quality fittings and a landlord that answers our calls. London. Such a bloody rip off. Makes me furious. Can your dad and mum not help?'

'They're still not on board with my life choices,' she said,

173

laughing away the conversation. 'I'm loving Bright Star. A bit too much All New Wild for my liking but beggars can't be choosers.'

'God, they're dreadful. I think Greta's quite taken with them.'

'Come on. She's taken with *everyone* even remotely famous.' Alexia giggled. It was true. Setting aside the fan club stuff, Greta was still dazzled by fame, whereas Alexia felt fatigued by it. She wanted to rip off the veneer to find out what was underneath. She got the feeling Greta wanted only the veneer.

'What I find amusing is how they're marketing them as not being a boyband, when they so obviously are. They were put together by Geoff's team through auditions in Soho. Just like musical theatre. Just like *X Factor*.'

'I know. Oh my god, is that a market on the canal? Can we?'

'Sure.' They hugged their hot ciders and wandered down to the canal. The boats were berthed three deep, as was usual for this time of year. Most were selling worthless clobber – second-hand clothing, trays of over-baked goods, small, boat-sized second-hand furniture – but one loud and raucous canal boat had a small bookshop set up inside, and on top a guy with a spongy beard was playing jazz trumpet over a pre-recorded backing track while a tall, skinny lady in a 1970s jumpsuit handed out glasses of sparkling wine at three pounds a pop. It was bustling with life.

There was something comfortingly familiar about this place, though Alexia felt so far from Manhattan.

'I'm boarding the bookshop!' She stepped onto the canal boat and ducked under a dark beam into the romantic dream world below. Books upon books, second-hand, thumbed, scribbled on, ripped, loved, devoured. She ran her finger along the spines and examined the amusing hand-scrawled dividers, which included 'Bend and Stretch' (containing a book about yoga and a collection of 1980s fitness magazines) and 'Feminism and Optimism' (*The Vagina Monologues* and *Let's Talk Sex* by someone called Davina McCall). There were sections called 'Science Things', 'Books That You'll Love More Than My Uncle Wayne Did' and 'Books About Stuff You Might Do For a Living If You Have a Trust Fund'. Alexia smiled wryly – that was the film-making, photography and fashion section.

She pulled out a book called *Direct Cinema: Film-making Style and its Relationship to Truth* from 1972 and turned to the lady drinking prosecco by the barge entrance. 'How much?'

'Whatever you like,' she said, motioning to a bucket next to the door. After a few more minutes, and a couple more books, Alexia fished out a handful of gold coins and tossed them in. When she emerged, Clint was chatting with a friend in a multi-coloured shell suit, flip-flops and a neon sweatband.

'Alexia *is* American.' Clint nodded as she approached mid-conversation.

'Hi, Alexia,' the stranger held his hand out. 'I was just saying I'm having a weekend in New York.'

She looked his outfit up and down, trying to figure out

whether it was some kind of practical joke. 'Oh, that's great. Looks like you'll fit right in.'

'I don't normally dress this way. I was at a birthday party last night – just on my way home now. Fancy dress. Eighties theme.'

'I like the headband. It's a nice touch,' she said. He was strawberry blond with a smattering of freckles across his nose, a fine cleft trailed through his full lips and he offered the most imperfectly warm and welcoming smile.

'Anyway, I really have to get on. Are you going to walk with me, then?'

'Yes,' replied Clint, turning to Alexia. 'I need to get on, doll, and Kym's walking in my direction.'

'No problem, off you both go.' She smiled.

'Got yourself a book?' Clint asked as he squashed his cup and searched for a bin.

Alexia hugged her books proudly. 'It's so awesome in there. I thought I could give this one to Lewis.' She held out a book titled *1001 Things to Do With Your Commodore 64*.

'Oh, a gift for Lewis?' Clint said, teasing. 'You two would make a ridiculously earnest couple. I approve.'

'It's not like that,' she snapped.

'Oh relax, Lexi,' Clint joked. 'I'm just teasing. I know you'll only ever have eyes for Lee. And Lewis has practically gamified Tinder, so . . . '

Alexia felt hurt, though she knew she had no right to. He was being playful, and the truth was everyone on tour knew

176

how she felt about Lee. She'd found it nearly impossible to hide, especially as he toyed with her so often and so publicly.

Clint gave her a kiss on the cheek. 'I'm kidding. Sorry. Forgiven?' He pouted, before pointing her on her way. 'Now: this way back to the market; this way along to Victoria Park, where Music in the Park was – and, in fact, near the lovely Greta; and this way to the station.'

'Got it,' she said, waving him off.

As she wandered back up the stalls, she stopped at a stand selling gorgeous handmade leather bags and fondled their buttery softness, shaking her head to stop the stall owner from trying to sell. She couldn't afford the hundred-pound price tags even if she'd wanted to.

Next, a record stall. She thumbed through the collection of mostly Motown tunes, looking for nothing in particular. Her mind wandered back to the years spent hiding out in the basement of her father's office block, where they kept file copies of old records. A surge of warm nostalgia rippled through her and she felt an uncharacteristic longing for a hug from him.

At the next stall there were some second-hand cameras. And not just stills cameras; old DV, VHS and film cameras. She was stopped in her tracks by a vintage Canon Super 8.

'Does it work?' she fired at the stall owner.

The lady smiled, her ruby-red lipstick absolutely breathtaking against her dark skin. 'It sure does. I shot with it just last week.'

'Oh my,' Alexia said. 'Can I?'

'Of course,' she said, eyeing the book poking out of her tote. 'You're a film student.'

'Not a student, no,' Alexia said, opening the battery compartment to check for rust.

'Tourist then?' she beamed.

'No, I work here. In London. In TV,' Alexia said proudly, peaking through the view finder. 'Can you get film for it here?'

'Yes. More and more stores are stocking it, actually. And you no longer need to send them to Amsterdam for processing.'

Alexia didn't know that was a thing. She looked at the lady and bit her lip. 'How much?'

'Four hundred and fifty pounds,' she said cautiously, and then added quickly, 'Comes with a case, though. And I can throw in a roll of film?'

'Oh jeez . . . ' Alexia's heart sank.

'Wanna see what it can do?' The woman pulled out her phone and opened the video section, hitting play on a short sequence of different scenes around London shot from an open-top bus. The shots of the Thames, the parks and St Paul's all drifted by with such beauty – the film was warm, so deeply real, the colours rich, and it gave the most delicious feel to everything it captured.

'Has a microphone here, it's steady as you like. Check out the zoom. And the lens is near mint condition.'

'Ahhhh, god.' Alexia was being seduced. It really was an absolute beauty. Far better than the straight off the shelf, brand new, soulless kit she had back in New York. 'It's just so expensive.'

The lady slipped her phone away, looking vaguely annoyed. 'Yeah, I'm afraid they are. It used to be you could pick one up on eBay for next to nothing, but now every hipster in Hackney wants one.'

'You know what? Screw it. Do you take card?'

CHAPTER 19

50 Ways to Leave Your Lover

Early starts are the worst. Greta grumbled, pulling her tights on and lacing up her Doc boots. She flung open the door of the houseboat and peered down the canal. The sky was dark, except for a small red glow in the distance. By the time she got to London Fields it would be light.

> FROM ALEXIA: Lewis wants coffees. Can you get?
> There's that place Climpson's on Broadway Market.

> TO ALEXIA: Got it.

'You off, darling?' Granny called out from her tiny berth. 'Can I make you some tea? There's leftover liver dumplings in the fridge. Oh damn. Actually, I think I left them on the roof. The dog will have got them.'

'I'm fine, Granny.'

'Did you do it?'

'Yep.'

'All of it?'

'Yep. Cold turkey. I'm done.'

'Oh, I'm so pleased, let me give you a hug …' The boat creaked as her legs hit the floor, and Greta heard a sigh as she stretched achy muscles and tired bones.

'Go back to sleep, Granny,' Greta whispered, shutting the cabin door. 'We'll talk about it later.'

'Okay, baby girl. I love you.'

Greta ran as fast as she could through the darkness, the smell of algae and fresh human wee thick in the still air. There was a new obstacle course every morning – a car tyre here, a mattress there, but she only needed to sprint 100 metres of terrifying canal footpath until she was up the steps and onto the relative safety of Mare Street.

They were filming a behind the scenes of the video for All New Wild's song 'Uncontrollable You' and Greta was, for once, looking forward to a day away from the office. Especially today. The first day of the rest of her life. The day she could say she was no longer a Keeper.

She rushed up to the cafe, bought a tray of flat whites and bounded towards the set. She felt lighter. Happier. Free. She was looking forward to telling Alexia and calming the murky waters of that relationship, too.

There was a huge film truck parked just to the side of the

street, and folks were milling around waiting. Everyone was always waiting on set. Waiting for the technical team to fix a cable. Waiting for the weather. Waiting for the sound guy to check something. Waiting for some poor hapless runner to arrive with some duct tape. Waiting for the DOP to re-set for the ninetieth time because a pigeon photobombed the shot. So, there they all were. WAITING.

'Hi, guys!' Greta said cheerfully, throwing Alexia an especially wide smile. 'Hi, Alexia – I got you soy milk, is that right?'

'Thank you, Greta,' said Alexia, without making eye contact. She looked tired and a little pale.

'Everything okay?' Greta said uneasily.

'Clint's furious about something. We're waiting to find out what,' Lewis explained, while he and Alexia exchanged serious, ominous and secretive glances. 'But, yeah, thanks for the coffee.' He smiled, pulling down on his fluro-yellow Space Invaders cap.

Greta slipped back into her usual on-set unease as she looked at Lewis and back to Alexia. *Why are they being so quiet? Best I stay quiet, too.*

'Anyone doing anything for Halloween? Because the houseboat fits like twenty and I was thinking of having a party. Is twenty a party? Maybe more like a gathering. We could go out afterwards? Moth Club maybe?'

That wasn't quiet, Greta, you bloody idiot.

Alexia looked bemused. 'I didn't think you guys really did Halloween?'

'It gets bigger every year. And who can resist the chance to dress up as a slutty horror nurse or slutty cartoon character or slutty Marvel hero or a slutty witch or a slutty ... '

'Ha! Sounds just like New York, actually,' Alexia said, thawing slightly. Their first real connection since the last shoot. Greta felt a surge of hope.

Clint came striding across the field, his beard actually flapping in the wind it was so long now. With a tripod flung over his shoulder and his jacket billowing behind him there was a definite air of ...

'Hi, Gandalf,' Lewis joked.

'Gaydalf, thank you very much. I just got off the phone with Kevin,' Clint said, throwing down the tripod with a huge thump, and holding up a copy of the *Sun*. 'There's been another leak.'

'Where is it?' Lewis said.

'Look at the front page.' He pointed to a shot of Dee and Charlie cosying up on a couch under the headline 'Hands off, YOKO! Fans rage at Dee Marlow for breaking up The Keep.' Greta recognised the image immediately and felt a sudden chill come over her.

'How is that a leak?' Lewis said again. 'It's a photo. For heaven's sake, you look totally stressed.'

'That *photo* is a still from our rushes.'

Greta looked back to Lewis, whose eyes narrowed, and then down to Alexia, who was busying herself sorting through the gels, without so much as a cursory glance at the catastrophe unfolding.

'How is that possible?'

'It's not possible. I brought them back from tour and they've only been imported locally at work.'

'Damn it.'

'Kevin's pissed. Apparently, Alexia, your dad's been on the phone and they're talking about pulling the filming contract for The Keep unless we plug the leak . . . '

'My dad?' Alexia shot up, eyes wide. 'My dad called?'

'Yeah, of course.' Clint furrowed his brow. 'I mean, it affects them, right?'

'There can't be a leak!' Greta said firmly. 'There's only the four of us with access to that footage.'

'Well,' Lewis removed his cap and ran his hand through his hair. 'Not exactly. The rushes are sometimes saved to a shared server if our local drive is full. Which is, frankly, all the time!'

'So we were hacked?'

'Well, if not hacked, at least a hundred people have access to the shared drive. It's an explanation. Who imported the footage?'

Greta felt a cold rush come over her as she shot a look at Alexia. 'Me. But that was ages ago. I haven't been in the suite since . . . well, since Alexia started.'

'Don't worry, Greta, no one thinks you're some kind of covert operative stealing Keep footage for money.'

'Huh?' *He's joking. Laugh.* She giggled. It was high-pitched and went on a fraction of a second longer than she would have liked. She tried to turn it into a cough. *Oh my god, Alexia knows about the fandom ...*

'What I mean is, did you save it to a shared drive?'

'Maybe.' Greta racked her brain. Her palms began to sweat. She felt a bead trickle down the side of her neck. *Danger! I don't like where this is going. I have to shut this down. Take the heat. Stop the questions.* 'You know, I think I did.' Her voice shook, her lip started to quiver.

'Damn!' Clint said.

'Jesus. How angry are the label?' Lewis asked.

'Pretty angry.'

'Alexia, can you talk to your dad?' Lewis suggested.

'Sorry, guys,' Greta said, biting her lip. *Don't look at Alexia.* 'I'm so sorry.'

'I can talk to my dad,' Alexia chipped in, 'and don't get mad at Greta. I was the one doing the editing. I should have moved the files across to the local drive.'

'This is bad, though. That's twice, right? That something has leaked from London – The Buzz must have had a local source on their story,' Clint said. 'I don't get it.'

'Well, the other thing was just gossip. Bound to come out. Max and Lee spoke about it at Music in the Park in front of all of us,' Alexia reasoned. 'I mean, it could have even been one of them.'

'True,' Clint nodded.

'I'll speak to Dad,' Alexia said firmly. 'It'll be fine. You know, people talk. When the initial anger dies down they'll probably be grateful for the attention.'

'I'll call Kev,' Lewis said.

'It's not the end of the world. This stuff happens all the time,' said Alexia. Greta marvelled at how relaxed and laissez faire she was in this crisis, given how she'd reacted to the fandom stuff. 'And even if it's meant to be a secret, the PR people will just spin it and milk the publicity. It's what they do.'

'Yeah, but it shouldn't come from us,' Clint said. 'It's unprofessional. We'll lose our contracts if we can't be trusted to keep footage and information secure, and then there will be no more music department.'

'I know,' Alexia agreed. 'I'll talk to Dad. Don't worry.'

Clint tossed the newspaper on the ground and picked his tripod back up, nodding towards the crew, who were suddenly full of life. 'All right. Here we go. I thought this was a walk and sing. Are they doing a walk and play now? He's holding his guitar. And is that a wind machine?'

Lewis spat out the last of his coffee. 'We were warned about this, remember? They want to be seen with instruments as much as possible so they don't get called a boyband.'

Greta laughed. 'I think it's the label that wants that. Nav would be quite happy with any boyband association.'

Nav stood in the centre of the path getting his make-up done. Someone held a light reader to his face. And then, tumbling out of the trailer parked on the road, came six backing dancers dressed as high-school cheerleaders.

'Well done you,' muttered Greta, looking at Nav proudly.

They headed towards the set to start their behind-the-scenes filming. Greta followed behind, as usual, holding the clip-board, sashaying around, making sure people were out of shot, release forms were signed, and the talent was happy.

She watched Alexia working; her demeanour was focused, serious. Greta wondered why she hadn't outed her. She was desperate to say thank you again, and reassure Alexia the new leak had nothing to do with her. Around mid-morning, she got her chance.

Alexia wandered off to make a quick phone call, and Clint and Lewis decided it was time to set up for some All New Wild video blogs. Greta watched and waited for Alexia to finish the call and rushed over when she saw her slip the phone into her back pocket.

As Greta jogged the short distance between them, she saw Alexia hunch over and rest her head in her hands. 'Alexia!'

Alexia looked up slowly, wiping her red eyes. Swollen. Bloodshot. She forced a brief smile.

'I wanted to say thank you,' Greta stammered. 'Thank you for not saying anything. I realise it looks bad but I promise you I didn't do anything. I promise. I would never betray you guys. You have to believe me. Wait ... Why are you crying? Are you okay?'

Fresh tears appeared in the corners of Alexia's eyes and she immediately looked in the opposite direction, chin up, head firm. 'I know you didn't do it,' she said quietly.

'Are you okay?' Greta said. 'Oh, Alexia, what's wrong? You look really upset.'

'I'm fine,' she said, miserably.

'And I signed over the fandom last night. To a girl from Devon called Ella McKeep. I'm sure that's not her real name. But anyway, I gave her all the logins and passwords to the fan feeds and told her to change them so I couldn't get in. I'm out.' Greta swept her hands in a 'no more' gesture and pursed her lips. 'Done,' she reiterated. 'Finished. Over. Complete. Doneski. Finito ... um ... That's all I got.'

Alexia nodded again. Unsure how to address the crying, Greta shifted a little on one foot and stared across at the boys. Even after their post meal-deal chat, she'd gone on seeing her fellow intern as invulnerable. Unreadable, even. 'Are you triple sure you're okay?'

'Yes. That was my dad.' She sniffed. 'He's mad at me.'

'Oh. The leak. But it's not *your* fault.'

'No, about other things. My mom ... ' her voice trailed off. 'She doesn't want me to be here. Doesn't think I can hack it. I need to make this work.'

'Well, there's a full-time job at the end of this. Will that help?'

'Don't *you* want that job?' Alexia wiped her eyes.

'Honestly? I don't know. I'm not ever going to be a DP, let's face it. I know you think it's ridic but I enjoy looking after people. Fangirling. Being all star-struck. It's fun. The bit I like is that. Making sure people are happy and feel special and adored. That's not a job though, is it?'

'It could be.' Alexia shrugged and forced another weak

smile. Greta felt a surge of affection for her strange, serious, earnest American friend. Because they *were* friends. Maybe a little bit dysfunctional, but it was early days. There was another little surge when Alexia said: 'I'm sorry about Lee. I was ... unfair.'

'That's okay. At least I met him. That was, like, my biggest dream. What happened to him, anyway? I was hoping after that hugely successful kebab supper, where I charmed him completely and made him laugh on no less than two occasions, he might ask me out for a date! He told me I was sweet, you know?' *Too far, Greta!* She couldn't put the last part back in her mouth.

Alexia's hunched shoulders straightened and she bristled a little, and Greta watched the vulnerable, relatable Alexia slip away. 'My dad asked me to help get him home, so I did. He's a mess.'

'A mess?'

'Yes. Jessica stuff.' Alexia looked away from Greta.

'*Really?*' Greta wanted to know more, but stopped herself from appearing too interested. That was the Keeper instinct still lingering – and that wasn't Greta any more.

Alexia stood up and pointed to the boys, who were waving like mad. 'I think we're back on.'

CHAPTER 20

Disintegration

Alexia slumped on the edge of her bed. She wrapped the thin blanket around her shoulders and looked down at the pile she had made on the floor. She yawned, and contemplated attempting to sleep again, but knew the moment her eyes closed, the wired feeling would return.

Her Mulberry handbag. The only pair of heels she brought with her to England – Miu Miu. A blue jacket by Tom Ford. Her wristwatch – a birthday present from Tiffany & Co. Her US iPhone. And a dress by RED Valentino she was loath to part with. Total cost retail: over ten thousand dollars. If she could get just half of that from reselling them she would be able to cover the rent and the bills for a little longer, plus have enough to eat. She looked at her chipped nails and vowed to go clear. They'd look better anyway.

Now she had to get downstairs without bumping into

her landlord, who seemed to be permanently stationed at the stall outside her house with a cup of tea, shouting at the neighbours, the council, the mini cab drivers and that swaggering prick Jez who lived in flat two. She bundled all her things up into a canvas bag and opened the door to the hallway. It was quiet, so she snuck out of the back entrance and into the alley.

She jumped as her UK phone buzzed. Everything seemed to make her jump now. Her heart rate was permanently elevated and her chest was often tight.

She looked at the screen. Theo. Again. She rejected the call.

The money for the first story had been great – two thousand pounds in all – but when Theo had handed her the second envelope a few weeks later, Alexia had been aggrieved to discover that it contained a measly 500. *That's all stealing that photo from work was worth?*

Theo had shrugged. 'I paid far less for an upskirt of Kate Middleton,' he explained. 'But you can always become a fulltime source. Put you on salary?'

To make real money from Theo she would have to give him information more regularly, once a week at least. There was no way she could face becoming a full-time source for The Buzz – the idea made her feel ill.

She wrapped her scarf around her neck and bristled against the cool air. This was better. Selling this meaningless stuff would buy her another month or so, and then there would be the chance of the paid job at Bright Star. And, if she worked a little harder on her parents, there was maybe a chance of assistance from them in the meantime.

She pushed into the designer vintage shop and the bell above the door gave a friendly ring.

A small dog barked less friendlily from under a rack of fur coats, and a glamorous lady with pencilled eyebrows, tight black braids and a glorious technicolour tea-dress appeared from through a door at the back of the shop. 'So sorry. My damn shoe strap snapped,' she muttered. 'Can I help you, darling?'

'Hi. I have some things to sell.'

'Wonderful. Come over here and let's take a look.' She motioned towards the large counter at the front of the store. 'We're only taking winter clothes.'

'Okay.'

The woman's long, bony fingers, heavy with junk jewellery, turned each piece over. She carefully inspected the seams of the bag, the wear on the soles of the shoes, searched the lining of the jacket for tears and shook out the creases from the dress. Alexia felt a pang of sadness – she'd told herself that each item was meaningless, but as the woman inspected them for flaws she couldn't help but feel her character was undergoing the same scrutiny. She was taking a long look at herself, at least.

'Pretty. From last season?' the woman questioned, holding the dress up to herself and sashaying over to the mirror.

'Yes.'

'Okay. I think ... one hundred for the bag, two hundred for the jacket. I don't think we'll sell that watch here – it's a specialist item – so I'll pass on that. Maybe 75 for the dress as well?'

'And the shoes and phone?'

'Yes, the shoes. 50? We don't sell iPhone, darling, try one of those pawn shops nearer the Highbury end of the road.'

Alexia felt winded as she did the mental arithmetic. 'Four hundred and fifty? But, there's over seven thousand pounds worth of stuff there.'

'Well, maybe when you bought it, and this is a second-hand store, darling. After I add my mark-up, less cost of running the store and, obviously, the risk the pieces won't sell – that's what I'm prepared to offer. I mean, if you want, I *could* take the watch as well – make it an even six hundred?' she said, clicking open the till and slowly pulling out a few £50 notes.

She smiled at Alexia, showing yellow teeth and receding gums. The effect was to deflate the last vestiges of the glamour Alexia had seen at first glance. Six hundred pounds was never going to make a dent in her living expenses. It wouldn't even cover a fortnight's rent.

'You could always try eBay?' the woman said.

'I thought it would be more,' Alexia said, making a last stab at haggling. 'I mean, you've got a dress way older and in worse condition than that in your window for two fifty.'

'That's because the risk is all mine. I *can* sell on your behalf, which means no money upfront, then we split the profit twenty-five per cent to me, seventy-five to you when it sells. I hold stock for one month.'

Alexia sighed. She didn't have time for that.

'Okay,' she said flatly. 'Six hundred it is.'

'Wonderful news, darling. Well, would you look at that. I only have about two hundred in the till. I'm going to need to pop out back.'

Alexia had walked aimlessly for over an hour. She'd made it down through Clerkenwell, past the Barbican, and down to the Thames. She walked the full way down to Tower Bridge, and realising she'd never bothered to cross, she forced her way through the Saturday tourist traffic and headed to a grassy bank on the other side. She sat down, pulling out her water bottle, and looked back towards the Tower of London. She'd rarely been south of the river since she'd arrived. It was true – people really stuck to their postcodes in London. Texts arrived from Lewis and Clint. The pre-production meeting for *Weekend Kitchen* must have finished. The whole team had been roped in as part of money-saving changes from the executive board.

FROM LEWIS: Feeling better? Are you going to be at the live show tomorrow?

FROM LEWIS: Not to worry you, but Kevin's been asking where you've been.

FROM CLINT: Lady, where the hell you been at? A
lot has happened. We need to speak tomorrow.

She really needed to call Clint back. She hadn't spoken to him
since the call last week when she'd tried to take him up on his
offer to crash on the couch. He and Julian *were* moving to a
studio as it turned out, and crashing on the couch would literally mean sleeping in their bedroom. She couldn't face that,
even if Clint had insisted it would be fine. And for how long?
A week wasn't enough.

She really needed to make this call. She dialled her
dad's number.

'James.'

'Alexia. Darling, how are you?'

'Fine. Is Cassie there?'

'No, she's out shopping for that retreat she does.'

Every year, her mother went upstate with her two best girlfriends for three days of yoga, meditation, silence and clean
eating. She always returned bleary-eyed and hungover.

'Thanks for getting Lee back, by the way. Don't know what
happened with that Jessica. The kid's in a bad way.'

'Can I ask you something and will you promise not to
tell Cassie?'

'I can't absolutely promise, no. I can try?'

Alexia thought about it for a moment, and weighed things
up. Her dad was nearly always good for a secret from Mom.
She'd been playing them off her whole life.

'Remember when I called you about that business with work a little while back?'

'Yes.'

'And you asked me if I needed any help?'

'Yes. What help do you need?'

'I need money, Dad. Without somewhere to live I can't do this internship. It's only another few weeks until I find out if I get offered a proper paid job. I can see the finish line, I'm so so so close.'

'I thought you had enough to see you through?'

'I thought so too, but it's expensive here.'

Silence for a few moments, and then a huge sigh from her father.

'Are you in trouble?'

'No,' Alexia said brightly. 'I just need a little extra then I'll be fine on my own, I promise.'

More silence on the end of the line. There was going to be a deal struck here, Alexia could feel it.

'I'm not comfortable with this, Alexia. No parent wants their child to be stuck without money a million miles away, but, equally . . . why can't I tell your mother?'

'Don't you want me to achieve my goals, James? Dad?' Alexia said, frantic. 'Don't you care that I'm happy?'

'Alexia, I can hear your mother at the door. I'd really like to speak to her about this. I'm not prepared to do this behind her back. I'm sure she'll agree to helping you out. How much do you need?'

'A few thousand. But I don't want Mom to know. She'll be too pleased I couldn't do it myself. I can't stand the thought of her swooping in with that look she always gives me.'

She could hear her mother arriving in the background now, the rustle of shopping bags and the thud as they hit the kitchen island. A seagull landed on the edge of a bench just in front of her, picking through the feathers under its wings before squawking and flying off. She had to be quick.

'So, can you do it? James? Just say yes or no. I need a few thousand pounds. Probably four.'

'Alexia!' *Damn, Cassie will be listening in now.*

'I didn't think about how expensive it was going to be.'

'You didn't think about a lot of things.' Her father's voice was raised and getting hot. She could imagine her mother with her arms folded, lips pursed, shaking her head in disapproval.

'Fine. Forget it. I'll figure it out. I have to go . . . '

'Wait. Are you going to come home for Christmas?'

'Yes. I mean, that was the plan. *If I can afford it.*' She knew how manipulative she was being, but didn't care.

'No, I mean for good.'

'Ah.' Alexia shook her head and ran her free hand up and down her thigh as if to smooth the pending confrontation.

'Come, Alexia. I've given it some thought, and maybe we can set up a production arm at Falls Records or something. Take that work Bright Star does internally. You could split time between that and college.'

'Dad, just . . . no.'

'Alexia, I want to help, I really do.'

She stared at a little patch of blue, listening to her dad try to convince her of this and that. For a moment, she felt a surge of regret. It had been months since they'd rubbed along together at breakfast, making muesli and giggling at her mother's stories. Her phone beeped to tell her another call was waiting. She looked at the screen – Mr Coleman. 'Dad, I have to go,' she snapped.

She switched lines. 'Hi, Mr Coleman. I know I'm late with rent.' She put the phone on speaker and placed it on the grass next to her. Just that act of not touching made it feel less intense.

'I knew I shouldn't have let an eighteen-year-old move in. What was I bloody thinking? I can't throw you out. I have a daughter your age. I'm too bloody worried about you. What are you going to do?'

'I'll have the money to you by Friday,' she said.

'You even *lie* like my daughter. But fine, fine. Friday.'

'Thanks, Mr Coleman.'

'Yeah. Okay. Friday though. It had better be Friday.' Alexia could picture him wagging his finger, speaking just a little loudly so everyone in the vicinity could hear him 'doing business'.

'I promise.'

'You know what? Don't promise. Just get me the money.'

He hung up. 'I'm sorry.' Alexia whispered into the dead line.

She took a deep breath, and dialled Theo Marlon's number once more.

Chapter 21

Nowhere to Run

'Welcome *back* to *Weekend Kitchen*. Welcome back to *Weeeeeekend Kitchen*. Which do you like more?' Giles Punter-Rooney was staring straight down the barrel of camera one as a hairdresser sprayed liquid hair onto his bald patch. 'No hang on, maybe a bit more informal. Welcome back, *friends*, to *Weekend Kitchen*.'

'Definitely not friends,' said Kevin, watching him on one of the eight monitors in the control room, pressing his finger on the playback switch so Giles could hear. Giles looked momentarily hurt. Kevin spun around in his chair. 'You're late. You know this show is live, right? That means, alive. Living. Happening now.'

'I'm sorry,' Alexia said. Sorry. It rolled off the tongue these days.

'It's fine. Too late to put you on the teleprompter, though,' he snapped. 'Can you assist Karen? She needs help with the food – the stylist has food poisoning. Irony, my American friend, or not?'

'Sure,' Alexia said sheepishly. She ducked out of the control room to concerned stares from Lewis and Clint, who were sitting at the back getting briefed by the director.

She knew she'd been a flake this past week, avoiding Greta's relentless lunch invitations, sneaky days off ... yesterday's secret afternoon meeting with Theo. She found it easier to keep her distance from everyone, just in case ...

'Who ate the bloody smoked salmon?!' shouted Karen, about six inches from Alexia's face. And then, quietly sinister: 'Who the hell. Ate all. The smoked salmon? It's for the "brunch" segment. We're done with avo-bloody-cados!'

Karen was red-faced and furious. Her painted eyebrows leaped forwards to make two huge, accusatory arrows, pointed right at Alexia.

'I just got here.'

'Then you're late.' She pointed to the dressing room. 'Go and make yourself useful and lipstick the bastard strawberries so we can finish the Victoria sponge for segment two.'

Alexia slipped into the dressing room obediently and was pleasantly relieved to have a menial task to do that morning. Anything to get her mind off the conversation she'd had with Theo. She hadn't wanted to go back to Theo ever again, but when she imagined the price of a parental bailout being a life-long lecture from her mother, she felt like she had no choice.

Her mother. Why was it so damn hard to get her to understand what she wanted? Why couldn't they just bloody help her? Why the control?

She peeled the lid back on the punnet of strawberries, chose a suitable lipstick from the open make-up bag to her right and began to gently colour the outside flesh. After about twenty minutes and thirteen strawberries, she began to feel calmer.

'Alexia.' Lewis slipped into the empty seat beside her. 'Hey.'

'Hi, Lewis.' She smiled at him. 'You've shaved.'

'Oh. Yeah. I do, every Saturday.'

'What's up?' she said, painting the last strawberry. Her hands were suddenly clumsy and it shot out of her grip and onto the floor. 'Damn.'

'No worries. I think you've done enough,' Lewis remarked, holding up a printed-out recipe and image of the finished cake. 'Looks like they only need three for the top.'

'Better start on the mashed potato for the gourmet milkshakes,' she said, standing up and looking for the powdered mash on the shelf above the trestle table.

'Do you want to talk about anything?' Lewis said abruptly.

'No.' Alexia's response was curt. 'Why would I?'

'You just seem like you're not here right now. You never helped finish The Keep programme. You never answered my texts the other day. You've been off sick a lot. I just want to check.'

'No,' she said. 'There's nothing wrong.'

'Nothing wrong,' he repeated. 'Okay.'

'Are you going to come to Greta's Halloween party?'

'Oh. When is that?'

'Tonight.' He sighed. 'She's been so excited. You should definitely come. Come with me.'

'I'm not going to be one of your dates, Lewis,' she said sharply.

'I don't mean like that,' Lewis retorted.

'I have to work … on my documentary idea.'

'Oh yeah? Which is what?'

Alexia opened a bottle of water and added it directly to the packet of powdered mash and watched it swell. She grabbed a pencil and stirred it into a thick gloopy paste and then eased it into a long, clear glass. 'No one eats this, do they?'

'I don't think so. Giles might pretend to drink it on set.'

'Oh, here's the smoked salmon,' Alexia said, spying the foily corner of a packet of fish beside the microwave. 'Eww, it's a little warm. And it's been left open for god knows how long. It's gone all oily and smelly. I'd better go and give it to Karen.'

'Okay, Alexia,' said Lewis, standing up, 'you don't have to talk, but remember that I'm here and Clint is here. And come tonight. Come and just hang.'

'Okay, maybe. Sure.' She nodded, unconvincingly, slipping out of the door into the safety of the hallway and straight into Karen's clipboard.

'JESUS CHRIST! Don't you look where you're going?'

'I found it!' Alexia said, sticking the fish under Karen's nose. Karen smiled momentarily – a curious, lip-curling, waxy smile that offered mostly teeth, very little eye and zero sincerity – and then she immediately recoiled in horror.

'Dear GOD! That smell? And where have you been?'

'Putting lipstick on strawberries,' Alexia said, suddenly feeling the need to giggle.

'Get onto the floor. We need you to hold up cue cards. Some imbecile, I'm sorry, some intern, broke the teleprompter.'

She made her way down the hall, past a hapless runner holding up a melting baked Alaska, trying in vain to solidify the cascading ice-cream by standing directly under the air conditioning vent (which was fighting a losing battle with the wall of heat coming from the studio in full lighting and mid-cooking mode). Really, everything seemed a right mess on set today.

When the red light was off, she pushed through the heavy doors and onto the stage floor. Giles's make-up was being touched up, and the guest for the next segment was being walked to his place.

She looked for the cue cards, and saw a sweaty Greta standing next to the first assistant director, who was trying to explain how to use them.

'Hi, I'm here to help with the cue cards,' Alexia said.

'I broke the teleprompter,' Greta said feebly.

'Here they are,' said the 1AD. 'Here is the list of things you need to write on them. Please write big and clear so he can read them. Then hold them up, in time with his reading. Got it? You need to hurry. We're back on soon.' He spoke slowly to Alexia, as if he was explaining astrophysics to an eight-year-old. She'd been around enough of this kind of condescension to know how to ignore it.

'I think we can manage that,' she said, shortly.

'This one can't manage much,' he grumbled at Greta, storming off before shouting, 'Three bloody minutes!' at the top of his voice to everyone in the studio.

'I'm so bloody useless. Why do they have to make me do this production stuff? I'm terrible at it,' Greta said.

'What happened?'

'I fell over on it during the segment. That's where my arse landed,' she said, pointing to a broken lever on the floor. 'Didn't you see? Giles stopped talking for about twenty-three seconds. They nearly cut to an ad break.'

'Oh dear,' Alexia snickered. 'Giles doesn't seem like the ad-libbing type. Let's get the cards ready. It'll be fine.'

'Where were you yesterday?' Greta asked. 'I missed you for our Tesco meal deal walk and talk.'

'Sick,' Alexia said, pulling a huge black marker pen out of a canvas pouch. She wrote carefully – *Next up! Kerry Katona talks aubergines, sourdough and the Omega 3 Myth.*

'Surreal,' Greta remarked, then, after a short pause, 'So I guess you heard about the new leak?'

'No,' Alexia slowed her scribbling, her hand unsteady. 'Another leak?'

'Yes. But it's really serious, Lexi. It's about Lee. No one told you?'

'No.' Alexia felt her heart quicken again as she concentrated on the words on the cue cards. A set dresser flounced in with a wooden board holding smoked salmon carefully displayed next to some dense sourdough.

'ONE MINUTE!' shouted the 1AD again. 'WHAT'S THAT SMELL?'

'Someone called Bright Star for a quote,' Greta said. 'Dear god, is that the fish?'

'What?' Alexia dropped the marker. It rolled across the floor and landed in front of Giles, who shook his head at her, tutting. A runner skated in like a ballboy at Wimbledon and it was gone.

'Yeah. The Buzz actually wrote in the article that someone from Bright Star gave the information. Like they *named* the source as Bright Star.'

'Are you serious?' Alexia felt sick. The bottom of her stomach dropped out and she felt dizzy.

'Thirty seconds!'

'Are you okay?'

'Yeah, I feel a bit queasy. Sorry. I'm still not fully recovered from—'

'The flu? Is it the flu? Granny had the flu just last week. So did the neighbours. It's terrible in the canal boat community, with all the dampness and bad personal hygiene.'

'Ten seconds.'

'Alexia, seriously, you look awful.' Greta put her hand on Alexia's shoulder and felt it immediately stiffen. 'Are you okay? You've been sick so much lately . . .'

'Yeah. I just . . . ' Alexia held up the first cue card and tried to focus. 'It's fine, I think it's the smell of that fish.'

'Are you sure you're all right? Alexia, you look like you're going to vom,' Greta whispered.

'Live in five, four, three . . . ' The 1AD held up two fingers, then one.

'Welcome back to *Weekend Kitchen*. I'm Giles and we've got a very special guest here today. She's a pop singer, a mother, a reality TV star, sourdough fanatic and now author of a book on wellness – it's Kerry Katona.'

'Hi, Giles.'

When the segment was done, Alexia dropped the cue cards. 'I think I'm going to throw up.'

'Go,' said Greta. 'Come tonight if you feel better?'

Chapter 22

Blend

'Granny? When are you leaving?' Greta shouted from the roof as she carefully placed tea lights inside a pumpkin carving of 'The Scream'. One of Granny's artist friends from *Seas the Day*, a boat and squat five berths down, had carved twelve art-inspired designs, all beautifully detailed and very playful. She dropped a light into a carving of 'The Great Wave Off Kanagawa'. It was incredible.

'You're not twelve years old, Greta. IT'S MY HOUSE.'

'It's a boat,' she said, falling into their well-worn banter.

'It's my boat!'

'It's actually MY boat.' Greta laughed.

'Only when I die!' Her granny appeared dressed as Vivienne Westwood, a frantic mix of punk rock, plaid and boobs. She looked incredible in the bright-red wig against her rich olive skin.

'Wow, Granny. You look amazing.'

'What are you wearing?'

'I'm Harley Quinn. Well, an extra sexy Harley Quinn.' She tugged at the T-shirt tied under her bust while she twirled her blue pigtail wig. 'I dunno. There wasn't anything left at the shop.'

'I wish you were a feminist.'

'I am, Granny. I even say it on my Twitter profile.'

'Do your homework.' She waved an admonishing finger at her.

'When are you leaving?' Greta repeated.

'I'm off now, child.' She kissed Greta on the head. 'I've left you some extra booze in the ice buckets. You know the drill – don't let anyone get too drunk and fall in. And if they do, which they will, give Ivor or Ulrich over there on *The Dirty Oar* a shout.' She waved at the immaculately turned out canal boat two across. 'They're always about.'

'I know, Granny.'

And with that she was off. Greta went downstairs and fixed herself a cold shandy and then pulled her phone out. It was tempting, in this final quiet moment of the day, to read up on Lee and the latest shocking Keep story, but with each day that passed she was finding it a little easier to step back. Instead, she found her carefully selected playlist, plugged in her phone and hit play. The Cure's moody pop hit 'Catch' filled the space and Greta was ready. *This is it. My real-life social debut*, she thought dramatically. *The moment everyone*

realises how awesome I am and fawns around me like they do with
people like Alexia.

Greta sighed when she thought of Alexia. There was something amiss there, but she couldn't put her finger on it. She
was worried about her. And her reaction to the leak today was
extreme, even though the news was shocking.

Lee had taken off to LA to see his girlfriend Jessica because
she was having an affair with a co-star in her new film. But
worse news for Lee – she was pregnant. The image of Lee
at the Taj Mahal had run all over again but now it had new
poignancy, and photos of Jessica out on the town in LA with
her co-star ran next to them. It was a deeply personal story
and one that Greta felt uncomfortable knowing.

But the worst part was when The Buzz called Bright Star's
office for further comment on the piece. Greta had been covering reception and had taken the call while she was cutting
up mature Cheddar for her ploughman's dicnic (Greta's term
for a desk picnic which had yet to catch on).

'Hello, Bright Star Productions.'

'Hi. It's Moe here, calling from The Buzz. I want to get a
comment on this story we're running.'

'Sure, okay. What is it?' Greta had been excited, without
thinking it through.

'Who am I speaking to?'

'Greta.'

'Is it true that Lee Bow from The Keep has been in town
and in your offices?'

'Ooh, yes!'

'And that he'd been in India recovering from the news of his ex-girlfriend's pregnancy.'

'How do you know?' she'd gasped.

'Is there anyone there that can give us an official comment?'

'Ah, I don't think so.'

'That's fine. Can I just confirm your last name Greta?'

'Greta Georgiou. With an "i". It's Greek. I'm sorry I can't help you.'

'You already did.' *Click.*

Greta obviously marched through to the music department to tell Lewis straight away, only pausing for seventeen minutes of code-red panic and a sudden desperate trip to the toilet.

She walked right up to him, putting her forthright, practical hat on – a hat which, while only a figurative tool, still sadly never seemed to fit. She looked around the office and crouched down next to Lewis, then stood up again, then decided crouching would give them most privacy, but crouched too low just as Lewis swivelled his chair and found she was precisely at crotch height. She decided to just sit on the floor. *Don't look at his crotch.*

'Lewis, nothing to worry about, but I believe we may have a situation that is utterly catastrophic on our hands.'

Lewis had been reassuring once she'd explained – it wasn't Greta's job to field those calls, the PR team would take care of it, not her fault, be more careful next time – but she was utterly terrified nevertheless. *Another leak.* And another reason for Alexia to think it was her. Lewis and Clint had spent most of the rest of the day in hushed meetings with management, and Greta could tell this was serious. It had to be. And now that the story was actually out, she was completely on edge.

'Hello there, my precious.' Clint two-foot hopped down the five stairs into the boat wearing a floor-length grey robe and wizard's hat. 'Julian's upstairs admiring the pumpkins, thought I'd slip some beers in the fridge. Does this thing have a fridge?'

'Oh, you gave me a fright! Of course. In here.'

'Everyone's a bit jumpy.' Clint nodded. 'But let's not talk about *that* tonight.'

Greta smiled. 'Thanks for coming ... Gandalf?'

'If the beard fits ... ' He grinned, twisting the top off a beer. 'Though Julian has just called me Daddy, so I might need to lose it.'

Feet tapped on the roof overhead and the wood of the boat creaked. 'Shall we head up?'

Soon enough, the others had arrived. Julian was dressed all in black, hair teaser up high and holding a pair of scissors. 'I couldn't be bothered making the hands work. Too much faff. How could I hold a glass? Call me Edward Scissors-in-my-hands.' He kissed Greta on both cheeks. 'Or Julian's fine. Fabulous to meet you. Oh, and I hope you don't mind, but you told Clint we could invite a few friends ... '

Three hours later, the boat was full. As was the empty boat

next berth over. And the canal path. Julian had, it appeared, invited half of the Hackney music scene. A three-piece jazz band were set up by the lock house and streams of Hackney's finest milled about self-consciously, looking for beer and hook-ups under the stars, the thrill of Halloween silliness in the air.

'My granny's going to skin me alive,' Greta complained to Lewis, who hadn't bothered with a costume, apparently.

'I'm Norman Core. Get it?' Lewis said, running his hands over his windcheater. 'Normcore. Come on, I never wear this much beige.'

She grabbed a net from a hook above one of the portholes and tried to fish out one of the several bottles of beer that was bobbing up and down in the water. A small black pug squirrelled between her legs.

'Jesus! Who brought the bloody dog?'

One of three Batmans picked the dog up and shrugged. 'Sorry, lovely,' he said, kissing his dog, 'it's not exactly Shoreditch House, is it, darling? You poor little thing.'

'You met Amelie, right?' Clint popped up beside her with his arm around the pretty girl from Music in the Park. *Also not dressed up. What is wrong with these people?*

'Hi, Amelie. I'm so glad you could make it,' shouted Greta over the noise, as the canal boat pitched to the left.

'I only live over the back there,' Amelie pointed towards a row of terraced houses across the canal.

'She's been a bit down, so I asked her along. Boy troubles,' Clint said in a loud slur.

'Shut up,' Amelie said, rolling her piercing blue eyes. 'You're getting drunk. And annoying.'

'Sorry to hear that,' Greta shouted.

'Sorry?' Amelie shouted back. 'What did you say?'

The music was turned up even louder, Donna Summer reverberating through the boat. Greta repeated, 'I'm sorry about your boy troubles. Is it Max?'

Amelie baulked and shook her head. 'No no no no. Okay, I need dry land,' she said, pointing to the empty bench seat on the canal path next to an overflowing bin.

'Yes. No worries! I wish I could leave, too,' Greta said. 'This is an absolute nightmare.'

'THAT'S RIGHT! It's a nightmare. It's Halloweeeeeeeeeen!' Clint said, spinning in circles down the boat and into Julian's arms, kicking a pumpkin into the water and forcing the Stay Puft Marshmallow Man to adjust his wee stream onto the boat next door.

'PLEASE! Wee in the water, at least,' Greta wailed, slipping backwards onto her arse and into a pool of something lumpy and sticky. 'I hate this. Parties are awful. Retract invitation. Retract. Ahhh!'

'Greta, you're hilarious. Do you know that?' Lewis laughed, helping her up.

'I'm stressed! All I can think about is the clean-up and grovelling apologies I'll have to make to my neighbours. Argghh. I have to change my pants.'

'Don't be stressed. It's fun. A great party, actually,' Lewis said, laughing. 'Hey, do you think that Tank Girl is single? Or do you think she's with the Super Mario dude?'

Greta shook her head, pushing her way downstairs towards her bedroom, recovering her phone from near the stereo en route, where it had been casually tossed aside to make way for someone else's far cooler playlist. *A quick regroup in bed. Is it rude to have a nap?* She pulled the door to her room back to discover someone lying on her bed, already having a sneaky bit of shut-eye, so she snuck into the safety of her granny's little room.

I hate parties. Almost instantly, the door flew open and a greying city boy in a business suit swayed for a moment in the doorway, looking at Greta confused. 'Oh, hi. You don't know if there's a toilet in this place, do you?'

'Down the hall.'

'Cool boat.'

'It's not mine,' Greta said, exasperated. 'Please shut the door!'

Greta tore off her shorts and tights and tossed them into the corner. Then she pulled out her phone and considered a text, warning her granny. In truth, Granny was more likely to be pleased that Greta had real-life visitors at the house. *Ugh.* The guys on the roof started jumping up and down and the sound of buckling wood, banging glass and blatantly out-of-tune squealing was deafening. *Never again.*

'Greta?' said a familiar voice, 'are you in there?'

'Alexia?'

Greta jumped up and flung open the door. 'You came!'

Alexia was wearing a wrist-to-floor black wool dress with a white frill at the collar, her face lightly powdered and hair parted in two braids. *Nothing Halloween slutty about her, of course.* 'Wednesday Adams. I didn't have any other ideas. You look cool. Your wig's coming off, though. Are you supposed to be wearing pants?'

'Oh crap. Yes. I just sat in something,' Greta said, tugging on a pair of jeans she'd grabbed from her room. 'Are you feeling better?'

'Yep. I thought I'd better pop down and say hi,' Alexia said.

'It's great you came. I should venture back upstairs. Do you want some pumpkin soup?'

'I think I just saw someone feeding that to the dog.'

'Great,' Greta said with a frown, slipping her phone back in her pocket.

'This place. Do you really live here with your grandmother?'

'Yes,' Greta said proudly, before realising Alexia was rather more stunned than impressed. 'I know it seems weird, but it's actually awesome. And we're only ever here for the warmer months – we're packing everything up in the next week actually, which is why I can get away with having a party. She has a place in Dalston as well, a flat. Anyway, the boat's not so pokey when you get used to it.'

'Well, it's bigger than my place,' Alexia said. 'And living with your granny means no rent. God, the cost of rent! I had no idea how much it would chew through my savings. I really should be sharing.'

'Maybe *we* could get a flat? Together. Flatmates!' Greta said, wide-eyed. 'You and me! Wouldn't that be awesome? I could teach you how to be English! And you could show me Americaning.'

Alexia laughed, looking intrigued by the idea. 'What were you doing down here, anyway?'

'Nothing. Well, hiding.'

'Why don't we go up and join the guys?' Alexia gently suggested. 'You don't like parties? I thought you'd love them.'

'No, I *do* love them,' Greta said glumly. 'But other people's parties. I hate being in charge. I hate being a host. I'm an anxious mess.'

'Don't worry,' said Alexia. 'You stick with me. I am a master at surviving parties you don't want to be at.'

'Your parents?' Greta asked.

'Sometimes it felt like every damn week,' Alexia said with an eye roll. 'And honestly, I don't think they liked them either. Come on, brave face, Greta.'

'Okay, I'm ready,' she said, taking a deep breath. 'Let's go.'

Chapter 23

You Know I'm No Good

Alexia hadn't wanted to come. She had spent most of the day since *Weekend Kitchen* lying on her bed at home. Rent paid up until the end of the year, RED Valentino dress rescued from the vintage store, she'd felt both relief and a dark ball of anxiety in the pit of her stomach. She'd managed a short sleep after failing to be distracted by a little Netflix, but when she woke, the thoughts and anxiety flooded back.

She needed real distraction, so she'd decided to force herself along to the party to try to relax. After all, this hell was surely going to pass.

As she and Greta made their way up onto the top deck, Alexia was surprised to see the boys in a serious huddle on the canal path. Lewis stood with his arms folded, while Clint stood looking at his phone. Julian had his arm around Clint, but that was probably as much about keeping him upright as comforting him.

'Hey, Lewis,' Alexia said with a wave. He waved back, with a pursed smile. Alexia looked at Greta. 'He doesn't look happy.'

'Has someone died at my Halloween party?' Greta tried, jovially. 'Because that would be ironic. I think. Is that irony? Anyway, I did hear a huge splash earlier.'

She motioned to the water, and then caught sight of her granny's kitchen chair slowly floating away downstream. 'What is wrong with people!' she moaned.

'There's more Keep stuff. Jessica made a statement,' Clint slurred, shaking his head.

'What? What does it say?' Greta asked distractedly. She kept looking over to the boat, where it seemed that guests were finally starting to head off into the night in search of louder, more purpose-built party venues.

'We're off to the Dolphin,' a sexy zombie paramedic announced. 'Great party!'

'I haven't read it yet,' Clint said, swaying a little against Julian. 'Someone appears to have removed my ability to see close up.'

'Read it!' Alexia snapped. 'Sorry – I mean, can you read it to us?'

'Okay …' Clint said, staring at Alexia as he pulled his phone out again. 'Relax there, Miss Falls. It's here. It just says. Um, nothing actually. Jeez, I can hardly read it. It's a denial! I think. She wants privacy.'

Alexia looked forlorn. 'No surprises there.'

'It's so weird, isn't it?' Clint slurred.

'What's going to happen about the leak?' Greta blurted. 'Am I in trouble?'

'No, of course not, Greta. But we're going to start an internal investigation over the stolen still,' Lewis said with a shrug. 'Whoever it is that's been leaking to the press will be caught. And fired, I guess. I mean, it's a career breaker.'

'Alexia, did you know about Jessica?' Clint asked, sobered by the discussion.

'Personally, I think the leak didn't come from Bright Star. The information is too personal. It's not like the band chatted about it in some backstage video diary,' Lewis said.

'So why did they call us?' Greta countered.

'Did *you* know, Alexia?' Clint asked again. 'Because you know everything. Where all the bodies are buried. You must've known.'

'Of course I did,' Alexia said coolly. 'But Lee was here for a few days. He could have told anyone. God knows who he might have told in India.'

'But you must have been the only one at Bright Star who knew,' Greta said. 'I mean, did you tell anyone?'

Alexia glanced at Greta for a moment, wondering if Greta was starting to figure it out or if she could be this authentically clueless. She stared off into the darkness of the canal path, turning a ring round on her finger. She felt a calm come over her, and hardened herself for what was coming.

'Maybe not the only one,' Alexia said, looking back meaningfully at Greta.

'I think there must have been a hack. Did you put it in an email or anything?' Greta continued. 'I just mean, the leaks started when you came, and you know the band really well, so maybe someone has got access to your accounts or something.'

'It's true, it did all start when you came,' Clint said, his eyes fixed on Alexia.

She took a deep breath. 'It's time you came clean, Greta.' Alexia let the words fall out of her mouth without emotion. It might be all she needed to say.

'What?' Greta yelped.

'Greta – tell them what you do online. Tell them, or I will.'

Alexia couldn't look at her. She focused on the boat behind her, now empty but for a couple snogging on the roof.

'What?' Lewis said.

'Tell them about your other life, with The Keep.'

'*What?* No, it's unrelated. No! Why would you . . .'

'What is it, Greta?' Clint asked, confusion creeping across his face.

'That doesn't have anything to do with anything,' Greta stammered.

'What doesn't?' Lewis snapped.

'I ran some UK Keep fan club stuff, but it isn't . . . it wasn't what you think. I don't do it any more, and I would never discuss anything confidential. Alexia, you know. You saw.'

'I'm not sure what I saw,' Alexia said coolly.

Greta shook her head at Alexia in disbelief, then looked frantically to Lewis and Clint. She was searching for some kindness, some forgiveness, some understanding.

A tear appeared on Greta's cheek. A single, large tear that ran slowly down her face, removing all the powdered make-up in its wake. The anguish on her face was almost too much for Alexia to bear. She looked at the ground and shook her head. She didn't have to do any more. The damage was done.

'No. It wasn't me. You have to believe me.' Greta's voice wavered, fragile, like the single thread holding her words together could snap at any moment.

'What fan club?' Lewis barked, suddenly losing his cool.

'The UK one? The Twitter feed? @thekeepers1?' Clint pressed. 'You ran it?'

'Yes. Bu-but I d-didn't do anything. I would never ...' Greta took a step backwards and looked at Alexia. 'Alexia, please.' Her voice finally cracked as tears came cascading down her cheeks. 'No no no. I didn't do anything. I didn't tell anyone. I don't speak to people. You're my friends. My only friends. I only have friends online and I don't even speak to them any more. Please.'

With that, Alexia had to leave. She felt Greta's words like a slug to the gut. *You're my friends. My only friends.* What had she done? Suddenly the world was collapsing around her and she had to get away. Without a word, she turned and marched off down the path.

'Wait. WAIT!' Greta shouted. 'Alexia! Tell them. You know I didn't do anything!'

Alexia focused only on getting to the night bus a hundred yards away at the top of the canal path steps.

Her mother had always told her that when she felt anxious, alone or afraid, she should find a calm place in her mind and focus on it. She used to go to the basement of her father's office when she was a kid and play records on one of the old turntables they had down there. Alongside the file copies of major successes, there were boxes and boxes of records and CDs that remained unsold, by artists that didn't work out. People who had put themselves out there, and no one wanted to listen. Her father, with uncharacteristic sentimentality, had never had the heart to send them all to landfill, so they just continued to pile up. Alexia would go down and play them on her own. She loved the idea that someone had just thrown their thoughts, feelings, desires – all of them – into a record. It was so brave. So real. It was a room full of dreams; even if some of them were a little tarnished, they were still alive if she played the records. That was her happy place. But she couldn't get in there. She couldn't open the door.

'Alexia! Wait.'

She kept walking, up the steps and onto Mare Street, and suddenly felt suffocated by her tight plaits. She tugged off the bands, shaking her hair free. The full moon was bright and lit the damp tarmac beneath her feet in silver. If she didn't feel so black, it would have been beautiful.

'Alexia.' A hand touched her shoulder and she spun around.

'I get it,' Lewis said, out of breath. He leaned over and sucked in the chilly air and then stood up, adjusting his tone. 'I mean, everything makes sense.'

She stood waiting, knowing the pieces of the puzzle that he was putting together.

'Greta? I mean, I can't believe it. I hired her!' Lewis said, shaking his head, wiping the sweat off his brow. 'And all this time she was some kind of duplicitous arsehole. No wonder you've been so quiet and cut up, Alexia. I totally get it now.' He put his hand back on her shoulder. 'Don't beat yourself up. It was kind of you to try to protect her – how could you have known how far she'd go?'

Please stop talking.

'Is Greta okay?'

'I don't know.' He looked at her. 'Don't worry about her. Are *you* okay? You did the right thing, making her tell us the truth.'

Alexia couldn't respond. She wanted him to stop talking. What was done was done.

'I can't believe she could sit there in our office. It's such a goddamn betrayal. We're all screwed. I hired her!' he repeated.

Alexia couldn't listen any more. Inside she was screaming. She needed him to stop talking. *Please stop talking.* She felt the first tears start to appear, and then they all came ... all the tears.

Once the floodgate was open the tears didn't stop, falling

like a river down her cheeks, her body convulsing as the sobs became a wretched release. She held onto Lewis's jacket sleeves, begging him to disappear, willing herself home. Willing herself back to her house in New York. Back to her mother. Home.

CHAPTER 24

Had You Told It Like It Was (It Wouldn't Be Like It Is)

'Well, thank god it's over now.' Kevin smiled at Lewis and the two of them heaved sighs of relief. Kevin gathered the papers in front of him and tapped them into a neat pile on the meeting room table before slipping them into a plastic envelope. 'And I'm very sorry about the department, but even with the leak plugged, we're just not making any money. You guys knew it was coming.'

'Thanks, Kevin.' Lewis looked glum.

'No worries. I'm sorry it wasn't better news. But I think you'll get a lot out of your new roles at Bright Star. And of course, Alexia, I'm pleased we can keep your internship going, and welcome you properly aboard next month.'

Alexia cringed. 'Oh ... thank you.'

'No problem at all. I spoke with your father this morning

and told him the good news about finding out the source of the leak. We may not have a dedicated music department any longer, but our relationship with Falls Records is as important as ever. And I hope you don't mind, but I also told him the news that we'd be offering you this full-time role come December.'

I bet he took that well. 'Oh, thank you. That's great news,' Alexia said.

'Just don't blow up the edit suite or upset Karen, and the job's yours,' Kevin said. 'I'm serious on that last point, actually.'

So her father knew about her job before her. *Arggh*. Why did it feel like she was still under her parents' wing? It would have been better if Falls Records had pulled the contract completely.

Lewis was beaming at her; she could feel his smile boring into her temple and she wanted to reach out and push his face away. She didn't need friends being happy for her right now – it felt like he was dancing on Greta's grave. Kevin stood up and looked out of the windows to the green over the road. 'Not a bad day to catch the last of the autumn sun, or is it the first of the winter sun?' he mused. 'Anyone fancy *lunch*?'

'It's four o'clock,' said Alexia, confused.

'He means a pint,' laughed Lewis. 'We already have plans, though. A friend of Clint's has a showcase and we're going to support.'

Kevin shrugged. 'You just turned down pints on the boss,

but whatever.' He rubbed his beard. 'It's been a rough few weeks with all of this stuff, so let's at least go and have a beer in the staff room before you head off. Show of solidarity and all that.'

'I just have to grab my laptop,' Alexia said, 'and I'll be right along.'

'You better,' Lewis warned, before leaning in. 'Come on. It's time to get out of that dark mood and stop blaming yourself, Alexia. You did the right thing. If anything, you're a hero.'

Alexia sighed. She went to her desk and pulled out her leather tote, one of the few survivors of project 'sell off'. She looked across at Greta's empty chair. She should be there – chatting away incessantly about some inane nonsense while Alexia tried to concentrate on logging film or planning the next shoot. Her 'in' tray was empty, her computer removed by IT to be completely wiped, and her desk phone was disconnected. All that remained was a pad with some scribbled production notes and her pass. Alexia picked it up and looked at the slightly goofy photo of Greta. Only she would have a work pass photo with one eye closed and her tongue out.

Alexia smiled fondly, which made the waves of guilt rise up, guilt she was becoming expert at ignoring. She shoved her laptop into her bag, along with her phone and her make-up bag, just as Clint wandered past.

'May as well colonise the whole desk, hey?' he said,

smoothing down his eyebrows and pulling at his nose between his thumb and forefinger.

'Maybe. It feels a bit wrong,' Alexia murmured.

'Yeah?' Clint said, staring straight at her.

'Well, you know. I feel bad for her.'

'Yeah, me too,' he said firmly. 'See you downstairs?'

'Yep. Five minutes.'

Clint's tone had been clipped with Alexia ever since Monday, when Greta had come in to hear her fate. She had arrived just after 10 a.m. and was in a meeting room with Kevin, Lewis and someone from HR for no more than fifteen minutes. When she came out her face was red and blotchy and she looked thoroughly humiliated. A security guard stood over her as she cleared out her side of the desk.

'I just wanted to say sorry, Alexia,' she'd sniffed as she grabbed all her stuff, pointedly tossing the news article about Lee into their shared bin. 'I know it looks really bad, but I promise you I never did it. I never did it.' She'd shaken her head.

'Greta, it's okay,' Alexia had said softly. 'Please don't apologise.'

'I know how it looks. But it wasn't me,' Greta insisted. 'To be honest, I would never do something like that to Lee, or to anyone. I know it seems strange, given I must look like some stalker freak to you, but I wouldn't hurt him like that.' She'd sighed as she closed her satchel and swung it over her shoulder.

'I don't think you're a stalker freak.' Alexia had felt a strong urge to hug her, to confess everything.

'That's enough, Greta,' Lewis had said gently. 'Time to go.'

'I'll see her out,' Clint had said to the security guard. 'Is this really necessary?'

'BYE EVERYONE!' Greta had shouted across the room as she was led through the glass doors towards the lifts, before adding with a hint of humour: 'I DIDN'T DO IT! I'M INNOCENT! INNNOOOOOOCENT I TELLS YA!'

Everyone in the office had looked up at her and then, as the glass doors shut, all looked back down at their computers in unison.

After a perfunctory beer downstairs with Kevin, Alexia, Lewis and Clint walked briskly up the road to the Lexington. It was cold now – the clear day meant a chilly night. Alexia couldn't wait to get inside and warm herself up. 'What time is she on?' she asked, rubbing her hands together. 'God, it's gloves weather already.'

'She's on in about thirty minutes, I think,' Lewis said. 'Let's go get a seat.'

He held the door open and smiled at her as she passed through into the bar. There were a couple of armchairs empty at the back of the room and Alexia headed towards them.

The room was a veritable who's who of the London music scene. Everyone had gathered to hear this special new artist, and Alexia recognised the buzz that signalled the beginning of something special. And then she felt crushing panic as she realised that there could be someone there she knew, or worse, her father knew. She slipped into an armchair and bowed her head.

'Can I get you a drink?' Lewis asked. 'Then can we sit down and go through Tinder for me?'

'Yes please and no thanks,' she said with a forced smile. 'Oh god, half my dad's label is here.'

'Well, Amelie's apparently really good. A new star in the making.'

Alexia slipped even lower into her chair. Her eyes darted around the room as she counted the number of people who knew her or her parents. It was worse than she feared.

With Falls Records, there was never going to be a humble get-together. A number of their British signings were present, along with radio DJ's, bloggers and music journalists. Plenty of named faces mingled with each other, quaffing back complimentary prosecco and guffawing at nothing. Alexia hated this kind of thing, but she couldn't help thinking of Greta, who would have been climbing the walls with excitement. *Don't think about it. She lied, anyway. She shouldn't have lied.* Alexia could push the angst away long enough to focus if she reminded herself of Greta's own betrayal.

A couple of members of All New Wild were leaning on the bar, chatting with South London hip hop duo Crush. She spotted the UK label head, Angela, a formidable force whose waist-length black hair bounced every time she nodded. Her cerise lips were moving at a hundred miles an hour while she chatted with Mike Church, a sound engineer and producer who had occasionally helped out with The Keep. If Alexia remembered right, Mike was Amelie's dad.

The merch table set up near the toilets was piled high with copies of the new artist's EP. Perched next to it, swigging on a pint of orange juice, was her old boss, Geoff.

'*Oh god.*' Alexia half turned in the chair, willing herself to fall through and disappear.

'You know him?' Lewis said, plonking down on the seat next to her.

'He's my old boss,' Alexia nodded, realising she was going to have to say hello.

'You must know tons of people here,' Lewis said, looking around.

'Unfortunately,' she murmured.

'You're not feeling bad about Greta, are you?' he asked, putting his hand on her arm.

'No,' she replied flatly. It was a friendly touch, but one that plagued her with guilt. Itching to pull her arm away, she reached for the bottled water in the middle of the table by way of excuse. She wished people would quit being kind to her, it made her feel increasingly uneasy.

'Great news about the full-time job though? Shame we won't all be working together any more.'

That was the deal. When the revelations about Greta came out, Bright Star had used it as an excuse to disband the music team and fold them into 'general factual and lifestyle'. Alexia would be put under a new producer, working mostly on their food formats, Clint was going to work on the UK version of *American Star* as the behind-the-scenes digital producer, and Lewis was being moved to their growing documentary division – where Alexia wanted to be, but didn't dare push.

'Yeah,' she said.

'Don't worry, you'll be across with me in docos soon enough. Just do your time. You'll learn heaps under Karen, she's amazing. Scary as hell, but amazing,' he enthused. 'How are those ideas coming along?'

'I'd better go see Geoff,' Alexia said, standing up. 'I'll be right back.'

Alexia was expecting a bit of a fracas when she greeted Geoff, but not the full-face explosion that she got.

'What the HELL are you doing?' he boomed. 'Call your father. No, damn it, I'll call him. He's worried sick. I should toss you on a plane now, you little twat. If I'd have known you were going to do this, I would never have let you quit.'

'Hi, Geoff,' Alexia said, manoeuvring for his usual sweaty, one-armed, no-body-contact hug. But it never came. She stood awkwardly, realising he was truly concerned. 'What are you doing here?' she asked. 'Are you working with this new singer?'

'Amelie? No. I know her father.' Geoff shook his head. 'But I'm helping launch All New Wild,' he said, motioning to Nav and the drummer Alex. 'Boybands with guitars. And we've got to pretend they're a "real" band. Turns out it *does* get worse than the bloody Keep.'

He turned to face Alexia again, his face reddening with fury. For a moment, Alexia stifled a grin. This was the Geoff she knew – the cartoon angry man. Ready to pounce on everyone he loved.

'Seriously. What are you doing? I know you didn't like working for me and tidying up after that bunch of man children, but I hear you're doing an unpaid internship for that bloody leaky sinking ship of a production company?'

'Well, I get a little bit of money now, and it'll be a paid gig come December,' Alexia said, with zero pride.

'That's a relief.' Geoff shook his head. 'Listen, I don't know if your plans are long term, but I get it. We all like to rebel against our parents, but what were you thinking? If someone had paid for me to go to college I would have taken it. I wanted to be an architect at one point, you know, but no one was offering to pay for me.'

Alexia knew better than to try to convince Geoff of anything, ever. He wouldn't understand that these so-called opportunities felt like chains. She tried to change the subject. 'How are the boys? I mean, after everything.'

'Fine. Christmas single comes out in a few weeks, then, well . . .' Geoff stopped. 'Anyway. It should go down a treat.'

'How's Lee?' She squirmed, almost frightened of the reply.

'I don't know. Maybe you can tell me if you see him?' Geoff said, rolling his eyes. 'Okay, Amelie's setting up. I'm going to watch.'

'How long are you in town for?'

'I leave Friday,' Geoff replied. He cared. He managed a slightly warped and crooked smile. 'Call your father. He loves you. And your mom … Look, just call home. Have a chat. Include them. I know you think they're a huge embarrassment, but they're good people.'

'I don't—' Alexia began to protest.

'Oh, you do. Typical entitled little brat.' He shook his head.

'They won't let me live my life,' Alexia protested.

'Wake up, kid,' Geoff boomed. 'You took off with twenty-four hours' notice to another continent to take an essentially unpaid job. Kinda worrying, if you ask me. Exactly what do you think they've done to you?'

'But they wanted me to go to NYU,' she complained.

'Day wanna me to goo to NYU,' he repeated in his best baby voice. 'Poor you, having university paid for by your parents. Getting a world-class education. What *a* drag. You should be a bit more grateful.'

'Aren't I allowed to do what I want to do? How about some damn independence?' She folded her arms, furious.

'Sure you are.' Geoff shook his head. 'Shutting people out doesn't make you more independent, though. Just more alone.' He looked at her and shrugged. 'You better make it count.'

'I will, I have this new—'

'Make. It. Count,' Geoff repeated.

The lights went down and Alexia tiptoed through the small

audience to find her seat, which had been filled by Clint, with Julian perched on the arm. Lewis stood up immediately to offer his chair.

'Here you go.'

'It's fine.'

'No, take a seat. Really.'

'I don't want to.'

Lewis stood awkwardly for a moment before putting his drink down on the table and turning to Alexia. 'Have I done something? This can't be just about Greta.'

'Why do you have to be nice to me all the time?' she snapped.

'Um ... because we're friends?' he said, incredulously.

'SHHHHHH!' Clint barked from his seat. 'It's our girl.'

Amelie stood on the small stage with just a couple of soft overhead lights beaming down on her. Alexia shook her head for a moment. Hanger-on to Max, daughter of a producer; it really was all about who you knew in this game. *Pathetic. And people wonder why I'm so determined to make it alone.*

But when Amelie began to play, it was clear she was no passenger riding on the coat-tails of daddy or her friends in the business. She looked nervous, maybe even slightly fragile, though the enchanting sound that came out of her was anything but. Deep, bluesy, like an old soul seeping out into the air, gathering in everyone around it.

Alexia was captivated. Amelie was doing it. Really doing it. There was no one in her way, no one stopping her. Alexia closed her eyes for a moment, and felt something shifting in her, a glimmer of hope, a faint hint of promise.

'She's still at school,' Julian whispered. 'Isn't my girl awesome? I work for her dad. She's like family.'

Alexia nodded, opening her eyes as they locked with Amelie's. As she sang, Alexia saw a sadness behind them and slowly felt a sense of creeping dread.

'Is she still seeing Max?' Alexia whispered to Julian, nervously. 'I mean, they were dating or starting to date, right?'

'Were,' replied Julian, looking glum. 'Poor doll. She doesn't like the celebrity stuff, and no sooner were they trying to get something going than that stupid story about Dee and Charlie and Max ran. Too much attention.'

'Oh god,' Alexia whispered, reeling.

'I think she should just focus on being a producer to be honest.' He nodded over at Amelie's dad, who looked so proud he might explode. 'Less attention.'

'SHUT UP!' Clint fumed.

Alexia waited for the song to finish. She realised this thing she created was never going to end. What she'd done wasn't insignificant. It wasn't a bit of bad press for a few people that would blow over. She had impacted on so many people's lives. The ripples of her actions were still spreading, rocking boats along the way. She thought of Greta again, then Amelie and Max. Then Lee, and then of Jessica, and wondered if there was something she could do, some way she could save this situation.

CHAPTER 25

From the Morning

Greta was glad to be leaving the boat for the Dalston flat. It was always fun being on the water over the summer but now that the nights were cold, and the frosts were coming, it was better to be on solid ground. Upside: drinking a cup of tea that is full to the brim. Downside: no gentle rocking to sleep.

As she tossed the last of her things into a cardboard box, she called out to Granny. 'Granny, I'm going for a walk round Victoria Park and maybe brekkie at the pavilion. Last one before we head.'

'Ooh, get the Sri Lankan breakfast!' Granny called back. 'Eggs, dhal. Delicious. And bring back some rosemary from the communal garden, would you?'

'You got it.'

Greta skipped over the fence and onto the main path, heading down to the pond for a last goodbye to the swans and their lanky grey cygnets. The trees were hanging on to the last of their leaves and a sudden windy gust would finally strip them bare.

'Goodbye my grumpy, aggressive, beautiful friends,' she said, tossing the swans a handful of sunflower seeds. 'See you in the summertime.'

She dug her hands deep into her pockets. She loved her blue duffel coat and was happy to liberate it out of storage along with her Docs. She was winter gal, no denying. The air had that remarkable chill that the low autumn sun could no longer penetrate, and she pulled up her hood for maximum warmth.

It was starting to hurt less. All of it.

She walked slowly round the pond, over the old Victorian bridge and down by the Japanese-style gazebo to take a closer look at the geese and the coots.

'Farewell little buddies.' She waved, tossing the last of her seeds out onto the water, feeling slightly irritated when the seagulls arrived.

She wandered through the tabled picnic area on the far side of the pond and made her way towards the pavilion. A dog barked at a kid throwing stones into the pond. A mother screamed at her toddler not to climb the fence. A couple of schoolgirls loitered by a bench trying to out-selfie each other.

By the time she arrived at the pavilion she was starved. She made her way up the counter and ordered BLT on sourdough, a side of scrambled eggs, a large hot chocolate, an orange juice and a croissant. As she walked out, balancing her overflowing tray, she ran right into Alexia.

'Alexia!' Greta stammered. 'Oh my god. Hello.'

'Hi.' Alexia smiled.

She's smiling at me. Greta smiled back cautiously.

Alexia looked paler than usual, her hair pulled back in a tight topknot, with one huge lightning bolt earring almost brushing the top of her black tuxedo-style coat.

'I just went to see you ... at your houseboat.'

'Canal boat,' Greta corrected, 'or barge, is probably more accurate.'

'Your grandmother said you were here.'

'You came to see me?' she said, shuffling her arms as she started to buckle under the weight of her tray.

'Oh, are you with someone?' Alexia said, eyeing her enormous breakfast for one.

'No no. I'm just hungry,' Greta sighed. 'I like to eat. I mean, really. It's one of my favourite pastimes.'

'So did I,' Alexia said wistfully. 'I don't seem to have much of an appetite these days. Come on, I'll help you.'

Alexia grabbed the juice and the coffee and motioned Greta towards one of the outside tables. 'Is it too cold?'

'No, I love it,' Greta said. 'I love cold air, warm food, living on a canal boat in summer only. I hate parties and although I love a certain boyband, I find some aspects of that love problematic now that I'm becoming an adult. But, I'm still proud of my fandom and that time of my life. It was fun.'

'Ohhhh-kay.'

'Sorry. I've been writing down lists. What I like. What I don't like. A kind of *Who is Greta?* project. Granny said it will help me with my next job. If anyone ever hires me again. Or deciding on a course if I go to university. Could you see me at university? With a robe and hat? I'd look like a wheelie bin.'

'I'm sorry about what happened.'

'Don't you be sorry. It's not your fault. It's totally my fault for being ... well, for hiding all that. I'm a bit bored of saying it, but I never leaked anything to anyone. You can believe me or not. I guess it doesn't matter. I lied to everyone anyway.' Greta shrugged. She really didn't feel like going over it all again. 'What are you doing here?'

'I just wanted to see if you're okay.'

'Me?' Greta laughed. 'Yes. I'm going to be fine.'

As Alexia watched her closely, Greta started to feel a bit irritated and self-conscious. Alexia could still intimidate her with her mere presence. *Leave me in peace. I just want to eat my breakfast for two people in solitude. Gah!*

'Do you know what you want to do?' Alexia asked.

'You know? I don't. I know I loathe the technical side of TV production. But I like the music stuff,' she said, before taking an awkward bite of her enormous, overflowing and utterly delicious sandwich. It leaked out of the far end, sending bacony deliciousness cascading down both forearms.

'Have you thought of working at a record label?'

Greta nearly spat out her food. 'Are you nuts? There's like

240

two jobs a year and they all – ALL OF THEM – go to people who know people. Or whose mummy and daddy work there.' She instantly blushed. 'Oh jeez. Sorry. Not including you, of course.'

'Well, it's true,' Alexia said, nodding slowly. 'It is who you know, I guess. I got the Bright Star job through Clint, who I met while working for my dad's record label.'

'What have *you* been doing?' Greta asked. 'What happened after I was casually lobbed out of the building by Andre the Giant Arsehole?'

'They dismantled the department,' Alexia said. 'I'm working for the food team. Under Karen. You know? Karen Eyebrows?'

'Oh, Christ. Bummer,' Greta commiserated. 'The food shows are the WORST.'

'It's okay, actually,' Alexia said. 'Karen's actually really smart and I'm learning so much from her. It's a good gig. And it'll be nice to be paid properly soon. Oh god. I'm sorry, Greta.'

'Why are you apologising?'

'I . . . I don't know.'

Greta suddenly felt angry at Alexia. 'I'm not going to make you feel better by telling you it's okay, because it's not. I had a really bad time the last couple of weeks, you know?'

'I'm sure,' she said.

'What do you want? You want to be friends still? After everything I've supposedly done?' Greta said. 'I don't get it.'

'I did think we were friends. I really like you.'

'But how can you if you think those things of me?' Greta asked. 'I don't understand you.'

'Well, we all miss you. Lewis and I were talking the other day about how—'

'Oh god, spare me. Sorry, but spare me the reminiscing with old friends. You may have noticed I don't have a lot left, Alexia.' Greta motioned to the empty seats around her.

'I'm sorry.'

'You can stop saying sorry. Really. But I do want to know one thing.'

'Yes?' Alexia said, straightening her shoulders.

'Do you think I did it?'

Alexia's face gave absolutely nothing away, except for a small flicker in her eyes just before she replied. 'Well, the evidence certainly—'

'Yes,' Greta interrupted. 'Yes, it does point to me. But that's not what I asked. Do you really think I did it?'

Alexia looked at her again and Greta could have sworn she saw regret in her eyes. 'I don't . . . ' her voice trailed off.

Greta was no longer hungry, and she was fighting hard to control the anger that swelled up inside her. She stood up. 'Look, what happened isn't your fault. I don't blame you for outing me, but don't come here looking for comfort or whatever it is you're looking for. I got nothing.' Her voice cracked and she buttoned her coat and pushed aside her food.

She walked off, tears streaming down her face. As the icy wind hit her cheeks she felt the sting and wiped at them. She headed over to the main road and stood at the gates of the park for a moment looking around, deciding which way to go, when a bus pulled up to the stop right by the gate.

Instinctively, she jumped on, pushing down the crowded aisle and onto the top deck.

CHAPTER 26

Loser

'Alexia!' Karen yelled through her office door across the floor of the hectic production room. 'I need you to go and recce a location for this shoot. Now! Not in five minutes! Now!'

Alexia jumped – she always jumped now – slipping her pen and her untouched Moleskine notebook into her bag. There was an idea of sorts forming, but it would have to wait.

She stood up and walked over to Karen's desk, pulling out her notepad and waiting attentively for more instructions. Along with their dire live cooking show, they had just had word of commission for their new reality series called *Tinder Fox* – a reality show about app dating featuring a play-along-swipe second-screen game.

There was already so much to do – she'd never had a work-load quite like it – and none of it was going to propel her dreams of documentary film-making forward.

She had to find CVs for a new casting director first thing this morning. And an actual director. And a very good production manager, since the budget was 'tight as a nun's fanny' (Karen's words) and she didn't have the luxury of time since Channel 5 wanted the launch to happen before Christmas.

She needed to find a location for the studio part of the show – which required a lot of travelling about London. She was also ordered to clear all the 'crap' cluttering Karen's office from the celebrity pet show shoot, which had finally been cancelled after several exhausting seasons. And there was the ongoing juggling of tasks for *Weekend Kitchen*, *Scotland Truckers* and *The Great British High Tea Revival*. How she was going to find time – any time – to work on ideas for a short documentary for the Sheffield Film Festival was beyond her right now. The task list felt relentless and insurmountable – it was almost like being back working for The Keep. But still, she waited patiently by Karen's desk for more, like the people-pleasing asshole she always would be.

'We're calling it just *FOX*, okay? No Tinder. Until we do a deal with Tinder, don't mention their name. And don't tell anyone there's no deal.'

Alexia was lost. 'Sure. Where is the location?'

'There's a building down by Southbank with an eighth-floor space which is apparently perfect.'

'Will somebody meet me?'

'They're already waiting. Hurry up,' Karen snapped,

turning her head to address a snivelling presenter who had just appeared from nowhere and was lurking behind Karen's wilting fern. 'Oh dear god, Josh. It happened, didn't it? I told you never to sleep with a lighting director. They're the worst! Sit down, there's the tissues. THANK YOU, ALEXIA. Please leave now.'

Alexia nodded and hurried back to her desk, throwing her jacket on and slipping her phone into her back pocket. She scurried through the door, bumping into Kevin in the corridor.

'Settling in Alexia?' Kevin said with a broad smile, as Alexia desperately pushed the lift buttons.

'Yes, thank you.'

'Great all this awfulness has been cleared up, eh?'

'Yes,' Alexia said, pressing the button again.

'I hope we can do business with your father again some day?' He was fishing.

'I'm sure,' she said. 'I'm sure, we maybe can.'

Mercifully, the lift opened, and Alexia slipped in, pressing the button for the ground floor. 'I have to go, so sorry!'

She hurried down to King's Cross station and jumped onto the Tube. She got off at Southwark and rushed towards the river to locate the tower block in question. It was one of those characterless 1980s buildings that sat not far behind the Tate Modern. She walked up to the reception area, where there was a man waiting to show her up.

'Karen?'

'Ah, no, I'm her assistant, Alexia.'

'Hi, Alexia,' he said, looking disappointed. She knew the look – it was the one she would get when people were hoping to speak to her old boss Geoff, or The Keep, but ended up having to speak to her instead. It was boring.

'I just need to take some photos, and then I'll be on my way. Shouldn't take long,' she said quickly.

'Okay. Number twenty-eight. It's the door directly in front of the service lift.'

As the clunky old lift shut behind her and juddered upwards she surveyed the space. *Plenty big enough for kit to be moved upstairs.* At the eighth floor, the lift door opened and she was greeted with the most incredible view down towards the river. The space was totally clear, with floor to ceiling windows. The only things remaining were two old office chairs, wiring spilling out of some detached ceiling squares and a few discarded Starbucks coffee cups beside one of two thick support columns.

She quickly surveyed the space, taking mental notes of any potential issues while she snapped with her camera.

Potential all day sun. Good access. Parking. Good ceiling height. Bathroom. Power. Stunning views. Direct light.

She walked towards the window and stared out across the cityscape and, for a brief moment, had her thoughts to herself. Then Karen called.

'Well?'

'It's kind of retro, eighties office space, but it's really a great location.'

'Fine. Can you get back now with the photos and down to help Penny in accounts with some queries?'

'Okay. But I'm not really sure I'll be much help with that. I've only been working with you a week.'

'Alexia. Can you just get back, please? I know everyone held your hand before but you're in a different team now. I need you to be your very best.'

'Yes, Karen,' she said flatly.

'I mean it. Give me your best,' she said.

Alexia was taken aback as the line went dead. She had never been made to feel like she was on trial before. Clint had been so supportive, and there had been a kind of unspoken expectation behind it all.

She slumped down against one of the columns and stared out onto the city as her thoughts turned to Theo Marlon. The last time they had spoken he had been distracted, as they'd just received some dick pics and were trying to verify that they were of the health secretary, and he was taking a call every few moments. His lack of attention to the deeply private information she was giving away made it feel all the more dirty.

She wanted to understand how she'd gotten to this place. What started as a need for independence from her parents had morphed into a catastrophic fall from personal grace. She didn't know herself. She didn't like herself. And here – the outcome – taking this job she didn't really want – what was it all for?

As she wallowed in her sadness, she peered down at the

people going about their daily business, tiny little figures below who seemed full of purpose, and wondered if there was a way back for her. Her phone rang again – Karen. She ignored it and pulled out her notebook.

It was time to take back some semblance of control. Her mother had a six-point plan for doing this, which she desperately tried to remember. There was some kind of acronym. She racked her foggy, exhausted brain. Sleeping was definitely one of the steps. And forgiving herself. And meditating. And writing a list. She could picture the little framed quote on the back of her bathroom door, but just couldn't remember what it said.

But a list she could do. She could try to look at it objectively, and see if there was a way she could tackle each task and make some kind of amends for her crimes.

She started with the most painful and began to scribble, and once she started it all came spilling out.

Mom – need to call her. Tell her I'm sorry. Tell her that I love her and that I need her. (But don't want to go back to NYC.)

Dad – see above.

Need to come clean to Kevin, Lewis and Clint.

Greta. Apologise. Help get job back?

Lee. Apologise.

Apologise to Max, Amelie, Jessica, Charlie and Dee, and anyone else hurt by this.

Theo Marlon . . .

She looked at the list. The first two were going to be big, but maybe there was no hurry to get to them? Then again, if she started by telling Bright Star the truth, then she really needed to give her parents and everyone in points five and six a call to tell them first.

There was no guarantee Greta would get her job back, since the fact that she had hidden the 'conflict of interest' would still be valid, despite her not spilling any secrets. But she missed Greta. There was no denying it. She had been so spirited and feisty when she saw her at the pavilion, but so very hurt. Of all the people she'd hurt, this one was the one that upset her most.

And Theo. What did she want to do about him?

She felt a surge of anger begin to course through her as she thought about their covert meetings and hushed phone calls. The dismissive attitude to people's feelings. The belief that because someone was in the public eye, they were somehow not allowed their privacy. The way he'd thrown his head back and cackled when Alexia had mentioned Jessica's pregnancy and that it might not be Lee's baby.

He was a scoundrel. An asshole. A complete bastard.

And she was complicit in his game.

She looked back at the list again. And then, just like that, her phone beeped. It was him. Again.

TO ALEXIA: Coffee? Wanna talk follow-up. Good $$$

CHAPTER 27

I'll Be Your Mirror

Theo sat across from her at the little kitchenette table in her bedsit, red-cheeked and puffing from the couple of short flights of stairs he had climbed. For a somewhat slender man, he was unfit, and the clothes, the weird clothes – he was like a relic from the early 2000s boybands with his shiny pants and fur.

The trickle of sweat running down his temple belied the chill in the air. It had turned out that floor-to-ceiling sash windows were fantastic in the summer, but an absolute disaster when the chill set in.

She had rushed to organise the meeting. If Theo was planning a follow-up perhaps there was something she could do to put a stop to it. She felt a surge of nervous excitement as she turned to the boiled kettle and poured hot water into two mugs.

'It's cold in here,' he remarked, pulling his enormous scarf around his pudgy neck and folding his arms.

'This should help. Milk?' she asked, wondering if she was sounding too warm. Normally in their encounters she'd been cool, even a bit dismissive of him. It was a way, she supposed, of putting some space between them – of feeling like she wasn't as bad as he was.

'Lots. And sugar,' he said while he readjusted his stool. 'So, you don't flatshare at eighteen? No wonder you took a job on the side.'

'No. But I think I will,' Alexia said, her mind wandering to Greta and her sweet offer on the night of the party. It would have been great to live with her. As much as she valued her independence, she couldn't imagine anything better than waking up to Greta burning cupcakes, or staying up late watching stupid Disney films together. She would have given Greta a music education, centred on her beloved pop still, but widening her scope from boybands somewhat. Alexia smiled a little. Greta could help her really get to know London. It could have been fun.

'Then again, I'd have thought the daughter of a big music exec would turn her nose up at anything this side of Selfridges, right? Quarterly figures a bit down at Falls Records? Not dipping into the trust fund?' he smirked.

Alexia resisted the urge to throw his tea in his face and slid it across the small table instead. She wrapped her hands around her own, staring out of the window.

'Oh, not really,' she said. She wouldn't share even the tiniest thing about her family or herself with him. 'I'm here on my own steam.'

He didn't seem to hear anyway. He never seemed to hear anything she said that wasn't of value. His currency of communication was illicit information; not emotions, not heart, not consequence. 'So, what did you want, Theo?'

'Ah, yes.' He smiled. 'Well. We ran the story about Lee and his little lady love, Jessica. Was fantastic, only, Alexia, here's the thing. She's put out this statement denying it. So obviously, I want to follow up, since it makes us look like we got it wrong. And, you didn't get it *wrong*, did you?' He stared at her hard, and Alexia felt a cold chill come over her.

'Um, well, I just told you what Lee told me,' Alexia said. 'I mean, he's not a liar. At least, he wouldn't lie about that kind of thing.'

'Right. Well, how do you explain the denial?' Theo asked. 'I mean, one can deny an affair, or a drug addiction. But one cannot deny a baby. At least not for ever.' He cackled.

'I can't explain it.' This was not what she had been expecting.

'Okay. Have you got any more information on it then? To back up *your* claim? Any times, references, emails, text messages, phone calls? Anything that we can use to go back and challenge the denial? Did she have a miscarriage? A termination? Can you find out?'

Alexia gasped.

'I don't know. I can't find any more out.' Alexia's heart

picked up pace as the conversation began to run in a direction that was definitely not good. 'I can't help you any more than I did.'

'Not even for ... Well, I could give you a more generous sum.' He smirked, pulling his wallet out and thumbing through a wad of notes. 'You see, usually if we print a rumour and it's untrue, I don't care. People never remember the denial, they only remember the rumour.'

'I don't need any money,' Alexia said, suddenly feeling cornered and panicked. 'I'm speaking to my parents later today—'

'Uh uh, Alexia. I haven't finished speaking yet, so perhaps just wait a moment,' he cautioned her, placing a fan of fifty-pound notes on the table. 'I was saying it's *usually* okay if we get it wrong.'

'I understand,' she said quickly.

'Yes, but in this instance, Jessica's lawyers – of which there are many – are threatening to sue. So you see, Alexia, you *need* to help me by backing this thing up. Or, I'm afraid ... well. Hopefully we don't need to talk about what will happen if you don't.'

Alexia looked down and steadied herself as the reality of what he was saying began to sink in. So Jessica was threatening to sue, and Theo needed to prove the story was correct or he was going to throw Alexia under a bus. Alexia considered this for a moment. Libel threats were not *that* common in the world of showbiz. That much she knew. She had witnessed enough hushed giggles and private high-fives behind closed doors at Falls Records to know that they operated on the premise that 'all column inches are good column inches'.

'Are you sure? I mean, about Jessica?' she asked.

'Oh yes,' he said, as he trailed a finger down his cheek, across his mouth and pulled at his chin.

This doesn't make sense. Alexia's eyes narrowed on him.

'You know, we never did a deal properly, did we? No privacy contract or anything like that,' he reminded her.

'Um, no.' Alexia cursed her naivety. She needed to buy some time to think. 'I could go through my phone and see? I mean, my emails and texts from Lee.'

'That would be a good start,' Theo said. 'I'm glad you're not seeing this as a problem, Alexia. But rather, a small matter that we both need to concern ourselves with resolving together.'

She motioned to her bag, which was slung over the chair on the other side of the room. Her notebook poked out. Her empty notebook, which served only to remind her that this whole time in London – this whole last few months – she had not achieved what she had come to do. She had no story. She had nothing to say. No insightful narrative on life to turn into an amazing debut documentary. Something she could show her mother, and make her proud of her for taking off and chasing her dreams. Just this mess.

'Can I get my phone?'

'Please,' Theo said.

She opened her phone and scanned through to the last couple of text messages from Lee, just before he'd left London.

After she'd picked him up from his dinner with Greta, he'd promised to get in touch to hang, and never did, until a few days later when she helped with his flight home.

> TO ALEXIA: How do I call a taxi?

> TO ALEXIA: What's my pin number?

> TO ALEXIA: Thanks for the flight. Catch ya round dude.

She suddenly felt a sting of anger. Was he really worth protecting? After all she had done for him, his final text read like a dismissal of something, someone, who was worthless to him. Someone who had outlived their usefulness. She looked over at Theo and the money on the table.

'How did you start out? Like, doing this for a living?' she asked him casually. 'I'm just going through the messages now.'

'Gossip blogging? You want to start a blog?' he said, tapping his fingers in a roll across the table top, chin in his hand. 'You totally could do a gossip site with all your connections. Or you could work for me?' He grinned, raising his eyebrows. They'd been over that before.

'No, I don't mean the blogging. Or even the entertainment gossip. I mean this part. What we're here to do now. Buying and selling people's secrets.'

'Ha!' He sat back a bit and ran a hand down his belly. 'You

make it sound so seedy. This is a game, Alexia. They need me like I need them.'

'I guess so. But it's one thing to get a pap photo of something someone's doing in public, but quite another to actually buy secrets ... isn't it? Do you think about it, like, morally?'

'Morally?' he scoffed. 'They're not moral. Why should I be?'

She walked over with her phone, pondering the fascinating world of Theo Marlon and his dirty business.

'I'm sorry, there's nothing about Jessica there,' Alexia said.

'Well, we'll have to look at plan B then,' he said, sighing.

'Plan B?'

'Plan B,' Theo said with a grin, 'in which Alexia phones Lee to get more information.'

Alexia held up her hands to stop him. 'I'm not doing that.'

'Well,' he said, collecting the cash and folding it back into the wallet, 'I'm afraid, Alexia, if you can't come up with some more evidence, I'll have to issue my statement to Jessica's lawyers. And, well, I'll need to name names. I won't like doing it. You know, I like you, Alexia. But I'll have no choice.'

Alexia felt her hands go clammy and she slid her phone onto the counter near the window, trying to figure out what to do next. Could she really just sell Lee completely out like that? Betray him?

She pictured him with his floppy hair and his cheeky grin. The way he used to put his hand on her arm when he was desperate for her to help with something that was beyond her job spec. The way he showed overt affection in public, often revelling in her embarrassment, like she was his property. That grin that got him whatever he wanted – it suddenly wasn't quite so cute. She suddenly considered something that for so long seemed impossible. Was she over Lee?

'Alexia?'

'I'm thinking. Sorry.'

A garbage truck began to back up outside, and the noise in the room was problematic. *Beep beep beep.* She walked to the window.

'I forgot it was garbage day. Stupid,' she said, willing the truck to finish as the banging, clanging and thumping continued downstairs. She smiled a little at her landlord, who was 'helping' by handing armfuls of disgusting wayward rubbish that the truck's mechanical arm had missed to the two poor council workers.

She thought about Jessica again, and the denial she had issued about the pregnancy. Theo was right – you couldn't deny a pregnancy unless it really wasn't true. Or she wasn't pregnant *any more*. But Alexia felt sure that would be even more reason for silence. And surely Jessica was above responding to online gossip sites with lawyers over something like this. It didn't add up.

'Did you forget to put it out?' he said, sighing.

'What?'

'The rubbish.' He was annoyed. It was too much small talk for Theo.

She looked over at him, and suddenly it was so obvious. He was bluffing to try to worm more out of her. She no longer wanted to play the game, and he wanted to pull her back in – any way he could. There was no threat from lawyers here. He didn't have his hands tied. He was just an asshole.

The world of gossip columns and trading secrets was a life of deceit, disloyalty and dishonesty. She looked across at her notebook again. Was this the story she was meant to tell?

'Well, I can't call Lee right now,' she said, playing along, 'he'll be with his grandmother in Long Island.'

Theo sat up straight and raised a brow. 'Okay.'

'Can you give me a week or so and I'll see what I can dig up?' She needed to buy some time.

Theo smiled. 'You're back on board. Good to hear.'

'I'll do everything I can, okay?'

As the door shut behind him, Alexia realised she had been holding her breath. She sat on the edge of the bed, closed her eyes and let out a long, slow exhalation until her lungs were empty, and then took a long, slow breath back in. It was a trick her mother had shown her to help stabilise her moods. She repeated this several times until her heart rate slowed.

A few moments later, she opened her eyes. She was suddenly aware of everything around her. The smell of Theo's sickly sweet cologne lingered in the room. She threw open a window and let the cold air rush in. As the blast hit her face and the bitter wind stung her cheek, she smiled.

She needed to tell this story.

Chapter 28

Mama Said

'Can I help?' Greta stood patiently beside an older lady with a walking stick, who was having difficulty leaning over to reach for something on the bottom shelf.

'Oh, yes dear, thank you.' The lady smiled. 'I want that book there. The one about the grey shades. No no. That one on the end. I've read the first two. Very good.'

'Can I take it to the counter for you?' Greta said, delighting in the brightly polished nails on the lady's long and elegant fingers.

'No, dear. I can manage.'

On positive days, Greta liked to maintain that she worked in a dinky record and book store. On her more negative days, the blank description was more accurate: a newsagent in the departures area of Luton Airport. The CD section featured the top twenty and a round, spinning display of orchestral classics, Enya and relaxation music for fearful flyers. The book section was slightly more exciting – but frankly the store was about 60 per cent deals on chocolate bars and bottled water.

'Can I help?' she asked her next customer, who was red-faced and panicked.

'iPhone chargers?' he almost shouted. 'My phone. I have the boarding pass on it. Seven per cent.'

'They're at the till.' She smiled. 'Good luck with your flight! Where are you going?'

'Hell ... ' he said, smiling.

Hell ... thought Greta. *Helsinki!* She pulled out her phone and tapped HELSINKI into her notes section. Another place to visit. This list was one of her granny's recommendations for figuring out what to do next.

Helsinki was in Finland, which was the country of Santa and magical snow fairies and all sorts of wonder. In her head, she saw vast, snow-covered castles and intricate icicles hanging from wrought-iron lamp posts. Like *Frozen*! She picked up one of the Finland guidebooks in the travel section and thumbed through it: 'Kamppi Chapel of Silence in Helsinki offers a place where people can take a moment to calm ... '

'Chapel of Silence? Christ.' Greta felt suffocated by the mere thought of all that head space. 'Can I help?' she squeaked at a little boy, who was fondling the chocolate bars while his mother pursued the beach reads.

'I'm not allowed,' he said sheepishly.

Greta sighed, looking over at the wall clock to see if it was knock-off time yet. *Five minutes.* She did a little fist pump and headed towards the staff room, loitering as she counted down to 3 p.m. It was a long day, what with the 5 a.m. starts, but at least it was a job and something to occupy her time ...

As she sat on the train back to St Pancras, she pulled out her phone and checked all the usual online news and social channels. It was easier now, after everything. She felt less hyper-addicted and any news of The Keep had become a curiosity rather than an obsession.

She was sad to see that her Keep account had fallen into disarray, as younger fans abandoned the band in their tens of thousands for the Next Big Thing, which was All New Wild. She decided to see what All New Wild's fanbase was like and had a little dig around. *Not much here*, she thought, scrolling through a very sanitary and professional Twitter feed.

@ANWILD Pre-order our first single here.

@ANWILD British tour dates and tickets on sale here.

@ANWILD Here's Nav and Jonah playing with balloons.

Yikes. She tried a search to see if Nav was even on Twitter, but he wasn't.

As the train pulled into the station Greta was feeling ready to get back to Dalston and curl up in bed. She disembarked and wandered through King's Cross station to wait for the bus, but when the display time said eighteen minutes, she opted to walk instead. Her phone rang.

'Clint!' Greta said with surprise, almost dropping her phone.

'How are you?'

'I'm okay. I'm sorry I haven't replied to your text yet. I'm so glad you called,' she said sweetly, before adding, 'Although I'm not sure why?'

'Yeah, listen, I'm sorry I didn't before. I think I just needed to process . . . everything that happened,' he said carefully. 'I wondered if we could talk. I don't want to make you feel bad, there's just a few things that aren't sitting right with me.'

'About?'

'The Keep stuff. Not about you.'

Greta paused as she waited for a cyclist to turn in front of her before she crossed the road. 'I'm sorry, I'm walking. It's okay. I'm actually near you now. Coming up to the Lexington. Do you fancy meeting up?'

'Sure,' Clint said. 'I'll be there in a few moments, actually.'

Greta hurried up the street to the pub and pushed open the two heavy doors. There was a couple sat in the raised area by the toilets and one of the booths was filled with the bar manager and a supplier doing paperwork. It was mid-afternoon on a weekday, so hardly surprising.

Greta went up to the bar and palmed a handful of change onto the counter. 'Ahh, sorry. I've only got change. Do I have enough for a shandy?'

'Just have one on me,' said the barman, pulling on the tap before topping up her half-pint glass with lemonade. He ran his heavily tattooed and not at all unpleasant forearm across his forehead before plonking the drink down right in front of her. 'End of the barrel, anyway.'

She eased herself onto a sofa and waited. Nervously. Clint was there in moments. He came breezing through the door, nodded at the barman and strode directly to Greta with a determined look. He'd shaved off his beard, and without it he looked much younger, thinner and more ... professional, maybe?

When their eyes met, she felt a giddy sense of anticipation. She wanted to hug him, but she didn't know whether it would be well received. She didn't have time to decide before Clint sat down and grabbed both of her arms.

'Tell me. Look me in the eye. Did you do it?'

'No,' she said calmly. She had no reason to feel afraid any more. She had lost her job and her friends already.

'But you ran the fan stuff?' he said, letting go of her.

'Yes, I did. I was heavily involved in the Keeper fandom since I was thirteen. I ran unofficial social media. I went to countless gigs. I tried to meet them. I am the fangirl every pop star needs but slightly fears!' She smiled.

'And is that why you harassed Lewis for the internship at Bright Star?'

'You think I came to learn how to be a key grip?' she said sarcastically, and then, without wanting to sound rude, 'Of course it was to be near The Keep. Come on, it's like the ultimate job for someone like me. At least it *was*.'

'Do you see how that makes it difficult to believe you didn't leak all that stuff to Theo?'

'Of course I do,' Greta said.

'But you're saying you didn't.'

'I didn't!'

'Okay.' He sat back. 'I've been boring Julian senseless with all this. Last night I actually made post-it notes with timelines of all the leaks, who knew, when and where and stuck them on the wall.'

Greta smirked. 'You went all CSI on it.'

'Dude, I was obsessed. But seriously, Greta, you're the worst production intern we've ever had. But you're a nice, good person. It doesn't sit right with me.'

Greta blushed and felt a surge of hope as tears began to well in her eyes.

'So, on the assumption that you didn't do it, who did?' he began. 'We know the first juicy bit of info – that Max was quitting the band and that Charlie and Dee were together – was something all of us knew and maybe many others in the wider music circle. But assuming the leak comes from Bright Star, let's start with the four of us.

'The next leak, the photo, could have come from any of us four. Maybe we could include some random cleaner or runner at Bright Star if the footage was on the shared drive, but it would be unlikely they would know about the break-up *and* the Dee and Charlie scandal *and* the final leak: Jessica is pregnant but not to Lee.'

'Yep.'

'Well, *I* didn't know that,' Clint insisted. 'And, in fact, the information has turned out not to be true.' He stared intently at Greta to gauge her reaction. She felt immediately relieved, and then confused.

'Huh?'

'Yep.' Clint raised his eyebrows. 'Not only is she not pregnant, she never had an affair. That much is in the press. But the word on the grapevine is that she made the whole thing up to hurt him, because of all the stuff he got up to on tour. So, we can rule out doctors, nurses, her PA or any other staff that might have known something was going on – people from the film she's currently in – everyone. We can rule them all out because they would know she wasn't pregnant, that it was just a thing she told Lee to hurt him.'

'So that means that the only people who knew this were the people who Lee told directly?' Clint mused.

'Yes. Someone Lee knew, confided in. Someone close to him who also worked at Bright Star,' Greta continued, as the whole truth started to emerge.

'Someone who he was used to keeping secrets for him?' Clint nodded.

'Alexia!' Greta gasped. 'No!'

Clint held up a cautionary finger. It was like he'd slipped into an episode of *Sherlock*. 'Well, perhaps. But you went for dinner with Lee that night he was in town, right? So he could have told you?'

'Sure, he could have. But he didn't. Alexia turned up pretty soon after we got there. I didn't even get a photo with him.' She still wasn't quite done sulking about that.

'Let's look at the rest of the evidence. The leaks started not long after Alexia arrived at Bright Star. I know for a *fact* she was struggling for money.'

'Yeah, I never got that. I thought she was super rich? All that designer labels? Growing up in Manhattan? She's like someone from *Gossip Girl*.'

'Well, she *was*. But she totally bailed on her parents. I don't know who cut who off, but she was supporting herself.'

'She had a fight with them that day of the All New Wild shoot,' Greta said, wide-eyed.

'Well, yeah. She was struggling, I think.'

'Oh, that's awful. She could have stayed with me!'

'Well, when she mentioned the stress of the rent I did offer my sofa, I mean a few times and when she did try to take up the offer it was too late . . . anyway, it doesn't matter.'

'Her card got declined that other time,' Greta remembered. 'That day at the hotel with the burritos. Three cards. It was mega awkward.'

'It's all making so much more sense, isn't it? Theo Marlon must have paid her.'

'But, Clint.' Greta sat back, feeling a knot in the pit of her stomach. 'That means she framed me. She let me lose my job.'

'Well, I was thinking about that. I guess she didn't accuse you of the leak exactly, she just let you take the fall after outing you,' he said. 'So to speak. I mean, the company might have taken issue with the fangirl stuff anyway.'

'But why would someone . . . '

'I don't know. Maybe she was in more trouble than I realised. She's very private. It's hard to know what's going on with her. On tour, she was just so focused on the boys and was so good at her job. So eager to please. To be thorough and do her job. You've seen it? I only really got talking to her because she followed me round with the camera whenever she could, and she was so excited to come to London. I don't know – maybe I thought she was a better person than she actually is.'

'Oh, I don't believe she's not a good person. She was very kind to me . . . before.'

'She was totally smitten with Lee, of course. So some of this could be revenge of some kind against him. I don't know.'

'WHAT?' Greta's jaw dropped.

'Oh my god, yes. It was the unrequited love of the century. Everyone could see it on tour, the poor love. And he used to play with her a lot.'

'Jesus.' Greta cringed as she remembered the evening of the meal with Lee at Deniz's. Everything took on so much more weight. Alexia's face when she arrived at the restaurant – now it was clear what that look was – a perfect storm of anger and jealousy. The way she bristled whenever Greta mentioned Lee. It wasn't because she was being superior, or cool, it was because she was in love with him.

Clint stood. 'I need a drink. You?'

'Yes. A beer. No shandy this time,' Greta said glumly.

As Clint walked to the bar, Greta looked down at the floor and felt the tears well in her eyes once more. Maybe she did understand why Alexia had done this? True to form, Greta started to analyse her own behaviour, and in the four minutes it took Clint to return she had convinced herself that the only one to blame for this was herself.

'It's my fault,' Greta said. 'I was too insecure around her. I never made enough effort. And I went on about Lee ... a lot ... even after she found out about the fan club.'

'What? Don't be a dick.'

'No, really. I was so jealous when she came. Oh my god, I was *so* jealous. You guys all loved her so much. And she was this tall, beautiful American lady whose father was essentially our bosses' boss and I was just, well, intimidated.'

'That's daft, love.' Clint shook his head. 'Everyone loves you, Greta.'

'No they don't. I'm clumsy and I was lazy at work. I couldn't hack it.'

'I know you didn't like the technical stuff but you were a superstar with the talent,' Clint offered. 'And you were *so* nice to have around the office. You just need to find the thing you love.'

'Thanks.' Greta blushed, looking down at her drink. 'What are you going to do though? I mean, will you confront Alexia?'

'Maybe. I don't know. What will it achieve?' Clint looked up, shaking his head. 'Apart from anything else, we don't work in the same department any more. I never see her. She's gone super underground. And I also can't prove it.'

'What about Lewis? Have you spoken to him about it?'

'I tried. It's hard with Lewis. He can only see the good in Alexia. He was so happy to have another docu-geek friend to play with. Although I think he's starting to get frustrated with her, too.'

'So that's it then?' Greta slumped in her seat.

'I don't know, Greta.'

'Well I hope *we* can be friends,' she said meekly. 'Can you forgive me for hiding the fan club from you? I'm mortified. Mortified that I hid it, but also that I ever did it in the first place.'

'What? Don't be mortified!' Clint suddenly laughed. 'It's kinda funny. Julian thinks it's absolutely hilarious. He calls you The Kreep. With great affection.'

Greta let out a small chuckle. 'When I look at it objectively, it did get to creepy levels sometimes.'

'Well, you should think about putting it on your CV. Whatever the subject matter, you built up and managed a social media channel with thousands of followers. And if you want a job that doesn't involve you wearing sky-blue polyester –' he nodded at her work uniform, '– then please allow me to be a reference, at least.'

CHAPTER 29

Tony's Theme

'... you're told you shouldn't put yourself at the centre of the story ...' Alexia said straight down the barrel.

'What the bloody Dickens?' Mr Coleman lowered the camera and looked at Alexia, then over her shoulder to the fracas. The manager of Costcutter was hurling a bag at the owner of the Swedish bakery. 'Sorry, that bloody hipster baker just dumped his rubbish in Roy's bin. Again.'

'I SEE YOU!' Coleman shouted. 'Ima come down there and shove that rye loaf up your arse, mate.'

'Why are you so fixated on the garbage?' Alexia asked.

He looked at her, perplexed. 'Cos this is my home.'

Alexia tried really hard not to be annoyed, but this was their seventh attempt. She really should have known better than to ask Mr Coleman, but she didn't have a lot of choice. There was no one else that could help her do this crucial bit of filming.

She stood patiently while he reframed the shot, leaning his elbow on the back of the supermarket trolley to steady it. He looked at her, smile as perky as ever. 'Come on then, luv.'

She straightened out her coat and stared down the camera lens once again, shaking her hair out and . . .

'Action!' he boomed, just as she was about to speak.

She flinched. 'It's okay, I said you don't need to say that.'

'Spoil sport,' he teased.

'Stop calling me luv,' she snapped.

'Sorry, darling.'

She sighed, looking down at her feet to make sure she was 'in position'. She nodded. 'Let's go.'

'What started out as a way to make a quick buck turned into a dark exploration of celebrity culture. You're told not to put yourself at the centre of the story, but when the story starts with you, that's exactly what you have to do.'

The trolley wobbled the camera hopelessly, clanging and squeaking as they tried to do the tracking shot. Alexia groaned. 'Cut.'

'Hey, you got to say "cut",' Mr Coleman complained. Seriously, this guy was like a toddler.

'Sorry,' Alexia groaned. 'Can we try with the office chair again?'

'We can, but I think you're going to get the same result,' Mr Coleman advised, 'and I'm going to have to start charging.' He winked.

'Please don't wink at me.'

'Christ, you milleniams,' he said, shaking his head.

'Millennials. And only just!' She walked over to reclaim her camera and her dignity. 'Thanks for the help, Mr Coleman.'

'You're welcome. I'll be sorry to see you go, really. Brought a bit of class to the flats, more than Jez ever has.'

'Well, my time at Chapel Market is up,' she said. 'And anyway, I'll be around for another few weeks yet.'

She popped her camera back into her bag and smiled at Mr Coleman once more before heading down towards the office. It was Sunday, so the perfect day for a quiet, undisturbed session in one of the edit suites.

She took the bigger suite, as it also had a small but complicated audio desk which, aside from allowing an awesome mix of the final film, would also allow her to record a phone call. After plugging in her laptop and her camera, she quickly ingested all the pieces to camera she'd filmed, including this morning's footage. She flicked through her rough script and crossed off the last few sections. She had everything she needed; even if the picture was wobbly, she could just lift the audio and use footage or stills to illustrate her point instead.

She looked down at the timeline – her edit was almost finished. She spent the next two hours and three coffees slotting the newly shot stuff in.

All she needed now was to go through her old tour photos to fill a few black holes. She also needed to make some basic graphics. And make that last phone call.

When she was done, she leaned back in the chair and

stretched her arms and rubbed her achy wrists. It was just breakfast time in New York – time to have another of the conversations she'd been dreading. But first – another coffee.

She stood up and immediately felt a bit light-headed. *Sugar!* She fished a handful of coins out of her bag and headed to the dreaded vending machine for a chocolate bar before wandering to the kitchen. She flicked the kettle on, leaned back against the bench, her mind darting about. She realised she was jittery as her anxiety had made room for anticipation and – dare she think it – excitement.

The last person she expected to run into was her new boss, Karen, who came sailing into the small room with her arms full of paperwork. She was dressed casually – jeans, sneakers, her hair pulled back into a messy ponytail, and not a scrap of make-up on her face. She had planned to speak with her on Monday. *No time like the present.*

'Hello, Karen.'

'Alexia. Good to see you putting in the hours.' Karen dropped her paperwork on the small kitchen table and swung round to fill the coffee percolator.

'Do you have a quick minute?' Alexia said, rousing all her inner confidence. Again. 'I've been working on something and I'd love to show it to you.'

'Sure. Of course.' A smile. Eye contact. Kindness? Alexia was completely taken aback. 'I'm totally snowed under this week, but how about we put some time in the diary where there is some?' She sniffed a carton of milk and erupted.

'Jesus Christ. It's like brie in there. Why do people have to open eight cartons at the same time? What a bloody waste of milk.' It was torpedoed into the open bin with such force that the bin fell over.

'I'll get it.' Alexia scrambled across to fix the mess. 'Can I put some time in your diary then?'

'Of course you can,' she said. Karen was actually being warm. She turned to leave, but paused. 'I get busy, but I'm never too busy to help you grow in your role. It's my job. Never fear asking for help.' And, with a brief nod, she was gone.

Alexia felt a surge of excitement. Karen was the head of Factual Entertainment, so also supervised the documentary team: this was the best person she could turn to for advice. Especially since she was sure Lewis wouldn't want to speak to her again once they'd had their conversation ...

Confidence boosted by her chat with Karen, Alexia decided now was as good a time as any to make the call to Lee. She was ready to set that huge ball in motion and come clean. And once she did, there was nothing Theo could hold against her.

She finished the set-up, and when everything in the suite was ready she took a deep breath and dialled his number. Amazingly, he answered after three short rings.

'Alexia,' Lee said. 'How you doing?'

She could hear the sadness in his voice and wanted to reach through the phone and hug him. She wished she could be having this conversation face to face.

'Hey, Lee. I'm sorry to call you so early. But I knew I'd catch you.'

'It's okay. What's going on?'

'Where are you?'

'Ah. Actually, I'm back in New York as of yesterday. We're going to London, did you know? In a couple of weeks. We should catch up.'

Alexia knew that wouldn't happen after this call. 'Sure, Lee.'

'Christmas lights, Christmas single, then ... Well, I'm not so sure we're going to keep going. You spoken to your dad? Or Geoff?'

'I saw Geoff. But not Dad. Haven't spoken to him in a while.'

'It's weird not having you around, Lexi,' he said. His voice was soft and sincere. 'But then, heaps has changed.'

'What happened with Jessica?' she quickly blurted out. 'Last time we spoke she was pregnant, and now I read she's not?'

'Yeah. It wasn't true.' He coughed. 'Sorry, I've had this chest infection.'

'Did you manage to sort things out then?'

'Nah, not really. Basically, she lied to hurt me because she thought I'd cheated or some crap. I dunno. Games, Lexi, games. Anyway, we're done.'

'Done?'

'Yeah, after it got in the papers, you can imagine. She was like "I can't believe you'd tell anyone I was pregnant so early on. What if I was?"' He laughed, which turned into another cough. 'So I was in trouble for telling *her* lie. Ha ha! Ridiculous.'

'I'm so sorry,' she said.

'It was a dick move, I guess. Dunno how it got in the papers, though. I, like, told hardly anyone. A few random people in India, and the boys of course. But no one that would rat me out.'

'Well,' she said, taking a deep breath. 'That's why I'm calling.'

'Yeah?'

'Yeah, Lee. I was the source that told The Buzz.'

'You what?'

'I told The Buzz about Jessica and the pregnancy. I sold the story for just over four thousand pounds.'

'What? Why?'

'I needed the money.'

'I'm a bit ... What?' He coughed again.

'I'm trying to clean things up as best I can,' she said, biting her lip. 'I'm so sorry that you and Jessica broke up anyway.'

'Lexi, babe, what the hell? You don't do this stuff. You're the vault. We used to *call* you the vault.'

'I know. I don't know why. I wanted things to work out in London, away from my parents, and things were harder than I thought.'

'But your dad's my boss. Sort of. You must have money. Why would you do that to me?'

'I know. I'm sorry.'

'Man, this is way too heavy for a Sunday morning.'

'I'm so sorry, Lee.'

Click.

With that, Lee would be out of her life for ever, and she had now hit 'start' on the ticking clock. She had to get to everyone else, to come clean before Lee started talking. She didn't have time to mourn what had just happened, she had to push on.

She checked the recording had worked, and then she called Max. After a few attempts, he picked up.

'Alexia? Is that you? Is something up?'

'Hey, Max. Where are you?'

'Back in Memphis for a bit, working on some more music. Something the matter? You sound stressed.'

Alexia had practised detaching emotionally from these moments, but hearing Max's upbeat, friendly voice, and knowing what she'd done had somehow driven a wedge into his fragile new relationship, actually burned worse than what she'd done to Lee.

'Um, I have something to tell you.'

'Okay, give me one sec,' he said. 'Sorry, just had to grab my coffee. What's up?'

'The story about Dee and Charlie? I leaked it to the press.'

'You did what?' Max sounded confused.

'I told the story about how they were together on that tour, and leaked the photo,' she said, staring at the screen where the audio bars bounced up and down in time with her voice.

'What? Why?'

'Money. Theo Marlon – the gossip columnist – approached me when I was really struggling and . . . well, I'm so sorry, Max.'

Silence on the end of the line. Alexia's heart thumped in her chest as she waited for his reaction.

'Well, thanks for telling me. It caused . . . ' There was a huge sigh down the line, followed by a long pause. 'It caused me a big problem.'

'With Amelie. I know.'

'Yeah. It was kinda fragile already, and very new. And after all that stuff it got suddenly dirty.' He sighed again. 'She hates it. All the attention.'

Silence.

'It probably won't change anything, that you told me,' he continued. 'But I'm glad you did.'

'I just wanted to come clean and say sorry.'

'Yeah. Okay. Well, I accept the sorry, I guess.'

'Do you want me to call her and explain?'

'No. I'm Skyping her in an hour anyway.'

Max was one of the kindest, most reasonable people she'd ever known, but in his voice there was haste. He wanted to end the call.

'Hey, Alexia?'

'Yes.'

'I hope you figure it out. Whatever got you to this place. Was it really money?'

'Yeah. I'd fallen out with my parents and I had this internship and—'

'You're from a pretty wealthy family, Lexi. There wasn't an aunt or a cousin? This was your only choice?'

Alexia reflected on this, recognising her feelings of defensiveness and sitting with them for a moment. It was true, at first the idea of selling the stories seemed like an ultimately harmless way to make a quick buck. She even recognised some of those feelings of anger and contempt that drove Theo Marlon. The Keep took her for granted, and while she cared for them, she often didn't like them very much.

'I'm sorry,' she repeated. 'Maybe it wasn't only about the money.'

'Hey, listen, I have to split. I got practice and Dad's hovering around wanting me to help programme his new iPhone. Be cool, Alexia.'

Two phone calls down; Dee and Charlie were next. Then, it was time to call her mom.

CHAPTER 30

Matchbook Seeks Maniac

Greta was jittery with excitement at the backstage invite from Clint to come and see the filming of the *Great British Stars* live results show, and All New Wild make their live TV debut. She was surprised how much she missed the excitement of a TV set after all, but this was the first UK version of the show that launched The Keep, so it was super special.

She stood by a side entrance to Wembley Arena, which was more or less dead outside, but she could hear the intermittent roar of the crowd warming up inside. She looked around for Clint, who was coming to meet her.

Earlier, her granny had taken to her hair with a pair of curling tongs, fighting her unruly curls into a beautiful wave. She had time to do her make-up perfectly, a beautiful palate of maroon wintry hues that really set off her big eyes. She KNEW she looked good.

'Are you sitting in the audience or backstage?' Granny had asked. 'Because if you're backstage, tell that horrible judge Simon Cowell that he walks like a Lego man.'

'Wrong show, Granny,' she'd grinned. 'I look good, right?'

'Yes, darling. Though I'm not sure why you want to go back into the lion's den.'

'Things have changed,' she'd said simply. The conversation with Clint, though it had changed nothing with Bright Star, meant that she still had a friend. And she couldn't wait to see him.

'GRETA!' Clint walked over, smiling and waving. He was wearing a black T-shirt with 'CREW' in bright white writing, and a *Great British Stars* logo on his breast pocket. Around his waist, his utility belt was bulging with camera gear. 'You made it.'

'I'm so excited,' Greta said, giddy with anticipation.

'Well, hurry up, the show's about to start.'

He led her into the foyer area, waving his AAA pass to security as they pushed through the electric turnstile and through a corridor to a door marked 'Staff Only'.

They pushed through the door and down another busy corridor with huge windows looking down onto the packed arena. It was absolutely rammed, and the audience was totally pumped. The purple, red and blue lights circled the crowd from overhead and music was blaring as an MC boomed, 'Are you ready? ARE YOOOOOUUUU READY?'

'Oh god, I wish we'd been working on THIS show,' Greta said, her eyes wide.

'I thought you might like it. We'll make a TV producer out of you yet.'

'No thanks,' Greta said with a grin. 'I don't really like working in TV, in case you hadn't noticed.'

He pushed through a door at the far end of the corridor and led her down some stairs and into the backstage area. 'Last time I showed a girl around backstage, she ended up falling in love with the singer of the band.'

Greta beamed. 'Amelie!'

'Yes.' He nodded. 'She came to see The Keep in Hammersmith.'

'Oh, that's so cool.'

'I know, right? Shame about all the crap that went down.' Clint frowned, shaking his head. 'God, Alexia's got a lot to apologise for.'

They arrived at the crew room, where dozens of young media types wandered about wearing earpieces and clutching call sheets. Every now and then a contestant was ushered past with a small entourage and bundled into a dressing room.

'Oh my god, it's so big back here,' Greta said with her eyes wide. 'Clint, I've been dying to know. Did you speak to Alexia? Or Lewis?'

'Oh, yeah. Well, no,' he said. 'Alexia actually tried to call me a few times today. I just couldn't answer it.'

'She's called me too,' Greta said, surprised. 'I can't answer either.'

'Maybe she's ready to confess?' Clint said, with half a smile and a shrug. 'I spoke to Lewis and he's not seen anything of her since she moved departments. Apparently, she's been working on her own film day and night and is firmly under Karen's wing.'

'Right,' Greta said. 'The band marches on, as my granny would say.'

'Sorry, Greta, I just can't see a way to resolve it,' he said. 'Without outwardly accusing her.'

'It's just not fair,' she said.

Clint put down his gear. 'The truth will out, Greta.'

'Yeah,' Greta said, 'and in the meantime, I'm loving things at Luton Airport. They've given me the late shift now; I get to sleep in but I have zero life, which sadly works right now.'

'God. That sucks.'

'I pulled a sickie for tonight,' Greta said, eyes darting about in excitement. 'Please never tell them how utterly uncommitted I am.'

Suddenly, everyone began to busy themselves as the backstage crew fired into action. 'Looks like show time!' Greta grinned.

'I managed to get a seat for you in the family and performers' area near the front row, you lucky thing, or you can watch from the wings, up to you. Here's your pass, you know the drill. Your seat is 3K,' he said, looking at some scribbled notes on his pad.

'I might go watch the show – would you mind?'

'Of course not. Just through there,' he said, pointing to a door guarded by a big burly bodyguard.

She pushed through the door and out into the main arena.

The music was cut and above the stage a countdown clock showed the time until the show was live. She slipped down towards the family area, which was situated right behind the four judges' chairs, which sat on a plinth with a walkway around the outside that extended from the stage.

Family members wore T-shirts printed with images of their loved one's face and waved flags. Her stomach leaped when she saw two actors from *Hollyoaks* squeezed on the end behind Ellie Goulding, who would be performing later in the show.

'Excuse me,' she said, squeezing along her row and onto her seat. Right next to Nav from All New Wild.

'Hey, Greta,' he smiled. 'How's it going?'

'Nav!' She beamed. 'What on EARTH are you doing here?!'

He was perfection. Much more done up than last time she'd seen him – far more polished, more properly styled. His hair was hardened by gel and hairspray, but his signature stubble, though more evenly groomed, remained.

'I'm performing!' He smiled. 'Well, of course we are. Our record company practically owns this show.'

'No, I mean here. In this seat.'

'The whole band is here,' he said, leaning back and pointing to the boys, who sat next to him in a row. Alex, the drummer, waved at her. 'We're playing last, so we can watch the beginning of the show.'

'It's good to see you.' She smiled. 'How did the music video work out?'

'Oh it's so good. I'm really proud of it. I've been exerting a bit more artistic authority on the band actually, and they've been surprisingly accepting of my demands.'

'Look at you, acting like a superstar already,' Greta said, teasing.

'I've missed you at the last few shoots,' he said. 'What happened? The new crew are from the label and they're totally rubbish. They filmed our last YouTube diary on a phone.'

'Oh dear. No ring light?'

'No ring light.' He smiled at her, and she felt a little flutter in her stomach.

CHAPTER 31

What Went Down

Alexia stood at Karen's door, clutching her flash drive and waiting for her to finish her personal conversation. Today was the big, terrifying day; first she had to show Karen her film and then – more difficult conversations.

'Stephanie, you can tell Christopher that I'm totally unhappy. The kids need picking up at five thirty today, and I told him already I couldn't do it.' She rested her forehead on her hand. 'I'm exhausted, Steph. Please can you help? I have literally nothing left right now. I can't get to them at five thirty. Why does he always have to do this?'

Alexia considered leaving, but Karen waved her in, motioning her to take a seat in front of her.

'Steph, just tell him I'm hurt. Okay? And thanks for getting the kids. I owe you. Again.' She hung up and sighed, her eyebrows arched high up under her fringe until they disappeared, presumably trying to make an escape.

'I can come back another time.'

'No no.' She half smiled. 'It's life, Alexia.' She nodded to a picture of her two little boys on her desk.

'I have my entry for the festival here.'

'Wow, that was fast,' Karen said, folding her arms in front of her. 'You wanna show it to me now? Shall we watch it here or down in the edit?'

'Well, I have it here,' Alexia said again. 'Only, I wanted to warn you about the subject matter.'

'Yup?' Karen said as she reached out and took the flash drive before plugging it into her computer.

'It's quite personal. And maybe you won't like it.'

'Good. That makes it more interesting.' Karen smiled. 'Shall I watch and let you know what I think? Or do you want to watch with me? How do you want to do it?'

'I don't think I can be here. And, in any case, I have some stuff to get on with.'

'Lewis!' Alexia rushed down the corridor. 'Lewis!'

'Hello.' He turned around, a weary smile on his face. 'Long time no see. Where you been?'

He'd let his usual buzzcut grow out, and tight black curls were starting to form. He was holding a pile of digibeta archive tapes and was waiting for the lift down to the edit suites in the basement. His shirt was rolled to the elbows and his slender forearms strained under the weight of the tapes.

'I know. The last few weeks, they've been, um, weird. But I want to talk to you.'

He was one of the last. She'd done the band, next up was Bright Star and then ... her parents. She looked at her watch – there was a Skype call scheduled for just over an hour's time. Best get on and speak to Lewis.

He sighed. 'Yeah?'

'Please,' she begged.

'Okay. You can help me carry these, then,' he said, offloading half his tapes onto her. 'You look well.'

'Thanks.' She didn't feel it. She'd hardly seen daylight since she'd started making the film and her normally sharp, tidy appearance had begun to slacken. She pulled on her topknot.

The lift arrived and they both entered, standing in silence as it dropped to the lowest floor.

'What are you working on?'

'My vinyl documentary,' he said. 'You know – I think I've mentioned it a few times.'

'Oh yeah? How's it coming on?'

'It's nearly done, actually. I'm just looking for some archive footage to fill parts of it out. Did you know Bright Star used to do this chart show in the noughties? It was called *Counting Down the Beat*. I think. Anyway, did you know that the UK indie market led to the resurrection of vinyl? Sales turned around thanks to the seven-inch, in around 2006. Jack White sold forty thousand copies of his LP in 2014.'

'Really?' she replied. 'I wonder why we ever needed CDs?'

'Well, it was the introduction of that format that led to a surge of money for labels in the nineties. All your dad's money,' Lewis said with a grin. 'CDs were a complete rip-off, really. If a vinyl record is looked after it will last for centuries –and how long is the longest you've ever had a working CD? Five minutes, right?'

'Not long at all,' she agreed quickly, ushering the conversation along.

'Man, research for documentary making is so rewarding. I've really enjoyed becoming a specialist on a subject.'

He pushed open the edit suite, and Alexia could see his project up and the timeline fully populated.

'I'd love to take a look,' she said eagerly. 'But there's something I have to tell you first.'

'Sure,' he said, pushing a chair in her direction before turning to the computer.

'It's not very nice,' she warned.

'Okay. What?' Lewis said. 'Spit it out, Alexia.'

'It was me that leaked that stuff to Theo Marlon, not Greta.'

'Huh?' He looked round at her, brows furrowed.

'Yep.'

He didn't say anything for a moment, his eyes narrowed and he sighed as he pushed himself back in his chair to look Alexia right in the eyes. A sudden stranger. 'Clint was right.'

'Clint? I haven't spoken to him. He's next on my list,' she mumbled, ashamed. 'I'm trying to speak to everyone.' She was thrown. What had Clint known? Is this why he wasn't answering her calls?

'Well, he came to me a while back with this, so he's obviously figured it out.'

'He did?' She licked her dry lips. 'I'm sorry, I was trying to tell everyone as quickly as possible so you heard it first from me. But you weren't answering.'

'Alexia, I need you to leave.'

'Lewis, I'm sorry. I didn't know things would get so bad. I didn't mean to go so far.'

'Poor Greta. You let her take the rap. And I was such an asshole to her. Great.' His cheeks were flushed, right down to the neck. He held his hands up. 'Alexia – please, just go.'

Alexia opened her mouth to protest, but caught the look of pure hurt in his eyes. She stood up and turned to the door. 'Can I say one thing?'

'No.'

'It wasn't about lying to you guys. Honestly, I didn't really think about how it would affect you,' she said, as he turned his face back to the computer. 'Lewis. I'm sorry.'

'Please just leave.'

Alexia made her way back to her desk and opened her laptop. She checked her watch: 4.58 p.m. Time to make the call. She slipped into an empty meeting room, opened up Skype and dialled the number. It rang just once before her mother appeared.

'Alexia!' she said. 'Oh look at you, you look just beautiful. Are you all right? Have you been sleeping? Practising self-care? I've been beside myself. Oh, I hate this!' She put her head in her hands and began to cry. 'Alexia, please tell me what I can do. I miss you. I just want you to be happy and feel loved and supported. I got everything wrong, didn't I?'

Alexia had expected the call to be emotional, but she had definitely not expected her mother to break down to this degree.

'Can you just listen for a moment?'

Her mom looked up and rubbed her nose with a mono-grammed cotton handkerchief, dabbing at her eyes where the mascara was beginning to run.

'I was a total asshat,' Alexia said.

'Alexia!' Her mom's eyes were wide as plates. 'Language!'

'I was.' Alexia smiled as Oprah jumped up on her mother's lap and tried to lick the screen. 'There's a few things I need to get off my chest, but first I wanted to say something.'

'I'm listening, Alexia.'

'Leaving New York was partially about the job offer – it was what I always wanted. But it was mostly about something else,' she said, steeling herself. 'You gave me so many amazing opportunities that I know you and Dad never had. The private schools, the car, our amazing home, all those photography and film courses you paid for, the offer of paying for NYU.'

'I'd do it all again, Alexia.'

'I know, I know. I just wanted to say that there was a part of me that needed to see what it was like to do something

293

completely on my own. Sometimes growing up, it felt like there was nothing to fight for.'

'I know I spoiled you too much. Your father used to tell me that. That's why we arranged the job at Falls Records for you, so you could learn to work and earn your own money.'

'Yes, but don't you see? That was a job with James. With Dad,' Alexia said. 'The point I'm trying to make is that I needed to do this for myself.'

'I do understand, Alexia.'

'And I went about it all wrong, but I felt a bit cornered, I think. And it was wrong to push you away and pretend like I didn't need you.' Alexia took a deep breath. 'And I'm sorry for hurting you.'

'Oh.' Again with the tears, but this time softer. 'I'm sorry. You're my only child, and one day when you're a mother ... well. It's not easy letting go. Alexia, I love you so much. I wish you would let down that wall ...'

Alexia felt herself starting to close up, as she did whenever her mother became too emotional. 'Please, Mom. I just find all the heavy emotions too much,' Alexia pleaded.

'What do you mean?' Her mom sniffed. 'My emotions are my emotions. I can't apologise for them.'

'When you were ... sick ... I kind of shut off a little. I think because it was too much to deal with. You know, I was thirteen or whatever,' Alexia said, thinking her way through the words. 'Sometimes I just wish I could come to you, instead of me having to watch out for your feelings all the time.'

'I'm sorry. I didn't realise,' her mother replied. Alexia looked at her face – open, sincere – and she knew that she finally *was* listening. It was going to be a long road – but this was a first step.

'Don't be sorry,' Alexia said. 'How could you know?'

They sat for a moment in silence, before Alexia took a deep breath. 'I do really love you, Mom.' As they shared a short moment of mutual acceptance, Alexia began to feel a well of emotion inside herself. She had to calm her breath and look away, or she might cry too.

As if he sensed the time was right, her dad appeared behind her mother, resting his hands on her shoulders and giving them a gentle rub.

'Are you ready to talk to me now?' He smiled. 'I'm so intrigued. Your text message was very cryptic. Did I interrupt?'

'No, no. We're just finishing up,' Alexia said. 'Well. Maybe just starting.' She smiled at her mother. 'Dad, this is kind of about work.'

'Yes. You said something to do with the leaks?' He was grinning. 'I feel a little bit bad. We didn't need to pull those contracts with Bright Star over it, storm in a teacup really, but it made a good excuse to bring things in-house. Sorry, that's more than I should say.'

Alexia drew in a deep breath. 'Yes, about those leaks . . . '

CHAPTER 32

Starry Eyed

It wasn't snowing, but it should have been. London never snows like you see in the Richard Curtis films, with the girl and guy in the cute little cobbled square and the big flakes that fall and perch gently on noses and eyelashes. No, London does early winter with bitter wind and par-frozen rain, and grey tides overflowing from putrid drains that taxis drive intentionally through to soak pedestrians who dare to stray too close to the gutter.

Right on cue, a passing bus splashed a tsunami up onto Granny, who squealed with delight as they rushed into Liberty for shelter.

'Don't mind if I do, Greta,' Granny said, pushing open the door into the world's most spectacular Christmas wonderland.

'I LOVE LOVE LOVE Christmas,' Greta squealed.

'Well, it's still a few weeks away yet, my love.'

'But look at this tiny glass fairy holding a star decoration.' Greta held it up, grinning at her granny. 'LOOK AT IT. ALL OF THE FEELS.'

'Yes, it's thirty-nine pounds. Thirty-nine bloody pounds for a Christmas decoration. We're not the pope. We don't *care* to the value of thirty-nine pounds.'

'What about this?' Greta held up a novelty Santa toilet-seat warmer. 'For the guest toilet?'

'I don't need to sit on Santa's face,' Granny said far too loudly, causing the two young students on the other side of the display to giggle and scurry off.

'Granny!' Greta said. 'Why've you got to be so outrageous?'

'Because when you get old, you realise there is nothing to fear.' She laughed. 'Come on, let's go to men's perfumes.'

Greta waited impatiently while her granny squirted one cologne after another onto the underside of her wrist.

'So, tell me the rest of the story then,' she said, holding up a silk scarf with a vivid peacock print. 'This?'

'No thanks, I prefer that black one.'

'Gah. You need colour. Stop wearing those blacks and greys and dark winter berries, Greta. You'd look lovely in a bit of bright magenta or cobalt blue. Colour gives everything a boost, you know.'

'I know it's dumb, but I feel skinnier in dark colours. I need to diet.'

'Please promise me you'll never, EVER diet. I can't imagine

a thing so dull. And anyway, you're plenty slim enough, Greta. It's only other women who want a stick figure, you know.'

Greta blushed. She looked at herself in a long mirror and leaned forward to inspect her plum lipstick. She did look rather dull. 'What about a bright lippy?'

'Let's go to make-up,' her granny said excitedly.

When they arrived at the make-up counter, the lady behind it dropped everything and rushed over. 'Hello, Maggie.'

'Can you give my granddaughter a new look please, Janelle?'

'Granny, no. I don't want a new look, I just want a new lip.'

'Ooooh let me. Your skin is just divine. And those big eyes? They're crying out for a little contouring at the edges . . . Can I just . . . ' Janelle walked towards her, mouth open, licking her lips, like a cat to a canary.

The flattery worked a treat. A moment later Greta was barefaced with a headband on, in the first stages of a full-scale makeover.

'Tell me the rest of the story now, please,' Granny said, settling into the stool opposite her. 'You got to the bit about Lewis calling you. I'm on tenterhooks here.'

'Yes. Well, so he basically said that he was sorry. The conversation was fairly brief, but he asked me if I wanted to come to meet him at Bright Star and he was going to see if he could get my job back. Or at least, some kind of new job there.'

'Wow! Greta, that's wonderful news.'

'Yes, but the bosses there won't have it. Clint already did

some digging for me. They don't care so much about the leak, but the fact I didn't disclose the fan club stuff. He *thinks* that's the issue anyway – he had to speak to Human Resources who didn't give much away, except that they considered my case "closed".'

'Can you stop talking for just a moment while I do your lips?' Janelle ran a rose liner around the outside of Greta's lips, and then took out a shimmery gloss.

'This will be off my lips in minutes,' Greta said, admiring the colour.

'I'll get them for you,' Granny assured her, winking at the make-up assistant. 'So what's happened to Alexia?'

'Apparently she quit.'

'She did?'

'Yep. She's probably heading back to New York, I guess. Back to Mummy and Daddy and probably a fancy new job.'

'Oh, that's a shame.'

'A shame?' Greta looked at her granny. 'A shame? She totally ruined my life. She's been awful. She has no redeeming features. Except all the features on her face. She's beautiful. But she's been AWFUL. She really hurt me.'

'Perhaps, but it seems to me that she needed some help, too,' Granny said, pulling out her credit card to pay for the enormous make-up haul.

'Three hundred and fifty-three pounds.'

'Christ. I need to re-mortgage.'

'It's fine, Granny. Just the gloss will do.'

'It will not. And, I made a bomb on renting out the apartment through Airbnb this summer. Your idea. So consider this a small commission.'

Greta grasped her purple Liberty bag with glee. Granny also bought the scarf, a cologne for Greta's dad and a long, deep-green Sonia Rykiel cardigan embellished with large coloured sequins for herself. The cardigan was beautiful and all Granny.

'I think the rain has stopped now,' said Greta. 'And they're turning the Christmas lights on in, like, twenty minutes!'

'Oh, all right, let's get on and see this band of yours.'

The Keep and All New Wild were turning on the lights this year. It was a kind of baton-passing stunt by Falls Records, and a few months ago Greta would have been excited at the thought of Lee being back in town once again, but as the year had drawn to a close, it was a certain other singer she'd been daydreaming about.

Oxford Street was cordoned off for the event. She could see a huge stage in the distance lit up with blue and silver lights, above which huge glitter balls and snowflakes waited in the softly twinkling streetlights for their cue. The crowd of shoppers and Keepers stood in wait for the big moment, as The Keep's big-band style Christmas single blared over the speakers.

With steadfast determination, Greta pushed her way through the crowd, guiding her granny as quickly as she could. But something else was playing on her mind.

'What did you mean before, about Alexia needing help?'

'I just meant that it seems like she did something fairly awful, but as you said yourself some time ago that she'd been kind to you, perhaps she did it for some desperate reason.'

'Well, she was broke. And she wanted me away from Lee and out her way.'

'No, I don't mean just that.' Granny turned to Greta. 'Darling, you are such a wonderful girl. You have been through a great ordeal, and as usual you've made the best of it. You have your mother's determination and incredible, endlessly cheery spirit.'

'I get sad, too,' Greta said, as the crowd began to thicken to the point of impenetrability.

'Yes, darling, but I just mean that perhaps there's even more to it. Perhaps she's very down indeed.' She smiled at Greta, leaving the thought hanging.

'Like, depressed? Do you think Alexia is depressed?' Greta frowned.

'I'm not sure about that,' Granny whispered in Greta's ear. 'But it's more likely her motivations were born of self-preservation rather than a desire to do wrong by you. Though the outcome is the same. Just a thought, in case you do end up seeing her.' Granny pointed to the stage. 'Is that your boyfriend?'

Ahead, an open-top red bus had pulled up behind the stage and the crowd started screaming. Eight figures were waving from the top of the bus. Greta couldn't make them out properly. Was that Lee on the end, pulling his top up to show off his belly? Probably.

'I guess so! Argh. Can't we get any closer?' Greta craned her neck.

'Yes, we can. Hold the shopping.' Granny handed Greta an armful of shopping bags and pushed her way through the crowd. 'COMING THROUGH. OLD LADY. VERY TIRED OLD LADY. COMING THROUGH.'

Greta tried not to laugh as Granny parted the crowd like a boat cutting through water. 'COMING THROUGH!' she boomed, as the young fans hastily made way for this doddery old lady who was heaving and puffing like she might keel over and die at any moment. She winked at Greta, who knew that this was a tried and tested trick.

Within a few minutes, and just in time, they were near the front. The floodlights switched on and bright white light shone across the crowd, who began to scream.

'THE KEEEE-EEP, THE KEEEEE-EP,' the crowd awkwardly chanted, out of time with each other. Greta always preferred the short and sharp 'Keep', said quickly, over and over, in time with a single clap.

'Amateurs,' she grumbled.

'I really do need a seat,' Granny whispered. 'Can I see you at Selfridges champagne bar at the conclusion of this impressive display of the pinnacle of the arts?'

'Sure, Granny. An hour or so?'

'That gives me a good head start.'

'OXFORD STREET, London Town. You ready?' Lee's voice boomed over the crowd.

The rest of The Keep took to the stage and the crowd roared. Greta's heart leapt as she saw Charlie, Kyle and Art wave and blow kisses. They looked different without Max, without the matching outfits – more relaxed. They looked like a band about to call it a day and say goodbye. Greta smiled proudly at her boys. They had grown up together – them as a band and Greta as their greatest cheerleader. They'd given her something to channel her passion into, and now it was time for them all to move on.

Lee whooped into the microphone – he looked good. Healthy. Happy. The boys began to sing their bouncy big-band Christmas single. Even the tune was grown up. There were no fancy outfits, fewer gimmicks, more . . . individuality.

Greta beamed, hoping that Lee would look over her way and spot her in the crowd. But it wasn't his eyes that finally fell on hers. To the side of the stage, standing with a man in a suit and next to Nav and the boys from All New Wild, stood Alexia.

She smiled apprehensively at Greta and gently waved, then pulled out her phone and held it up to Greta, pointing.

There she was, standing on stage, and Greta was in the crowd. Nothing had changed. Nothing. Greta felt a surge of anger at the little vibration from her phone.

FROM ALEXIA: Can we talk?

Greta looked up at Alexia, who looked back, nervous but hopeful. 'Well?' she mouthed. Greta looked back at Lee and the boys, singing on stage. She tried to ignore the message and shrugged at Alexia, a polite smile slipping out before she could stop it. *Damn her for being here.* Her phone vibrated again.

> FROM ALEXIA: I'm sorry, Greta. From the bottom of my heart.

Greta pretended to be busy watching the show. Lee was singing his solo line down on one knee, serenading a girl up front to rapturous squeals. *They still got it.* She was proud. Her phone, again.

> FROM ALEXIA: I want to make it up to you.

Greta shot another look at Alexia, who had stepped down from the stage and was looking down at her phone, furiously typing another message.

> FROM ALEXIA: When you're ready, I want you to meet my dad. I have an idea.

Greta looked back at her again. Alexia nodded, waving her over. *What is she playing at?*

'Don't do it, Greta,' she said loudly as she began picking her way to the side of the stage. 'This is your dumbest idea ever. Why would you talk to someone who did such terrible things

to you? The girl's a backstabbing, lying, conniving, nasty...'
She pushed over to some velvet roping that separated the
crowd from the stage. Alexia made her way towards her, smiling apprehensively. '...no good, dirty...' She stopped and
smiled. It was fully automatic. 'Hi, Alexia.'

'Hello. Can you come with me?'

CHAPTER 33

Running Up That Hill

'I don't want to miss . . .' Greta craned her neck to see the boys as Alexia led her to the back of the stage.

'We'll be quick, I promise.' Alexia was holding her hand tightly – it was colder than hers, and she wanted to pull away, but felt obliged to follow.

When they rounded the stage, Alexia pulled her behind a huge speaker, careful not to trip on the huge black cables that lay everywhere. It was immediately quieter, though the sound became almost all bass and vibration that shook Greta to the core.

'Greta,' Alexia said flatly. 'I know you know what I did. I sold stories to Theo Marlon and let you take the fall. In fact, I actively manipulated the situation so you took the fall.'

Alexia spoke with such calmness that Greta was taken aback. Where was the gaping, weeping apology she'd imagined receiving one day? The grovelling? The tears? This was *so* Alexia.

'There is no excuse for what happened. And I don't want to caveat my full and sincere apology, but I would like to explain to you how it happened. Why I did what I did ... if you'd be willing to listen?'

Greta pursed her lips. There had still been a part of her that didn't want to believe Alexia had planned to frame her, and she felt a surge of anger at the stark and full admission. 'I don't think I need to hear it, if it's only to relieve your own guilt. I thought you wanted me to meet your dad?'

'Yes, there's also that. But first, I wanted to speak to you about all of this.'

'All of this?' Greta felt a surge of anger. 'ALL OF THIS? You ruined my life. You took away my job, I mean, fair enough I didn't really like most parts of the job, but that was for ME to change, not you. You took away my friends. The only ones I've ever had.'

'Clint is speaking to you, isn't he?' Alexia said meekly.

'He's *spoken* to me, but we had work in common, and that's gone. I'm not sure he wants to discuss stock-taking or the value of a good city guidebook with me.' She was almost shouting.

Alexia looked confused, Greta lowered her voice to its normal tone. 'I'm working at a newsagent at Luton Airport. It's like a bookshop that sells sandwiches and headphones and an awful lot of cheap chocolate.'

'Oh, I know the kind – the ones that try and sell you a newspaper with your bottle of water?'

'IT'S A BETTER DEAL. Whatever, regardless of that . . . ' Greta sighed, a break in the booming music ruining her momentum.

'LET'S HEAR IT FOR BRITAIN'S NEWEST BOYBAND SENSATION – ALL. NEW. WILD,' the MC shouted, the last word drowned out by deafening squeals.

'Boyband?' Greta's ears pricked up. 'I thought they weren't calling them that.'

'There's been some changes.'

'Ooh, Nav will be pleased.'

Their single kicked in, and as the music blared Greta turned to Alexia and set her voice to maximum volume. 'I'm just not sure what the point of this is. Talking to you. Now. What's the point?'

Alexia held her hand up to her mouth and shouted, 'Greta. There's an after party for this happening at MEATliquor. Do you know where that is?'

'Yes, of course. It does the best burger in London. Well, I'd take a Lucky Chip myself, but it really comes down to personal preference. I'm not in for a brioche bun, me. Too soft and way too sickly.'

'Shall we go now? We can talk before the guys arrive.'

The guys? Hang on! Greta's stomach flipped a little at the thought of seeing Lee again. And the rest of The Keep. Perhaps she could die happy after all. And an after party?

She'd never been to an actual after party before. Plenty of parties, and gigs and shows and that wrap party with All New Wild, but never an after party. So exclusive.

'My granny. She's waiting for me.'

'Where?'

'Selfridges. She doesn't have a mobile.'

'Well, shall we go tell her? Or bring her?' Alexia suggested. 'Lewis said your granny is hilarious.'

'She's nuts. And yes, we can bring her. But it means whatever you have to say will need to be said in front of her and she doesn't . . . ' Greta broke into a grin ' . . . mince her words.'

'Well, all right then.'

Alexia followed Greta towards Selfridges as All New Wild's performance carried on. Greta's muttering had reached drunken hobo proportions. 'Bloody, who does she think she is, cushioning this bloody apology with an invitation to an after party with The Keep. I don't care how cool she claims this will be.' The truth, however, was that she was excited.

They found Granny at the back end of the bar, perched on a dove-grey stool, her shopping at her feet, lecturing the waitress on the complex superiority of a good whisky.

'Ahh, there's my granddaughter. Greta, over here!'

'I see you, Granny.'

No one could miss her in the neck-to-floor embellished blue and green cardigan that hung open to reveal her dark-silver shirt and shimmering silver trousers. She looked a little like a Christmas decoration. Greta winced slightly as she introduced Alexia, who was all understated class in a simple Christmassy red dress, woollen tights and neat black pea coat.

'Alexia, Granny. Granny, Alexia,' Greta said. 'We're making up,' she added quickly, by way of explanation.

'It's nice to meet you.' Alexia smiled. *Nervously.* Greta wasn't surprised – Granny had that effect on people.

'Well, I've heard an awful lot about you, my dear,' Granny replied. *'Awful* being the important word, of course.'

Alexia hung her head and Greta jumped in to save her. 'Oh Granny, really. You don't need to—'

'Better to be clear, Greta.' Granny turned to Alexia. 'She's told me everything that went on, but I have a few questions for you, Alexia. Can I get you two a whisky? Or some of that god-awful champagne?' she said, motioning to a bottle of pale-pink bubbles on the counter.

'Champagne! Amazing!' Greta said, forgetting herself. 'But we have to be quick, Granny.'

'Very well.' Granny waved at the waitress, who poured out two glasses. Granny pushed out the stool next to her and offered it to Alexia. Greta sat on the other side of her granny, whose back was partially turned to her as she focused her attention on Alexia. 'So, are you alone for Christmas?'

'No. I'm flying back with my father next week,' Alexia said, meekly, eyeing Greta carefully as she spoke.

'But you're coming back?'

'Maybe. I'd like to. I'm talking through some things with my parents. I'll need their help. And a new job.' She looked uneasy as Granny casually pressed her. Greta craned her head around her granny's shoulder, feeling very much like she was imposing on a private conversation.

Alexia leaned forward and nodded to Greta. 'Speaking of which, it's part of what I wanted to talk to *you* about—'

'Well.' Granny turned her full body on the stool, blocking Greta completely. 'I'm glad to hear you're staying on. After all that you've done, better to stay and face it than run away.'

'I'm sorry,' Alexia said, blushing.

'Yes, I'm sure you are,' Granny said softly. She smiled and then tilted her head to speak over her shoulder. 'You're right, Greta, she is beautiful. Inside and out.'

Eh? What on earth was Granny doing?

'We are all human, Alexia,' Granny said, putting her hand on Alexia's shoulder. Greta leaned backwards to look round her granny and saw a tear flicker in the corner of Alexia's eye. She leaned back further, deeply fascinated, her champagne to her lips – and then she slipped, crashing to the floor, catching herself on the stool but forsaking her glass, which crashed to the ground and smashed into a million pieces.

She looked up at Granny and Alexia, then shook herself off and stood up slowly, with casual coolness, before slipping once more on the champagne that had collected on the polished floor in delicious, icy-pink pools.

'I think it's time we left, anyway,' Alexia said. 'I'm so glad to have met you.'

'Likewise, dear.' Granny nodded. 'Alexia, here's the thing.'

She put her empty whisky glass on the counter top. 'There's a room at my Dalston flat if you want to stay in London and take some pressure off. You need to mend whatever it was that broke with your parents, but I suspect that moving home long-term will not do that. Though Greta would protest, I believe you two can sort through this. We women must stick together.'

'I know. I just don't have a job any more.'

'You're a capable woman. You'll find another,' Granny said. She turned to Greta, who was standing and heaving loud, protesting puffs while tapping her foot in obvious irritation. 'Both of you are, and both of you will.'

'Can we go, Alexia? She's in the middle of apologising to *me*, Granny.'

'Off you go.' Granny waved. 'See you at home, dear. Oh, and take your new lippy!' She fished it out of the Liberty bag at her feet.

A few minutes later, they were in a dark corner of MEATliquor, and Greta was hearing Alexia out in full.

'It started as a way to make some money, but if I'm really honest, I also enjoyed it a little. There was a kind of revenge in it all. Annoying my father, and toying a bit with Lee.' She looked down at her drink and stirred the ice cubes slowly with her straw. 'I had these feelings for Lee and he was so dismiss-ive of me. He was never kind. I told myself I didn't really care about hurting any of them.' She looked at Greta, her eyes full of tears. 'But each time I did it I felt sick to my stomach. And then I truly saw the hurt it was causing.'

'But why did you blame me?' Greta said. 'I can't help but feel that was a little bit premeditated. Like you held back the information about the fandom in case you ever came under fire.'

Alexia breathed out and shrugged. 'I did. I'm sorry.'

'Is that it?'

'I didn't think it would matter.'

'*You didn't think it would matter?*' Greta was shocked.

'I just mean, you didn't really want the full-time job.' Alexia stopped herself, looking over Greta's shoulder. 'I only thought of myself.'

Greta became aware of the room starting to fill behind her. The bands would be here soon, and she wanted to wrap the conversation with Alexia up so she could meet the rest of them.

'Do you think Lee will recognise me?' Greta asked, completely changing the subject. Alexia sat open-mouthed. 'Look, it's fine. Really. I'll find another cool job, and—'

'But that's what I wanted to talk to you about. Why I wanted you to meet Dad. He's just arrived . . .'

'Oh-kay,' said Greta cautiously. 'You want me to meet your dad because . . . ?'

Before she could finish, James Falls was standing in front of them, pulling Alexia over for a hug. 'Is this *the* Greta? *The* girl?'

'Yes.' Alexia nodded, smiling shyly.

'Greta, I hear you ran The Keep's biggest fan site?'

'Ah ...' Greta's eyes popped open and she hesitated.

'Did you know it was one of the reasons for the boys' success? That we used to read the feed almost daily in the office?'

'Um, maybe.' Greta blushed, shooting Alexia a where-the-hell-is-this-going look.

'You're one of the reasons the boys won countless Teen Choice awards,' he crowed. 'You!'

'Um, yes.' Greta was now blushing wildly. 'I just ... well ...'

'Do you think you could show the same passion for another band?' James asked with palms up and a broad smile.

Greta felt a surge of excitement. He couldn't mean ... 'All New Wild?'

'What do you think?'

'You want me to run their fan feed?'

'No. I want you to run their official feeds, and all their social media. I want you to be their social media producer.'

Greta looked at Alexia, who was smiling nervously and biting her bottom lip. She gave Greta a nod of encouragement.

'Is this some kind of thing to make me not hate Alexia?' Greta blurted.

'Well, I can't make you feel one way or another, but she really pushed for me to meet you, so I hope that tells you something about her.' He nodded. 'So, what do you say? Can I see you before I fly back to New York, and we can go over everything?'

'Thank you,' she said aloud. *I can't believe you're helping me after I lied to everyone.*

'You'll be helping *us*, Greta.'

'I apologise in advance for what I'm about to do.' Greta threw her arms around James and hugged him tightly. He patted her back, gently laughing.

'Now, shall we celebrate your new job?'

As James walked over to the bar, Greta turned to Alexia, beaming from ear to ear. 'Oh, Alexia, this is amazing. I was actually already looking at All New Wild's online stuff and they really need help. Like, REALLY.'

'I'm so pleased for you. It's so *you*. Isn't it?'

She nodded, beaming with delight. 'Alexia, thank you.'

'Don't thank me. This is honestly the least I could do. And it was Dad's idea. When I told him everything that I'd done, he was really intrigued by your story and got totally excited when I told him about the fan feed.'

'And are *you* in trouble with him?' she asked, wishing that Alexia could feel as happy and carefree as she did right now.

'No, not in trouble. But I am going to head back to New York for Christmas after the screening. It's important that I do.' She shrugged.

'The screening?'

'Yes.' Alexia let out a huge breath. 'I've been busy.'

It felt like a lifetime before the boys filed into the bar. They'd spent the best part of two hours signing autographs and doing interviews with the press. First Charlie came gliding through in virtual slow motion, his white teeth shining as he high-fived and hugged various members of their entourage, who were milling around the door, waiting.

Kyle followed. He was even more beautiful in real life. Actual sheer perfection, his lean, muscular arms flexing as he shook hands with the two doormen holding back the velvet roping. Art strolled in clutching a book, as usual. He eyed Alexia with disappointment. They all knew what she'd done by now, and Greta couldn't help thinking that her friend still had some making up to do.

The All New Wild boys came filing through after him, with far less hubbub than their superstar American predecessors. Greta's excitement kept building.

Alexia looked across at Greta and smiled, but her face fell as Geoff arrived, grimacing at her like a comic-book villain. Another person she'd probably need to apologise to.

Alexia looked over to Greta again, who was beaming with delight now. She followed her gaze, expecting to see Lee on the receiving end of such a warm, adoring smile, but was surprised to see Navid from All New Wild.

They locked eyes, and she watched as Greta beamed with delight.

'I have to go and tell him my news! Do you mind?' Greta bounced off and into a warm, friendly hug from the singer.

'Please.' Alexia chuckled in her wake. She braced herself and headed towards Geoff, but her way was abruptly blocked by a waxy arm.

'Alexia,' Lee said, glaring at her. His eyes were narrow and he was swaying slightly on his feet. His breath smelled foul and sweet, of beer and cigarettes, and there were faint beads of sweat on his forehead. She felt a knot in her stomach as she turned to face the full force of his feelings. Alongside Greta, Lee was the one she'd caused the most damage to. And the one she'd cared for the most.

'Hi, Lee.' She leaned nervously back on the railing of the bar for support.

'I didn't think I'd see *you* here, Sexi Lexi.'

'I'm sorry, Lee. I'm so sorry.'

'Oh, about Jessica? Don't worry about that. Like I said, she was a drag.'

'Okay. But I'm still sorry.'

'Let's not talk about it.' He smiled, putting his hand on her arm. 'It's nice to be properly single again, anyway.'

Alexia froze, a feeling of dread filling her. 'Um, okay?' She pointed at Geoff. 'I was just going to catch up with him.' She tried to move, but Lee stood firm, smiling at her, his eyes glassy and his eyelids heavy.

'I thought *we* were catching up,' he said with a smirk. Then he coughed and looked over at the bartender, who was clearly eavesdropping as he repeatedly cleaned the same glass right next to them. 'Can I have a Coke?'

'Sure,' the bartender said, flipping the top off a bottle and dropping it onto the counter.

'No more booze for Lee.' He smirked. 'Daddy's orders.' He nodded to Geoff, who was looking over and shaking his head at Alexia. 'Where's that cute little girl you had working for you?'

Alexia stood perplexed for a moment. 'Greta?'

'Yeah. She's sweet. Where is she?'

Alexia looked at Lee and suddenly felt angry. He was just so ignorant. Selfish. These days were behind her now, and it no longer mattered what Lee thought of her. And it never mattered a damn to him how she felt.

'She's busy,' Alexia said curtly. 'And I have to get going.'

'So soon?' Lee said. 'You could never keep up with the party, Lexi.'

She pushed past him and headed for the door, stopping by her dad to quickly check on his plans. 'Are you meeting Mom?'

'Yes, at the hotel. Shall we come get you in the morning?'

'Perfect.' She kissed him on the cheek and left. It was the last time she would see the band, she was sure of it. But it was finally time to cut off that life, and repair the one she needed.

CHAPTER 34

Karma Police

Theo Marlon ran a finger through the gap between the glued seal of the envelope and the fold, tearing it open. Inside was a thumb drive and a handwritten note.

It's my last story. I don't think you'll like it, but you might want to take a look, anyway. Despite everything, I wish you the best. Alexia.

Theo turned the note over and looked at the simple black thumb drive with curiosity. 'Moe!' he shouted to his showbiz editor. 'There's something from that Keep source. At last.'

Moe hurried over while Theo leaned back and ripped the top off a stick of snack salami. A whiff of garlic smacked them both in the face.

'Can you make it work?' Theo waved at his machine.

Moe plugged it in and opened the drive's only folder. 'It's a film of some kind, called *The Source*.' He smirked. 'Subtle.'

'Ooh great. We need some more video. TMZ are all over us these days with their bloody video exclusives.'

'Just hit the spacebar,' Moe said. 'Give me a shout if you need me to edit it.'

A few minutes later, the sausage slipped out of Theo's fingers and onto the floor. His heart began to thump. 'Nooooo!' He shouted at the screen! 'NOOOOOO!'

CHAPTER 35

Changes

In the small theatre just off Redchurch Street, Alexia sat down low in her chair as her film played out. Karen sat to her left, occasionally smiling at her and nodding to gently reassure her during some of the more intimate content of the film. Alexia watched herself, her work onscreen, overwhelmed by the feeling that this had somehow been part of her journey all along.

The film was an apology. But it was also, according to Karen, a stunning debut film. She blushed, remembering Karen's face when she'd finished watching it in her office. 'It needs a hell of a lot of work, Alexia, but my god, it's fantastic. Also, I think you probably can't work here any more.'

The film was a gritty look at the ethics and the tricks of the gossip-column trade. It covered all the major sites and was a probing exposé, but the thread that held it all together was her personal story. She went into incredible detail about her meetings with Theo, showing notes, text messages and touching lightly on the impact those stories had on the people she loved. One such moment was her phone call with Lee, which had been excruciating to listen to as many times as she had.

In the original edit, Alexia had been hard on Theo, but Karen had talked her through separating her own feelings of anger and revenge from what was actually a sad story about a lonely man and his computer. In the final version of the film, Theo looked pitiful, rather than like some cartoon evil dude. *And that's way more cutting.*

As the film ended, applause started slowly with the credits. Within a few moments there was more applause, and then some cheering from the back row.

Alexia stood up and saw her mother smiling broadly from across the aisle. 'I love you,' she mouthed. Alexia looked up at the back row. *They all came.*

Clint, Greta and Lewis.

As Alexia took in their smiles and cheers, her heart melted.

'Alexia, that was extraordinary.' Her mother grabbed her by the arm. 'My darling, I had no idea.'

'I didn't know either,' Alexia said, blushing.

'It's been hard for you,' her mom said, her eyes staring into Alexia's. 'My darling, I'm so sorry I was so hard on you.'

'It's okay, Mom. It's living, isn't it?' Alexia reassured her. 'It was my journey. My journey so far.' She took a deep breath. 'Mom, before we head for dinner, can I just go and say goodbye to my friends?'

'Sure.' Her mom pulled out her make-up, grinning like a teenager. 'I'll just go touch up and meet you outside.'

Alexia walked up the stairs to the back of the auditorium, throwing her arms around Clint as he gave her a big smile.

'She's back,' Clint teased.

'Well done!' Greta beamed.

Alexia gave her friend a kiss and a warm embrace. 'Thank you so much, Greta. For everything.'

'It was truly fantastic, Alexia,' Lewis said keenly. He was reserved, but he had come. 'Can we take you for a drink? I have a date later, but I would love to celebrate with you.'

'My mother is here, so I have to go with her. But we'll catch up really soon. Spend some proper time together. I promise,' Alexia said, filling those words with as much affection as she could.

The four of them walked outside, the frozen chill of winter hitting them as snowflakes gently added to the white blanket spreading itself across the city. Alexia pulled her scarf tightly around her neck and rubbed her bare hands together. 'Winter is definitely here.'

'We never get a white Christmas. Must be something in the air.' Greta winked at Alexia. 'Maybe see you at home later?'

Home, thought Alexia, as she watched her friends leave fresh prints in the new snow. Her mother came out and put her arm through Alexia's. 'Come on, then. Let's discuss how this London adventure could continue to work so I can see as much of you as possible.'

'You got it.' Alexia smiled.